and of itself), the writing or the plot, I guarantee that YOU WILL FALL IN LOVE. It's inevitable.

Teenreads

A fantastic read – gripping from the first page

on P Clark

Kat Ellis is a young adult author whose novels include *Blackfin Sky, Breaker*, and *Purge*. She is a self-proclaimed sci-fi geek, and a keen explorer of ruins, castles, and cemeteries - all of which are plentiful in North Wales, where Kat lives with her husband. You can find out more about Kat at www.katelliswrites.com or connect with her on Twitter @el_kat

PURGE

First published in 2016
by Firefly Press
25 Gabalfa Road, Llandaff North, Cardiff, CF14 2JJ
www.fireflypress.co.uk

A CIP catalogue record of this book is available from the British Library.

Print ISBN 9781910080405
epub ISBN 9781910080412

This book has been published with the support of the
Welsh Books Council.

Typeset by: Elaine Sharples
cover image: Anne Glenn

Printed and bound by: Pulsio SARL

PURGE

KAT ELLIS

For Ian

CHAPTER ONE

Alteria Community

Like all the other communities on our cesspool of a planet, Alteria looked like an egg some giant bird had crapped out of the sky and left floating on the ocean. I watched through the sub's porthole as the underside of the ark loomed closer. From underwater, Alteria's shields were like mirrored glass. Small pockets of air bubbles bounced off them, fizzing uncertainly at the electric charge before making a break for the surface.

I felt a tug on my arm and found my sister frowning at me.

'Turn on your implant. We're about to dock,' I lip-read, and reactivated my audio implant. Immediately the compressed sounds of the sub's engines, the groaning metal of the hull, the shifting and chattering of the other passengers – it all crowded in on me, making me feel sick.

The sub surfaced and docked, the hiss of the airlock engaging like nails scraping against the inside of my skull. I understood why Ari was feeling twitchy. So far, my custom-made implant had fooled all the bio-scanners in other communities, but every time we moved to a new ark we faced this moment – the one where it might all go horribly wrong.

'Ariadne Coulter and Mason Coulter.'

We grabbed our stuff and were ushered past the guy with the tablet. I glanced at the tiny green eye of the scanner above his head – flashing, now that it had something to inspect – and kept right on walking. The hairs on the back of my neck bristled as the scanner beam passed over me. With every step, I expected the alarm. It would start with flashing lights, maybe a siren blaring. Then a heavy hand would fall on my shoulder, a security squad raising their weapons to point at me.

Being deaf wasn't the problem. But it marked me as someone who had survived the blast at Cardis, and everyone knew the only survivors there were the Rats who massacred that entire community. Rats were wasters, outcasts-turned-terrorists who would attack and seize any ark not strong enough to defend itself.

If people found out I was deaf they always joined the dots the same way: I'd been at Cardis. I'd survived. I must be a Rat, right? Except I wasn't. I just had a habit of being in the wrong place at the wrong time – which was kind of hard to explain when you were being marched through an airlock at gunpoint.

There were no blaring sirens this time. No lights, no guns. It was almost disappointing.

Inside the airlock, the place was a beige assault. From the carpeted floor to the speckled walls to the ambient lighting, it was a study in conformity. I knew instantly that this place and I were not going to get along.

I took in the glass-fronted mezzanine arcing across the lobby, ignoring the curious looks Ari and I were drawing from passing Alterians. A plaque – discreetly beige with mocha lettering – hung beneath the walkway. It read, 'In the Supremacy of Our Knowledge We Find His Truth.'

Oh, shit.

'Ari, tell me you didn't…'

My sister's teeth were showing, but the smile wasn't really a smile.

'It was the only decent community that would take us both, baby brother.'

She spoke without moving her lips, not-so-subtly checking I still had my implant turned on. It annoyed the crap out of me, and Ari knew it.

'Yeah, *decent*,' I muttered.

Ariadne was an engineer, so with her squeaky-clean Citizen record, she basically had a free pass to any community on the planet. She was useful. *Wanted*. I, on the other hand, was not a Citizen yet, and had one or two dark spots on my record. Or seven. Whatever.

With a twinge of guilt, I realised how limited our options had become if Ari had had to choose *this* community. One where we'd be expected to worship whatever mythical being this herd of weirdos had picked as their saviour.

Just remember – stay clean, stay out of trouble, and you'll be out of here soon.

I repeated the words in my head like a mantra, willing myself to believe them so that the walls would stop moving in on me.

Two doors at the opposite end of the lobby swooshed open, and we were beckoned inside by a guy in a hazmat suit. A *beige* hazmat suit.

I stepped forward with a sigh.

Ari and I were quarantined at the gate for four days, undergoing scans and treatments and tests. Even without seeing her, I knew Ari would be content to submit to all this. She was good at putting up with things.

The technicians looked like they'd been born wearing their starchy tunics and superior expressions, and it obviously bugged them to be handling a dirty outsider like me. Once I was fairly certain I wasn't going to set off any terrorist alerts, I let myself enjoy needling them. I filled their little jars with a whole spectrum of bodily substances, handing each one back with a feral smile. On the fourth day, my shit had apparently assumed the correct shade of beige, and Ari and I were released into the general population.

The first thing that struck me was the near-perfect

silence. The Alterians glided about in slippers that you never heard coming, except for the snap of static as they came within arm's reach. Even the doors swooshed open and shut with an almost audible apology as their red-eyed sensors identified and eradicated any unwanted elements – certain bacteria, toxins, random filth – from your body. With its sledgehammer approach to religion and cleanliness, Alteria was equipped to purge all undesirable substances from the community.

This didn't bode well for me.

'Welcome to Alteria,' the standard-issue message started blaring through an unseen PA system, ruining my moment of peace. 'We seek knowledge in His name, and welcome you as you join our mission to be the first to set foot on New Earth…'

I switched off my implant, sick of hearing the same trumped-up speech. Every community said the same thing, and not every community could be the first to blast off this shithole planet.

After making the dire discovery that the Alterians' library of so-called entertainment consisted mainly of scientific articles and videos of nerds debating philosophy, I spent my first couple of days at the new community avoiding orientation and experimenting with the doors' purge units. This mostly involved stuffing myself with food and leaving rooms to see if it would be purged right out of my stomach. Didn't work that way, although I didn't use the bathroom for four days.

Having purge technology built into every door was definitely a novelty. In other communities, it was reserved for medical use – and in my case, for making sure my bad habits went undetected. I'd never lived in a community that could afford to waste money on such unnecessary tech. Here, they seemed dead set on eradicating every last molecule that might stain their spotless utopia. It was beyond uptight.

When my experimenting got old, I went exploring until I'd found all the major work hives within the ark's structure: Engineering, the Command Deck, Waste Processing, and – most importantly – the Chemical Facility. There were always one or two chem workers in every community who were Pi dealers. It just made sense. They had access to the ingredients, and high enough security clearance to get away with it.

I'd arranged to meet one of them, a woman called Angela, at the Recreation Room. Noticing the enlarged pupils that gave her away as a regular Pi user, I'd carefully introduced myself to her outside the labs the previous day.

I spotted her as soon as I walked into the Rec – a large, too-bright space decorated with affirmations and religious murals. Without speaking, she gestured for me to follow her into what looked like a storage closet. I hesitated a moment. We hadn't discussed payment, so I had to weigh how much I wanted the drugs before stepping inside. Pretty badly, it turned out.

I followed her, closing the door behind me. When I turned around, Angela's head was just disappearing through an access hatch in the floor. I leaned over the hole, staring into darkness.

'Are you coming?'

I jumped as her face reappeared three metres below me, lit by the neon glow of a wrist device the Alterians called a *vox*. I hadn't bothered wearing the one they'd allocated to me. I took a deep breath, tapped a spot next to my right ear to switch the implant off, and followed her down. Without the echo hammering at me from all sides, it was doable.

We spilled out into a space the same size as the Rec upstairs, but the room itself couldn't have been more different. Neon lights pulsed in rhythm with the music I could feel vibrating up through the floor. I couldn't tell what it was, but I would have bet some serious credits that it wasn't the upbeat faith music playing in the room above.

Towering stacks of steel crates rose up to the ceiling with dancing bodies writhing in between, like a giant razor-toothed mouth swirling with bacteria.

Angela's hand appeared on my shoulder, and I got the impression she'd been trying to get my attention for a while.

'It's safer…' she said, but I lost the rest as she ducked

her head and started unpicking a seam on her tunic. Tunics were the clothing of choice for the God-fearing Alterians, I'd noticed. From the looks I kept getting in my jeans and t-shirt, my lack of tunic was obviously seen as a major insult.

I leaned against one of the crates while I waited, the deep bass of the music throbbing through my chest like a second heartbeat. Considering Alteria's strict line on cleanliness, it was both surprising and not to see so many people down here. My eyes roamed from twitching limb to twitching limb, feeling uneasy as their wide black pupils stared back at me.

That was when I saw her.

She moved like a wraith in the pulsing lights, the whites of her eyes glowing blue, then green in time with the music. Even from far across the room, I could tell she felt my eyes on her. I probably stood out as the only thing in the entire room that wasn't moving.

She smiled and tossed her hair so that it whipped around her, turning her body to the music and extending every limb in rhythm. I followed the lines of her body, watched the light weave and curl around her bare arms, around her wrists and her fingers.

'You like her?' Angela asked. I jumped, noticing that the heavy bass of the music wasn't just a vibration anymore. I'd reactivated my implant at some point, so fixated on watching the girl that I hadn't felt the crushing weight of sound. Rather than shout, I nodded. Angela smiled with her thin lips.

'You and she have a common interest,' she said, pressing something small and hard into the waistband of my jeans. 'I took the liberty of transferring twenty credits from your account earlier today. Keep the stuff in the container; it'll mask the contents from the door sensors. And remember to purge,' she added, shaking her head and leaving before I could respond.

I pulled my t-shirt down to hide the lumpy container and slunk over to the hatch. Back in the stark light of the Rec, nobody seemed to notice as I slipped out of the storage closet and headed straight for the exit.

After a full day's Pi abuse, I was starting to feel spectacularly funky. Getting high gave me access to the only vast expanse I could find, locked away in my cramped quarters with my implant turned off. It also helped blank out the never-ending announcements issued over the PA system about how close Alteria supposedly was to being ready to launch for New Earth.

Bullshit.

Despite the high level of tech surrounding me, I just couldn't picture this godly crew sailing off into the cosmos – even if it was supposedly 'in pursuit of His all-knowing grace'. But whichever community was actually the first to be ready for the big off, I would be in it. I would make it happen.

An ugly flashing light above my door alerted me to the fact that someone had pressed the buzzer on the other side. I had enough presence of mind to get rid of the drugs in my system with a handheld purge unit I'd made out of scrap I'd nicked back in Parisia, then switched on my implant and opened the door.

A thin streak of a guy peered down at me over a beaky nose. A good nose for snorting with, I thought. I obviously hadn't quite shaken the brain-fug from the Pi.

'We seek knowledge in His name,' he said.

There was a good, long moment of staring before I remembered that this was a standard Alterian greeting. I wracked my brain, trying to remember how I was meant to answer. I settled for 'Hi'. He actually tutted at me.

'I'm Lyle, your assigned counsellor. And the correct reciprocal greeting is, "In truth we know His grace".'

'Oh. I'll remember that,' I lied, which cheered him up. He smiled at me thinly underneath his beak.

'It would have been prudent to remember to attend your orientation, as well.'

This was why he was here? Dickhead.

'Yeah, I completely meant to go to that, but I...'

'There is another orientation session starting in ten minutes,' he said.

There was no pretence that he was *asking* me to go – I was being herded.

'Maybe tomorrow,' I said.

'No. Now.'

He angled his body in a way that was obviously meant to encourage me to leave my quarters and follow him. After a long, awkward silence, I left my quarters and followed him.

'You should consider getting some more suitable clothing from the requisitions section. It's on the tour.' Lyle smiled at me efficiently, then grimaced as he looked me up and down. I was wearing dark jeans with a plain white t-shirt – not flashy, but not exactly stand-out shitty either. I gave him the same up-and-down appraisal, letting my thoughts about his beige tunic and slacks show on my face.

We walked in silence until we came to some kind of restaurant. Judging by the gaggle of lost-looking people outside, this was where the orientation session started.

'Have fun,' Lyle instructed with a bow from the waist. I had the urge to drive my knee up into his face while he was down there. 'Be bold in the pursuit of knowledge.'

I had no clue what the correct parting phrase was, so I gave a sarcastic salute as I weaved my way into the orientation group.

The restaurant was more of a self-service refectory, really. A very smooth-surfaces, fixed-seating kind of place. But even with all the loud colours, it still somehow managed to look beige. I thought about turning around and leaving, but a sharp twinge in my stomach reminded me that I'd been too busy bingeing in my quarters to eat for the last thirty hours or so. It wouldn't hurt to fill the void.

Trying to find a way around the swarm, I came face to face with the wraith.

She was at the front of the tour group, in a neat beige tunic with a neat name tag. It called her *Eden*.

Without the lurid artifice of the lights in the secret room below the Rec, she was as immaculately beige as the rest of them. Almost. Her quick hazel eyes checked me out, a smirk playing around her mouth. She was so *pristine* compared to the first time I'd seen her. Her hair was now braided, trailing down her back like a black mane, her skin darker than mine against her tunic. But her lips were painted a luminous shade of yellow – one small, significant rebellion.

In that moment I knew three things for certain.

One: Eden was way out of my league.

Two: the girl had 'trouble' stamped through her like a stick of rock candy.

And three: I was going to do whatever it took to spend time with her. Preferably naked time.

Fighting a grin, I joined the tour group. Eden performed the tour around the social facility with an enthusiasm that wasn't quite convincing. Her words, her smile, seemed automatic, but her eyes said she was thinking about something else entirely. Something *bad*. I immediately liked that about her – the duplicity.

Once we reached the upper levels, she handed the tour group over to another guide who took them to the supply area, where furniture and other clutter could be ordered. I hung back, watching. Her movements were fluid, and I noted that even in the muted light of the ark, she still held an almost chemical appeal. The next moment I was standing next to her, with no memory of having moved. Pi had that lingering effect sometimes.

'Hello … Mason, isn't it?' she said as she looked up, like she hadn't been aware of me at all until that moment. Her voice was soft, deeper than when she was giving the tour – almost a purr in her Alterian drawl. I nodded. 'Lyle said I should report you if you didn't complete the orientation.'

She must have known I'd skipped out on my allocated session, and from the way her mouth curved into a wicked smile, I had a feeling she knew why.

'It was a good tour,' I said, cursing myself for not being able to think of something interesting to say.

'If you say so. You were the only one even pretending to pay attention.'

'I'm sure I saw a few eyebrows shoot up when you mentioned the tour would end with a cavity inspection to check for barnacles.'

'I said no such thing. But maybe I'll add that to the next session.' Her smile faded as she glanced past me. I turned to find Lyle standing across the room, his arms folded over his chest as he studied the faces around him.

'Is that arsehole here to check up on me?' I said, bristling. Eden's mouth had a pinched look that hadn't been there a second ago. Instead of answering the question, she edged closer so that she was out of Lyle's line of sight.

'He told me I should stay away from you, Mason Coulter.'

My heart sank. Lyle had access to all my past counselling notes, and had probably told everyone about my *history*. But before I could come up with a way to explain myself that didn't make me sound like a complete bastard, I noticed she was grinning.

'But I don't usually do what he tells me,' she said. 'Maybe I'll call on you sometime, find out if you're the bad influence he seems to think you are.'

Eden cast one glance at me from under her thick black lashes and I knew I was in deep trouble.

CHAPTER TWO

Alteria Community

'Be among the first to venture forth in search of His great truth! Ensure your place in time for our launch to the new world! Apply for your Citizen card today!'

I groaned inwardly at the reminder, delivered as enthusiastically as it was via the PA system. At seventeen, I still had to complete my final term of Prep Therapy before I could apply for a Citizen card. Because being a good Citizen required *preparation*, according to every counsellor I'd ever met. And *preparation* always involved mindfuckery in one form or another. But once I had my card, I'd be able to move from one community to another when I wanted to, pretty much. I wouldn't have to rely on my sister's status or some arsehole counsellor's approval to get past the front gate. With the planet all gone to hell, each community was supposedly working towards building their own colony ship to travel to New Earth – a planet just six months away at the fastest possible speed, according to the last scout mission report. The arks had once held the remnants of the old nation states, all separate and eyeing each other suspiciously as they always had. But after six generations of people haggling their way from one ark to another, they were now just sardine tins filled with more or less skilled sardines, depending on the desirability of the tin.

I didn't care which tin I was in. Being stuck inside an ark was hell, but it wasn't the worst hell available. The Rats were forced to live in small pockets of the irradiated wasteland, and being shoved outside to die a lingering, painful death with them wasn't exactly my number one choice. That was why I needed to finagle my way off this crumbling rock. I'd be one of the first people to walk outside in more than a century without feeling the acid-like burn of the sun – it would just be another sun, on another world. I imagined being able to turn on my implant without hearing the faint crackle of the radiation shields, and not having to worry about someone catching me and screaming 'TERRORIST!' in my face. Yeah, that'd be pretty sweet.

I made my way down to my first group counselling class. The room was a mixture of Perspex furniture and that weird suede-like carpeting which lined the floors and some of the walls, like a comfortable beige mould.

Eden was sitting in the middle of a group of girls, obviously the leader of whatever clique she had going on. I vaguely recognised a couple of her friends from the secret room beneath the Rec, as they'd been orbiting Eden then as they were now.

I caught her eye as I walked in. There was a flash of slippered feet as she stretched them out from beneath the clear desk and crossed them at the ankles. A glance at her face told me she'd done it purely so that I'd get a good look at her legs. I tried not to grin as I went to sit at my allocated desk. Eden didn't say much during the session, just sat picking at her brightly coloured fingernails and staring out of the window when the counsellor wasn't looking in her direction.

'Mason?'

I flinched, realising I'd been caught staring at Eden when I should have been writing a log in my journal or something. When I looked up, I found Lyle peering at me like a vulture. I hadn't even noticed he was the one leading the session.

'Counsellor?'

'Are you feeling unwell?' he asked.

'No, Counsellor.'

'Then please try to concentrate,' he said, bringing up an idea stream on the central monitor. Words and images pulsed together, creating a subliminal imprint that would make forgetting the lesson almost impossible. Well, unless you had a little Pi to help the memory on its way. This stream about the schedules of reinforcement in behaviourism was a lesson I'd already had seared into my brain back in Nepalia, so I dared another glance at Eden.

17

Lyle turned with almost preternatural speed and glared at me with his small, beady eyes. 'Whatever behaviour you got away with in other communities will not be tolerated here. Do you understand me, Mason?'

I focused every ounce of the rage I was feeling into my glare before answering. 'Yes, Counsellor.'

He gave me his underwhelming smile again. 'Good. And call me Lyle. I prefer to be free of barriers in this classroom.'

What a twat.

Across the room, Eden crossed her eyes and mimed blowing her brains across the desk. I laughed sharply, then tried to stifle it with a cough. When I looked at her again, Eden had ducked her head as though concentrating intently on her monitor, but a slight hitch in her shoulders gave her away.

'Distraction diverts us from the path of enlightenment,' Lyle snapped, then turned back to the idea stream.

Letting my second tab of Pi dissolve under my tongue later that afternoon, I felt the drug surge through my body. I spiralled through the suddenly liquid air of my quarters, the inevitable contact with the walls creating tingling sparks where they touched the bare skin of my upper body. As the momentum of the wave dissipated, I ended up staring at the shielded glass of the window.

In the darkness outside, my own face looked back at me.

It was surrounded by dazzling points of light. My reflection stretched his arms wide, communicating to me how free he felt to be outside, floating with the stars.

Lucky bastard.

Tilting my head, I watched my counterpart's face become a smooth white marble. I leaned closer and felt the warm tingling of my breath as it bounced back from the window, misting my reflection. When I came back into view, my face was almost back to normal. Only my dark eyes now shone white. They were two brilliant stars locked behind the glass, blinding me to anything but their light. After a moment, the twin lights seemed to harden – like they, too, had turned to marble. They dropped from my reflection like eggs from a nest. I jerked forward to see them land in the water and smacked my head against the window, reactivating my audio implant at the same time, and found that my door buzzer was blaring.

Jolting upright, I purged the Pi from my system with the handheld unit and kicked anything incriminating under my bed.

'Door unlock,' I said, activating the mechanism so that the door swooshed open as I strolled over to it, throwing on a shirt and feeling a little light-headed after nutting the window and purging in rapid succession. I'd expected it to be Ari checking up on me, but instead found Eden waiting outside.

Her pupils were so dilated that her hazel eyes looked

black – an unnerving counterpoint to my very recent hallucination.

'You look a bit Pi-eyed,' I said.

'Ha!' She laughed, a bit too loudly. 'You're funny.'

'Do you want to come in?' I said, worried that someone would hear her and call Security.

'Na-ah.' She wagged a finger with a vivid purple nail towards the sensor unit above my apartment door. 'Don't want to alert the old man. I think you should come out to play.' Before I could say anything, she pulled me out through the doorway into the corridor. 'You don't mind, do you?'

'Not at all,' I said, just as she reached up and touched my lips.

'Open,' she said, sliding two fingers into my mouth. I could taste the bitterness of the Pi coating her skin and felt it course back into my system. I closed my eyes and floated up towards the ceiling.

'Follow me,' she whispered, so close I could feel the heat of her skin, and yet far away at the same time. Her footsteps rattled off down the corridor, magnified by the drug. My eyes and feet followed shortly afterwards as Eden's magnetic pull kicked in.

As I wasn't yet familiar with the layout of Alteria, I couldn't tell where we were heading as we ran along corridor after corridor, careful never to pass through a doorway. I trailed my fingers along the fuzzy walls. The friction burned my fingertips, the lettering of the affirmations zipping by and reminding me to 'welcome knowledge and know nirvana' before turning into whippy little black snakes which chased and snapped at my fingers. I pulled my hand away and focused on following Eden.

After what felt like hours but could have been seconds, we came to a stop at a door marked *restricted access*.

'Come on,' I beckoned her away, 'we can't go in there.'

Eden smiled, her eyes and teeth once more pulsing blue and green. I blinked a few times, and they returned to their normal white.

'We can with this,' she said, pulling a card from her tunic. 'We can be like ghosts.'

Like wraiths, I thought. Then I saw what she was holding. It looked like a security override card – I'd been around enough security guards to know. 'Where did you get that? What's in there?' I asked, my words coming out tangled.

'It's okay,' Eden said. 'The card scrambles the door's ID sensor for a few seconds.' She leaned forward, and her skin became fuzzy with golden auras. 'I stole it from my dad. He's Chief of Security. Didn't I say?'

Before I could answer, she had swiped the card against the access panel, turning the display screen to static.

'Take a deep breath and run,' she said as the door opened into darkness.

Some way ahead, I heard a dull roar. As Eden ran

forward into the darkness, I realised I only had a couple of seconds before the ID sensor came back online and recognised me – as well as the Pi in my system. I took a breath, tapped off my audio implant, and ran after her.

The rushing wind enveloped me as I was launched straight up. Faster and faster, the air knocked from my lungs like I'd been sucker-punched. After a few seconds it grew brighter in the tunnel. I angled myself in the airstream towards the source of the light, and up ahead I saw stars.

Strange, I don't remember there being stars inside the ark.

I reached out, ready to grab the stars, only to feel a hand taking mine. Eden pulled me out of the airstream and we both landed in a heap.

The ground beneath us felt cool and prickly. Grass, I realised. We'd landed in the arboretum. There was an arboretum at the very top of every ark – a vast dome covering a zoo of flora, acting as the lungs of the entire structure.

'What the … hell … just happened?' I said, casually tapping the spot near my ear as I rolled onto my side. The hum of the shield buzzed back to life inside my head.

'We flew … through the air system,' Eden said. I already knew we'd just travelled through the central line of the air purification system, carried on a current of waste carbon dioxide all the way up the centre of the ark, but I'd asked her anyway, needing a moment for my brain to unscramble. 'But that's not what I … wanted to show you.

Look,' she said, her chest still heaving in a way that wasn't exactly terrible to watch. She laughed. 'No, look *there*.'

Eden pushed my shoulder so I lay flat on my back again, resting her head next to mine as she pointed up at the dome. I blinked at the stars spread like raindrops over the clear roof above us. They seemed to pulse, brighter than I'd ever seen them before. But that was probably just the Pi talking.

'Aren't they incredible? Like God's promise to us that there's more out there – more than we can even begin to understand,' she said. She was grinning, so I decided she was having herself a little Pi-epiphany. 'When I look up at the stars, I feel like I can see the future.'

I breathed deep, not saying anything. We lay side by side, her little finger just overlapping mine. The smell of plant life filled my lungs, somehow fresh and rotten at the same time, individual scents of the shadowy shapes around us all mingling together.

Eden sat up suddenly, then brushed herself off and pulled me up. My head felt foggy, but like it did after a purge, not when the Pi was working its magic.

'What happened to the Pi?' I asked her.

'Oh, the door took it,' she said, then must have seen the startled look on my face. 'Don't worry – the scrambler card makes sure Security can't ID the person it came from. Dad won't be sending his guys out after us. Come on,' she said, then disappeared into the wilderness.

I could see enough to find my way to a path winding around the perimeter of the arboretum, and followed the sound of her moving through the towering greenery. Finally, I came into a clearing. Square edges marked off excruciatingly neat plant beds. Eden stood in the middle of one, treading a ripe tomato into the soil with her bare foot. A smile crept onto my face.

'Have you got something against tomatoes?' I asked her.

'*Tomatoes.*' She mimicked my softened vowels and hard consonants.

'You're getting dirty.' I nodded my head to her bare foot, covered in the juicy innards of the fruit. For a second, I imagined her lying in the plant beds as I licked the residue from her toes. Just for a second.

'I'm helping the plants to grow,' she said. I didn't believe her. 'Spreading the seeds around.'

'I don't think – '

A wave of orange light swept over us. It only lasted a second, but it was quickly followed by a distant boom that made my implant buzz with feedback. My first thought was that a thunderstorm had somehow snuck up on us, but that hadn't been lightning. Another flash made it look like the whole arboretum was on fire.

'What's going on?' I said.

'It's just Rats.' Eden showed no trace of the cold fear now clenching my guts. 'It'll be over soon. Want to watch?'

Without waiting for an answer, she took my hand and

led me over to a point where the dome met the grassy floor. From there, we could see the ocean below us. Floating half-submerged, six or seven small vessels were in an attack formation.

Rat subs.

My heart thumped a tattoo inside my ribs. Everyone feared the Rats, but I had a special reason to loathe them. I'd survived the massacre at Cardis, where I'd been living with my family until Rats wiped out our entire community.

I'd been eight at the time. Hiding in a closet with my VR game gear on when I was supposed to be in class, I had no clue what was happening when a white-hot pain shot through my skull, and everything went quiet. The noise-blocking headset had saved my life, but not my hearing.

My dad and Ari had been off-ark when it happened, collecting sea samples for one of her school projects, I think – I hadn't really been paying attention when they told me where they were going – but when they got back to Cardis, they found the corridors littered with corpses, and me huddled next to my mother's body with my ears bleeding. The terrorists had used a sonic blast so strong it left the Rats themselves permanently deafened, even outside the ark in their shielded subs. That unexpected backlash was the only reason Dad managed to get me and Ari out before they swarmed the ark and took Cardis for themselves. The Rats didn't use sonic weapons after that. They never stopped attacking, though.

I could see their gun masts pointed at Alteria now, and I backed away from the clear barrier.

'Don't worry, the shields can handle it,' Eden said as another orange blast lit the arboretum. The missile hit the side of the ark a few levels below us, the flames billowing across the outer shielding just a few metres from our faces. Sparks trailed off into the night before petering out. But I felt no heat, no shaking through the floor.

'What the hell kind of shielding do you have here?' I asked. Eden shrugged.

'The good kind. Look, they're bringing them in now.'

Something shot out from the side of the ark, a dark tail trailing behind it. It hit the nearest vessel, punching through the side of the Rats' corroded hull, and started dragging the sub towards Alteria's docking bay.

'Is that a grapple?' I asked, leaning forward to see better, but only succeeded in turning my hair into a ball of static against the inner shield. It snapped and hissed through my implant, and I shut it off before I even thought to check whether Eden was watching. But she wasn't looking my way. She stared out at the vessels being hauled in one after another, a thoughtful look on her face.

'They're lucky,' she said, her mouth moving silently now, although I could read her lips perfectly well from this angle. Even so, I had the feeling she was talking more to herself than to me.

'What do you mean?'

Eden glanced at me sharply, then her mouth softened into a smile. 'Right now, they believe we're their enemies. But soon they'll be a part of our community.'

'You take in Rats?' I didn't even try to hide my disbelief. Nobody took in Rats. They were the screw-ups who'd been turned away from every ark and left to die in the dust. That was why they hated the communities enough to want to annihilate them, or take them by force.

'We have been lately,' Eden said, and turned back to the barrier. There were no more vessels out there now, every last one seized and swallowed, as though the ark were some kind of kraken.

The ocean rippled gently. I could almost believe the Rats had never been out there at all.

'But don't worry, Mason. They're not allowed to mix with us. You're safe here. We're all safe.'

Perhaps I would have believed her if she hadn't been gripping my hand so tightly.

CHAPTER THREE

Sector 24

Beth blinked through her dark goggles, trying to make out any sign of life outside the vehicle. It had always been a wasteland, but now all she saw was the burning crater where the most recent bomb had hit, the already bleak expanse swallowed by a blanket of dust and smoke. Nothing grew there. The trees were all withered and twisted, any grass that might once have covered the ground long since taken by the breeze. The charred landscape held the scars of civilisation at its least civilised, now nothing but dirt and debris.

'We should go,' Saul said from behind her in the roach's cab, his breath moist on Beth's neck. She edged away.

'We can't just leave Michael out there.'

'Don't see why not. It's not like he's a real person.'

She could hear Saul's sneer without even looking at him. Another blast rocked the roach, further away but still too damned close. The armoured vehicle lurched on its six legs, but managed to regain its balance.

'Not. Yet.' Her mouth set in a firm line, one hand hovering near her gun. Saul rolled his eyes.

'Fine…' His voice trailed off as Beth hurried past him to the rear hatch of the roach. Saul followed just in time to see Michael striding out from the dust cloud. His feet moved steadily despite the rising wind, as though the body draped across his shoulders weighed nothing.

Michael carried the unconscious boy past Beth and Saul, laying him flat on one of the bunks at the back of the roach. As soon as his weight hit the bunk, the boy's eyes flew open. Sucking in panicked breaths he scanned his surroundings until his gaze settled on Beth.

'I'm here for you!' the stranger whispered urgently.

Beth gasped and stepped back, but the boy had already lapsed back into unconsciousness.

'What did he mean, Michael? Why did he…'

But even as Michael faced them, Beth and Saul had already fallen silent. They weren't watching Michael now. Everything was still, even the wind, as they stared blindly for five-point-two seconds. Then they blinked, movement returning to their limbs. They looked curiously at the young man on the bunk as though they had never seen him before that moment.

'This is Noah. We rescued him from the enemy. Now he will be staying with us.'

Michael's companions nodded mutely before taking their places in the vehicle as though nothing unusual had occurred. Michael started the roach. It creaked and groaned as it picked its way, insect-like, over the terrain.

Michael never forgot where the mines were, no matter how the ground shifted and tore apart beneath them. He never forgot anything.

Unlike the others.

Noah sat up with a jerk, headbutting the metal plating above the bunk with a dull clang. Ignoring the sick-making movement of the vehicle, he leaned back on his elbows and scanned the compartment. He saw two men. One was driving the vehicle, the other wedged into a bunk across from him. There was also a girl sitting up front, humming tunelessly along with whatever was playing on her headphones as she checked her gun clip. Through the windshield, Noah watched the dull landscape beneath them, punctuated by flares of light as missiles obliterated what already lay wasted.

What is this hell I'm in?

He flinched at the colossal *thud* as something hit the roof of the vehicle and bounced off.

'Dud scud,' the man on the opposite bunk said.

'Where am I?' Noah addressed the space rather than anyone in particular. The driver grated a lever upwards and pressed a switch on the dash, making the vehicle jerk sharply to the right.

'You are currently on board a roach,' the driver called

over his shoulder, 'an extreme-terrain vehicle, travelling north through Sector 24, Northern Hemisphere.'

Noah understood the words, but what they meant for him, in this situation, was a mystery. His stomach flipped over as the vehicle seemed to defy gravity for a second. It landed sharply, almost throwing him from the bunk. Through the rear window he glimpsed a wide split in the earth falling away behind them, its edges crumbling inward like teeth in a rotting skull.

'Why am I here?' he tried again.

The driver remained facing front, but lifted one hand to snag the wire of the girl's headphones from her ears. 'I'm a little busy here. Can you take care of him for a minute?'

Her eyes darted to Noah, lighting up orange as yet another fireball mushroomed in the distance.

A girl who looks like she's already seen too much at … *sixteen? Seventeen?*

She interrupted Noah's thoughts before he could decide. 'I'm Beth. Look, I'm sorry, I know how weird this feels. Michael here,' she pointed with her thumb towards the driver, 'will answer all your questions when we get back to the house. At the moment, though, we're travelling through a field of concealed mines, with the enemy raining down pearly-gate specials on our heads, so he needs to be thinking about that and not turning around for a chat, 'kay?'

'Michael!' the tall guy yelled as the vehicle jerked suddenly. Noah flinched away from him. 'Stop driving like a little bitch, can't you?' He strode forward to the control station, pulling the girl from the passenger seat. She shot him a fierce look like she would rather fight him for the seat than withdraw, but finally took the vacant spot on the bunk.

The driver spoke without moving his eyes from the view out front. 'Saul, I'm trying to retrace our previous course through this minefield, but there has been some ground disturbance since we last came this way. It is making it difficult to find a clear path.'

'Where are you taking me?' Noah tried again. 'Who's trying to kill us?'

Michael looked at the boy just as the vehicle tilted sharply to one side. He faced front again with neck-snapping speed.

Saul turned on Noah with a snarl. 'Say one more fucking word, pal. I dare you.'

'But I…'

In three strides Saul had reached the bunks, grabbed Beth's gun, and cold-cocked the boy back into unconsciousness. He handed the gun back to Beth before returning to his seat.

'What?' he asked testily as Michael shot him a disapproving glance. 'He's just another problem we don't need.'

*

Noah sat rubbing the lump on his head as the roach settled outside a very old and partly burned-out house. There were a number of small outbuildings surrounding it, like it had once been some kind of farm.

He clambered down from the roach after the others. The vehicle's hull was pitted and blackened in places, as though it had crawled up from some fiery pit, and six thick legs shot out from the sides. It looked very much like the insect it had been named after, Noah decided. He backed away from it warily.

'Where are we?' Noah looked around to see Beth striding towards the house.

'This is our place. It's not much, but it's safe enough,' she said, without breaking her stride. Noah made an effort to keep up with her.

'I don't understand… I don't recognise this place… Hey!' He caught her by the elbow. Beth looked down at where he touched her arm, instinctively pulling away, but giving him a puzzled look as though she'd only just noticed he was there. 'Just take a minute, please,' he said, 'and tell me what's going on. Preferably without pistol-whipping me.'

'Ask the robot,' she snapped, exhaling through her nose impatiently. 'I really don't know what to tell you.'

'Robot?'

She pointed to the driver. 'That's him. Michael!' she

called. 'Come and talk to this boy. He's getting on my last nerve.' Beth walked off ahead with a look that told him not to try speaking to her again anytime soon.

Michael gestured towards the door Beth had just disappeared into. 'Please come inside,' he said, 'and I'll explain what I can.'

Noah closed his eyes, trying to gather his thoughts into a logical order.

'So, I have been ... *rescued* from the enemy holding camp in the middle of a war?'

'Yes,' Michael replied. They sat around a fireplace, in front of which Saul lay snoring.

'But who *are* the enemy, and why can't I remember anything about this war? Or even about myself?'

Noah sat in a drawing room which, despite the general grime and disorder of the place, was remarkably intact. Old portraits stood in shattered frames on the mantle – people he didn't recognise – but their clothes appeared to be the same style as the ones which he and the others all wore.

'The enemy are insurgents. Those who would seek to destroy knowledge,' Michael said, as though he had spoken the words so many times they had lost all meaning. 'Their weapons create pockets of gamma-4 radiation. Anyone exposed to one of these pockets suffers intermittent memory loss.'

'So I was exposed? That's why I can't remember anything?'

Michael nodded.

'Gamma-4 has a staggered impact on the brain. It wipes an individual's memory sporadically, although it happens less frequently over time, and should eventually stop altogether.'

Noah considered this. 'How do you know who I am?'

'Pull back your right sleeve and look at your wrist.'

He did as instructed, pulling his sleeve up past his elbow to reveal a word and a series of numbers in block markings across the underside of his wrist. Above the tattoo, a red band of skin stretched around his forearm. It looked like it had been tied with a burning rope. Noah ignored it, focusing instead on the tattoo. He thought he saw some trace of confusion pass over Michael's face, but it was gone so quickly that he couldn't be sure.

'That's your name and serial number,' Michael added. 'It says when and where you were born.' He held up his own wrist, showing that he too had a mark. 'Mine's blue, which means it's more of a production date than a birth date.'

'This says my name is Noah?'

Michael nodded, frowning. 'Tell me, do you have *any* sense, any memory, of who you are? Of how you got that mark around your arm?'

Noah thought about it, then shook his head. 'Should I?'

Michael continued, ignoring the question. 'Nothing

feels … familiar to you?' He nodded towards the boy's clasped hands. 'What about your serial number? Does anything seem unusual about that?'

Noah saw nothing familiar or particularly unusual about it.

'I knew someone else called Noah,' Michael said. Noah rolled the name around in his head. Was it familiar? Not at all. But it would do, he supposed. 'He had the same birthdate as you,' Michael continued. Noah looked up to find the android studying him with his pale eyes. 'And he looked like you, only … different.'

'You think I might be him?' Michael made a non-committal sound. 'You're not sure?'

'Not sure, no. When he left, I didn't expect I'd ever see him again.' Michael extended his hand. 'But either way, I'm pleased to meet you, Noah.'

CHAPTER FOUR

Alteria Community

Lyle had a private room for one-to-one Prep Therapy sessions. When he signalled for me to come in, he was busy poring over my transfer scripts.

The room was small, with only two chairs and a desk. As Lyle was very tall and lean, he had the look of a grasshopper crouching behind his desk. A frosted false window faced me, indicating that this room was on the interior of the ark, with a light behind it pretending to be the sun.

After running through the standard faith greetings I'd reluctantly memorised, Lyle gestured for me to have a seat. I tried to appear relaxed. A little bored, even. But the truth was I'd been on edge ever since seeing how Alteria dealt with Rats, and the casually brutal way they'd seized those vessels and hauled them inside the ark. It was as though Alteria had been lying in wait for them. I'd never been in any community that could withstand a missile assault like that – like their bombs were no more than tumbleweeds.

Knowing how strong Alteria's defences were should have made me feel safe, protected. For some reason it didn't.

'I've been reading through the notes of some of your previous sessions,' Lyle said. 'There is a lot of interesting information here.'

I said nothing.

'Shall we pick up from where you left off with your last counsellor?' he asked with a friendly head tilt – a gesture vastly overused by shrinks in general. 'I believe you were discussing the difficulty you seem to have establishing yourself within the communities you have lived in…?'

'I'm settling in fine here.'

Lyle sat silently for a minute and waited for me to continue. Finally, he checked the data pad.

'But that hasn't always been the case, has it? I would like to hear where you believe things may have started to go wrong for you.'

Well, there was no good way to answer that. There had been a six-month period when I was thirteen that all my counsellors liked to fixate on. The six months had started when I first started dabbling with Pi – which was unfortunately on my record – and ended when my recklessness got my dad killed. It was after Dad died and Ari became my guardian that I got my implant, and the headaches and nausea that came with it, and my Pi abuse became a full-time retreat. That wasn't written in his data pad, though. At least I hoped not.

I looked at Lyle, slouching in his hard-backed office chair. 'I'm not sure what I can tell you that I didn't already tell my last counsellor.'

He gave me a cold look, exhaling through his nose so hard I expected it to whistle.

'Why don't you tell me what happened around the time your father passed away?' he said, then jabbed a finger at his data pad. 'It appears things became more turbulent for you around that time.'

This particular dark spot in my life was every counsellor's second port of call, so I wasn't surprised. But none of them knew what had really led to it.

There'd been a grungy little cubby back in Parisia, hidden away in the bowels of the ark, where the users went to get high. Everyone knew it was there, but as long as the users stayed out of sight and didn't venture out among the general population when they were off their cakes, they were left alone.

Dallan, Eli, and I had gone down there on a dare the first time. It was a filthy little hole, full of half-naked addicts doing a variety of disgusting things to each other under the drug's influence. They mostly ignored the three wide-eyed boys staring around, until one of the sweaty hags grabbed hold of me and kissed me hard on the mouth. I'd pushed her away, freaked out, but not before a tiny amount of Pi was transferred through her sour spit into my mouth. Suddenly, I was floating, my insides turned to candyfloss. The ugly weight of missing my mother lifted. It didn't matter that I'd had to hide a part of myself away for the last five years, terrified I'd get my family exiled to the wastes outside just by being deaf. The constant awareness of the glass cage surrounding me was gone, and I felt free.

I knew the risks. You had to get it out of your system within hours if you didn't want to risk major organ failure, and getting hold of the tech to build a handheld purge unit wasn't easy. There was also the danger of being caught with it ... but the relief Pi offered outweighed all of that. With one disgusting kiss, the drug had me.

We spent a lot of time hanging around that cubby over the next few weeks. Different people wandered in and out, none of them particularly bothered that we were there, but not offering us any of their Pi either. I kept an eye out for the woman I'd seen the first time, but she never reappeared. Dallan had even asked one of the regulars where we could get hold of some stuff, but the guy just laughed and told us to piss off.

As I was the only one who'd tried Pi at this point, it somehow fell to me to get hold of some for Dallan and Eli to try. We lounged around, waiting for an opportunity.

I'd almost given up hope when I noticed a man sitting nearby, his back propped against the wall, eyes closed. He was sweating so hard he'd left a grease mark from his head on the wall panel. I was mid-retch when I noticed it: a whole capsule of Pi just sitting there in his limp, damp palm. It was practically waving to me.

I gestured to the others to make a discreet exit and waited for them to disappear. When I was alone with the guy, I casually walked over and stood with my back against the wall next to him. With the toe of my boot I nudged his hand to see if he would stir. He didn't. I took one last look to check that the exit was clear, bent down, and took the capsule out of his hand. Without looking back, I walked as casually as I could to the door.

Pulse thrumming in my temples, I expected the vibration of heavy footsteps to rattle through the grille flooring at any second, a sweaty hand clamping on my arm. But none came. As soon as I was out of sight, I broke into a run and went to meet the lads, ready to be hailed a hero.

'I've put all that behind me now,' I hedged, not sure how much detail there was in the file Lyle was studying.

'Right, I see.' He looked again at the data pad, searching for more scabs to pick. 'How did you feel when you found out that your father was deceased?'

Pretty fucking bad, obviously.

'It was a difficult time,' I said. His eyes flickered to mine, seeming at last to sense some hostility.

'I believe there may be a lot more we need to work through regarding your self-destructive behaviour after his death.' Lyle leaned forward, waiting for me to pick up the thread. When I didn't, he pushed on. 'Are you still using contraband substances?'

'No,' I lied.

He smiled in a way that made his nose eclipse his mouth. 'Of course, you realise that *any* mind-altering substance is strictly prohibited in Alteria?'

It sounded like a question, but I knew it really wasn't. 'Drugs are prohibited in every community.'

The smile grew impossibly smarmier. 'A person not in control of his own mind is not pursuing His Eternal Truth.'

I could think of several decent counter-arguments to that, but I knew when to keep my mouth shut. Mostly.

After a moment's silence, Lyle decided to change tack. 'How are you finding life here in Alteria?'

'Just dandy.'

'And you are making friends?' Lyle looked at the false window as if he were asking the question with only casual interest.

'Yes.'

'Are you forming any … intimate relationships?' he asked, still focused on some fascinating portion of the false window.

'Not at the moment,' I replied carefully. I had no idea whether casual sex was also 'prohibited' in this freak-show community. I'd gotten a pretty strange reaction when I'd walked into the medical bay and asked for condoms, though – I swear the kid covering the reception had blown dust from the pack before he handed it to me. It only occurred to me later that Alteria's purge system would take care of the need to use condoms entirely.

Lyle took a good few seconds to consider before he asked his next question. 'Tell me, Mason, how many people *have* you had sexual intercourse with?'

Most counsellors asked this at some point, although they were generally less blunt about it.

'Today?' I asked, raising an eyebrow.

'In all.' Lyle's voice betrayed a hint of annoyance – a tiny fracture in his control. Interesting.

'I don't see why that's important,' I said.

'Isn't it?' He made a note on the data pad.

I sighed, and picked a number that I thought sounded reasonable. 'Five.'

His eyes zeroed straight back in on mine. They were pale blue in colour, so pale that his irises looked transparent. I hadn't seen anyone else with eyes like that in Alteria. Their translucence felt like a statement: *I'm an open book, no secrets here.* I wondered if Lyle wore coloured contact lenses just to give that impression, the pretentious twat.

'Five?' He practically spat the word.

Not a reasonable number, then.

'That isn't what it says here.' Lyle pointed to the data file.

'So you didn't need to ask,' I said.

Lyle leaned back in his chair, a flush creeping up from the collar of his tunic. 'You should know that such … *indiscriminate* behaviour will not be tolerated here. While disease and unwanted pregnancies aren't a concern, thanks to our superior technology' – my guts churned at his smug expression – 'moral purity is as important as the physical. Habitual transgressions are met with the most intensive rehabilitation. Do we understand one another?'

I nodded. The silence grew dense between us.

'All right, Mason, what would you like to talk about?' he said at last.

I didn't like the way he said my name. His lips formed the word with the same expression people use to spit.

'How about the importance of personal space?' I offered.

'These sessions *are* your personal space, and it is important that you make the best use of them. I'm sure you are aware that you can only apply for a Citizen card if you complete your final year of Preparatory Therapy with a clean bill of mental health.' He paused, giving me a thin smile. 'I am sure you wouldn't want to repeat the year.'

The prick had me backed into a corner, and he knew it. I sighed.

'Fine. Let's talk.'

CHAPTER FIVE

Alteria Community

It was almost an hour later when I took the lift up to the arboretum, squinting as I stepped through the doorway into the fading afternoon light. Before I started running along the path that circled the immaculate jungle, I could hear my own breathing a little too loudly inside my head, terse and shallow. But it felt necessary, somehow, so I didn't turn off the implant.

I ran anticlockwise, starting to feel better as my breathing settled into the same steady rhythm as my footsteps. I kept running, losing count of the laps after an hour or so.

When I got back to my quarters, there was a message written on my door. *Gift inside*, it said. It had the yellow imprint of a kiss underneath. My heart, still beating fast from my run, pushed up the pace another notch as I pressed a command on the interface panel next to the door and checked for signs of life inside my room. None showed up on the scan.

Damn.

I deactivated the door lock, noticing that the message disappeared as the door swooshed open, taken by the purge system. Inside, the lighting had been set so that most of the room was in darkness. Only a section of the wall was highlighted near the bed, now transformed from its previous beige uniformity. The painting was abstract and beautiful. In the centre, the life-sized spectre of Eden already seemed to strobe blue and green as I moved closer, just as she had the first time I saw her in the Rec. Parts of the painting were clearly imprints of her actual limbs, conjuring mental images of her naked, covering herself in paint in my quarters. I wished I'd taken a shorter run.

Reaching behind the wall panel for a tab of Pi, I kept my eyes on the painting as I let it dissolve under my tongue. The colours started to move on their own now, fuelled by the drug in my system. The image danced in time to the pulse pounding in my skull. She was there, inside my head, and it felt amazing.

I watched from the bed as my wraith's hair flickered against the smooth lines of her upstretched arms. She undulated like a flame, closer and closer. I let my eyes drift shut as she reached out to me, sinking into the imagined feel of her – the hot spark of electricity. Not one part of me doubted that Eden had known the kind of evening I'd be having with her gift. It made it so much easier to imagine that the hand touching me was hers and not my own.

When I awoke, the dim light of early morning hurt my eyes, and I jolted upright. I'd forgotten to purge the Pi from my system.

I snatched at the panel covering my secret purge unit, trying to ignore the stabbing pains in my chest. I'd souped up my patch'n'piece unit so that even the minutest trace of Pi would be purged instantly through my pores, but I still ran it over my body a few times to be sure. Once it was done, I checked the read-out on the unit. I stared at the display, not understanding what I was seeing.

Pi particulates purged = zero.

What the hell? Was it broken?

Something shifted on the bed next to me, and I jerked, knocking the purge unit off my bedside table as I turned to see who or what was in my quarters.

The painted Eden had returned to her original position on my bedroom wall and the real Eden was lying propped on one elbow beside me. I could tell she was fully clothed under the bedsheets, her stolen security pass discarded on the floor.

'I purged you when I came in last night,' she said silently. It took a few seconds for the words to hit home. Eden had purged me. If she hadn't, I'd probably have massive internal bleeding by now.

Shit.

I pretended to rub sleep from my eyes so I could

activate my implant with my thumb, and I missed a little of what she said next.

'…nasty if you don't purge real quick. But you know that.'

I forced my bunched muscles to relax. I was fine, no damage done. There was no point making a big deal about it.

'Not that I don't appreciate the save, but … what are you doing here?' I said, throwing in a smile as an afterthought.

'I felt restless, and wanted to see you.' Eden shrugged. 'But when I arrived you looked kind of out of it, so I let you sleep.'

I raised an eyebrow. This wasn't exactly the first time I'd woken up with someone else in my bed, but I usually remembered how they'd got there.

'So we didn't…?' I let the question hang, knowing perfectly well that we hadn't spent the night having wild sex. Pi might leave me a little fuzzy-headed, but there was no way it'd make me forget something like *that*.

Eden's face flushed, but she tried to hide it with a yawn that somehow involved her whole body. 'Sorry to break it to you, but you were a complete gentleman.'

I brushed the hair from Eden's face with my hand, enjoying the small sound she made as she stretched and settled back down, her eyes drifting closed.

'Doesn't sound like me,' I said, but if she heard me, she gave no sign.

I waited until her breathing took on the steady rhythm of sleep, then slid out of bed. Now that I knew my organs weren't burned full of holes, I was starting to feel almost human again, if a little twitchy. I'd been in the shower a few minutes when I heard the computer's voice over the hiss of steam.

'CleanSweep activated.'

I turned off the water and listened. The static buzz coming from the next room told me that the computer was in the process of cleaning my quarters, but there was no sound of Eden's breathing. Making sure not to cross the threshold while the CleanSweep was doing its thing, I ducked my head into the doorway to the bedroom. Eden had already left.

As I watched, a coffee cup I had used the previous day was emptied of its contents and left clean on the floor. My bed sheets lost their rumpled appearance, becoming smooth and fresh again. Any dust or dirt I'd managed to accumulate in the past twenty-four hours was broken down by the CleanSweep, parsed to more useful particles, and sucked up into the air filters.

Then my painted Eden began to vanish from the far wall, her toes and ankles bleeding their colour and returning to muted beige. The sweep chased slowly up the length of her body, until at last her head and outstretched arms disappeared noiselessly into the light.

I'd almost finished faffing about in the bathroom when a message from my sister flashed up on the vox I'd left sitting on my bedside table since the day we arrived.

Meet me for breakfast – my quarters @9:30.

I finished dressing and combed my hair back in the mirror. After my night's adventures, the skin around my eyes looked sallow, some faint lines beginning to wear a path in the corners. With one hard night of bingeing, I had undone all the good work the doors had done with my skin.

Not looking so fresh, I said to myself. *Need to cut back on the Pi.*

I went down the hallway to my sister's quarters and pressed the intercom.

As usual, she'd filled her space with mounds of useless junk. Ari tended to theme the decor of her quarters around traditional colours and fabrics from the old countries that'd been around before the formation of the World States – a quirk she'd inherited from our mother. So far, over the course of our various moves to different places, she had recreated rooms from ancient Greece, Egypt, early twentieth-century Britain, Mexico, Jamaica and France. This time, she'd opted for a distinctly Japanese theme. It suited her, somehow.

As much as I wanted to get out, Ari needed to find a place to fit in. And this was her way of making a space for herself. I got it – really I did. Even if it meant I whapped my head on a low-hanging paper lantern on my way in.

'It feels like I've hardly seen you in weeks!' Ari caught me in a surprisingly strong hug, nearly choking me on the cloud of her white-blonde hair.

'I saw you yesterday.'

She leaned back and frowned for a second, trying to remember. 'Saying good morning in the corridor is hardly quality time.'

'Are we having quality time this morning, Ari?' I asked, smiling.

She gestured for me to take a seat at the breakfast table as she drifted around the room a bit more, not doing anything much – all curly hair and perfume. It was weird, but when she was in her own environment, my sister was the exact opposite of how you'd imagine an engineer to be. As a kid, even though she was five years older than me, she'd always been the one bugging *me* to play. Especially when we were supposed to be studying. *A champion procrastinator*, Dad had called her. And that part of her had never grown up. Put her in an engine room, though, and she'd instantly adapt to her environment, becoming as much of a well-oiled machine as the ones she worked on. She loved solving problems, fixing things. Maybe that was why she loved me so much.

'Ariadne, come and sit down.'

'Yes, breakfast,' she said, joining me at the table. I poured her some coffee and she smiled. 'It really is good to see you, Mase. I miss your ugly face.'

I gave her an open-mouthed smile, showing her my half-chewed toast. She groaned, then dived into her cereal. Looking after me by herself for the last four years had meant Ari'd had to develop a strong stomach – and infinite patience.

Still chewing, I said to her, 'It's good to see you eating properly.'

'The shifts here are much better. I get more time to look after myself,' she said, adding, 'and the amount of time I save not having to go to the bathroom all the time – well, I just couldn't do without the magic doors now.'

I laughed quietly. *Magic doors.*

Ari leaned in. 'Seriously, though, it's like the people here don't understand the value of their own tech. Who wastes money installing purge systems in *every door*?'

'People who are too uptight to shit?' I offered. Ari smacked me on the arm, but she was laughing. 'I'm glad you like it here.'

'I really do,' she said, then sighed as she looked down into her cereal.

'So do *I*.' A testy note entered my voice that I hadn't meant for her to hear. I knew what was bugging her, and that she hated having this conversation as much as I did. I'd caused her a lot of trouble over the years – not on purpose, but still. It was time to stop. Stop the drugs, the screwing around, all of it. Stop making her look at me with sad, tired eyes.

She'd had those eyes ever since she was thirteen years old, exiled to a grimy sub with just Dad and me. Ari had helped me practise my speech and lip-reading for hours every day, over and over and over again. She'd put up with my shit-fits, my crying for Mum as though Ari hadn't lost her too. She wore down my absolute lack of cooperation until I finally got it right – or at least good enough to go undetected for a while. That was usually enough. Sometimes my teachers would notice, but generally they wrote me off as *that boy who never listens.* Then Dad would quietly arrange for us to move on before they asked too many questions.

'You're a good kid, Mase. And sometimes things happen that are nobody's fault.' Ari paused, as though the lie tasted strange in her mouth. She reached across the table and put her hand on mine. 'But wouldn't you like to fit in, make a real life for yourself?'

I gave her fingers a quick squeeze. 'That sounds like a good idea.'

She sat back, her eyes narrowed. 'You make no promises.'

'I don't want to break them.' I wouldn't lie to her. 'I can apply for a Citizen card in a few months. Once I have it, they won't be able to make you leave because of anything I've done. I'm hoping you'll come with me when they announce which of the communities is going to be the first to set off for New Earth, but you know … I don't *expect* you to come if you don't want to. I know you're not in the same rush to leave that I am.'

She laughed. 'That really wasn't what I meant. I just want to see you keeping out of trouble, and, well … happy. And of course I'll come with you when it's time.' Ari waggled her eyebrows. 'Unless, of course, Alteria's the first to be ready to launch.'

'Yeah, right.'

I was feeling somewhat tense when I checked into the fight simulator at the leisure facility. The whole *last chance, don't fuck it up* thing kept running through my head, and that was usually a sign I was about to *fuck it up* fairly imminently.

I strapped myself in and selected some random martial arts programme, then started working my way through the levels, pounding hell out of one faceless opponent after another. This would normally help to clear my head. Today, I just couldn't shake off the fog. I felt too aware of the walls around me, the sound bouncing back and forth until it pinballed inside my skull, and I couldn't force myself to really let go. After an hour or so of trying to sweat out my frustration, I went back to my quarters and placed a call to Parisia.

'Mason,' Eli's voice grumbled from a dark screen, 'do you know what time it is here?'

'Sorry, man, I forgot about the time difference. I'll give you a call back in a few hours…'

'I'm awake now,' he cut me off. 'How've you been? *Lights on dim*,' he said, activating the lighting in his quarters. His coppery hair was longer than last time I'd seen him, spiralling outwards from his head like a lion's mane. Behind him I could see the peeling green paint on his walls, a dark patch where the hull had sprung a leak at some point, and felt a pang of nostalgia for my old home. 'You in trouble yet?'

'Not yet,' I laughed. 'What's been happening in Parisia?'

'You hear about Dallan?' Eli looked serious – which had me instantly on edge.

'No, is he all right?'

Eli huffed in air through his teeth, shaking his head. 'Sorry, man, I sent you a message but it must have bounced while you were still in transit.' He cleared his throat awkwardly. 'A couple of weeks ago, Dallan got himself messed up on Pi and took a walk out of an airlock. Outside the *shields*. He got a nasty dose of radiation and some sun-damage to his eyes. They sent him away to rehab last week.'

Eli and Dallan were the best friends I had. The fact that I was only just learning this told me I'd been out of touch too long.

'Did he know what he was doing?' I asked.

Eli shrugged, his hair bouncing. 'I don't know, Mase. He's been doing a lot of Pi lately, but maybe that's *because* he's messed up. You know?'

'Yeah,' I replied. *Definitely time to give the Pi a rest.*

'But come on, brighten my day. What have you been up to?'

I laughed. 'This is going to sound so pathetic now. I met a girl.'

'There will be some hysterical sobbing here when your fans find out. So, are you…?' He made a gross gesture.

'No. Well, not exactly. She's … I don't know…' I searched for the words to explain myself in an acceptable way. 'She's just my kind of trouble.'

Eli laughed, showing off the gap in his teeth that girls said made him look sweet. *Yeah, sweet like a bloody shark.* 'You don't leave the drama behind, do you, Mase?'

'I know. I've only been here for a couple of weeks. Do I really want things to go down here the same as in all the other communities? Like with the riots I accidentally started in Nepalia? Or having to leave Daytonia because of that thing with the captain's daughter? Anyway, I'll never get my card if I mess up again.'

Eli shook his head, looking sage. 'You won't get a strike for having fun with a girl. Just keep it off the grid.'

'I suppose so. But how about you? How's life in the lab?' Eli had gotten his Citizen card the previous year, being much smarter than me – and slick enough to get through Prep Therapy with no problems. I had to admit that his final semester had probably gone much more smoothly without my bad influence. It wouldn't have surprised me if Eli's folks had thrown a party the day I got kicked out of Parisia.

Since getting his card, Eli had taken an internship at the biotech lab. He was currently studying how mice bred with genetically lengthened legs coped in a zero-gravity atmosphere. This was both weird and hilarious, and apparently a vital area of study for a people planning to colonise another world.

'It's good,' he said, looking more enthusiastic than he sounded – his voice carefully controlled through years of practice. It made him difficult to read if you didn't know him well. 'We're working on biomedical stasis chambers.'

'What? *Freezing* people?' I asked, surprised.

'Well, freezing rabbits, actually. And technically they're not frozen. They just don't age.'

I laughed. 'Because there's nothing worse than an old rabbit.'

'This is important research. It'll change how we travel to the new world, if we get it right.' Eli's eyes shone with excitement that didn't match his fake-outraged tone.

'Yeah, *if*,' I said.

He snorted. 'Well, I know how my work bores you, so if that's all the drama sorted, I'm going back to bed.' Eli rubbed his eyes to emphasise how he felt at being dragged out of bed early. 'Check in soon though, yeah?'

'Yeah. Let me know how Dallan's doing,' I added.

'I will, man. And keep me up to speed about the girl.

You know I only get to live out my fantasies through you, you handsome bastard. Eli out.'

'Mason out,' I said, laughing as the screen went black.

CHAPTER SIX

Alteria Community

I tried to ignore the snap of my ridiculous Alterian-issue slippers as I loped past a herd of Alterians discussing the morning's 'Lesson', which had just finished blaring over the PA system.

'…tolerate the likes of *him*,' one whispered, not knowing that my ultra-sensitive audio implant would pick up the snark. I shot the weaselly twat a glare and hurried to catch up with Eden.

I'd arranged to meet her after she'd finished her shift running tour groups. Alteria was now letting in enough outsiders to warrant two tours a week, and I wondered about the sudden influx. Judging by the sheer uniformity of the place, Alteria had been sealed tighter than a python's sphincter for decades. So why now, suddenly, were dregs like me being welcomed into the beige utopia?

Eden slipped through the doorway into the arboretum ahead of me. I caught a flash of taupe tunic, swishy black hair, and lips which were bright purple today. I followed her into the jungle, heading for our now usual meeting spot near the tomato beds. Hearing me close behind her, she turned around.

'Mason.' Eden reached up and touched my cheek.

'Why do you do that?' I asked before realising it sounded like I minded it, which I definitely didn't. But she just smiled.

'People don't really touch each other here,' she said. I must have given her some kind of *taking that sexually* look. 'I don't mean like that. I mean … it's just kind of sad that affection, intimacy – those things are looked at as being uncivilised or something. Like we're supposed to have moved past the need for that connection to other people.' I hadn't actually noticed that the Alterians avoided physical contact with one another, but that was probably because I'd assumed they were just avoiding contact with *me*.

'Some things are important enough to hang on to, even when everyone else has let them go, you know? Besides,' she said with a shrug, 'I like you.'

I brushed my fingers across her cheek the same way she had mine. 'I suppose you're not so bad, either.'

Eden laughed. 'Are we flying today?'

I shook my head. I'd decided to steer clear of Pi – at least for a while – after my meeting with Lyle. He'd pricked some paranoid reflex in me with his questions, and speaking with Eli had compounded the idea that it was time to get clean. It was also approaching the anniversary of my father's death, which tended to bring on Pi-related feelings of guilt.

'Let's mooch for a while,' I said, sliding down to sit with my back braced against a pear tree. Eden looked down at me, hands on hips.

'Why so melancholy?'

'I don't know. Just thinking.' I put on a smile. 'Tell me something to distract me.'

'What kind of something?' She came over and knelt next to me on the grass.

'Tell me what you're going to do with your life.'

She considered. 'I'm going to do lots of things.'

'So tell me one of them.'

'Well,' she said, 'I'm going to be a great artist.' There was no cockiness to that statement, but no false modesty either. Just a determination that made me want to kiss her until she felt it from her toes to her eyelashes.

'I did enjoy your work,' I said, remembering the painting she'd done with her own body parts. I cleared my throat and shifted so one arm rested on my bent knee. 'And will you do that here?'

'Yes, of course. I like being with my people in Alteria.' The way she said it – so matter-of-fact, without a moment's hesitation – made me think she'd either spent a lot of time considering this, or none at all.

'You haven't seen any other communities, though, have you?'

Eden shrugged. 'Were the other arks you lived in so different from here?'

I had the urge to snort, but didn't want her to think I was laughing at her. 'A bit, yeah.'

'In what way?' She leaned in, like she really wanted to know. Her hand rested against my thigh. I didn't know if this was accidental or a part of her attempt to drag me out of my grim mood, but it was working, anyway.

'Tell me why you love it here so much,' I said, avoiding her question. Telling her about the communities I'd lived in – and been kicked out of – wasn't a good idea.

Eden cocked her head to one side. 'It's not about the place, it's the people. Alteria is like one big family. We share the same faith, have the same goals. I can't imagine being anywhere without them. So yeah, I'll stay here until we're ready to launch. Then when we reach New Earth, I'll be an artist there. Just think, I could be the first to capture our new home on canvas.' I barely listened to the last part, my attention snagged by the mention of *faith*. I hadn't been raised to give much thought to God or divine plans or whatever. The idea of it all kind of threw me.

'You take Pi.'

Eden laughed at the blunt remark. 'Yeah, and…?'

'I mean, it's just that…' Eden waited. 'Uh, doesn't that kind of go against the whole Alterian faith thing?'

She seemed amused by my squirming. 'Not the way I see it. We believe in learning as much as we can about our universe, and every new discovery brings us closer to the Creator. Taking Pi gives me a different outlook on things, and I don't see why that goes against my faith. It's knowledge I wouldn't have otherwise.'

I don't think many people around here would agree with that, I thought, but kept quiet as she'd started playing with my hair.

'When we get to New Earth, I'm going to find a beach. There will have to be beaches there, don't you think? I've always wanted to walk on real sand.' Her gaze wandered to the clear barrier of the dome. 'What do you think it's like out there now, *outside*?'

Why was she asking me about *outside*? I studied her expression, looking for signs it had been a loaded question. It was possible I'd given myself away somehow, that she'd heard the subtle difference in how I spoke, or she'd seen me jabbing the spot next to my ear when I needed quiet. I'd come close to being caught before, plenty of times. Was she trying to prod me into a confession? Because if she suspected I was deaf, she had to be wondering why I hadn't been offered cloning treatment to repair the damage to my ears right away – it was something any community would do if a child became deafened the way I had. But after Dad dragged Ari and me away from the massacre at Cardis, no community would take us in. None of them believed Dad hadn't been involved in the attack. How else had we managed to escape? Never mind that we'd been forced to leave my dead mother there among the corpses of my friends, my teachers, every person I'd ever known. It took months living in that cramped, sweaty sub before Dad managed to lie our way inside another ark, and by then he'd drilled it into me: *Never let anyone know about your deafness, about what happened. If you do, we'll all be outcast.*

I took a deep breath, still trying to figure out Eden's motives for asking about the wastelands. But all I saw in her face was curiosity.

'I don't think there's anything worth seeing out there anymore,' I said. 'But I wouldn't know. The only *outside* I've seen was through a sub window, going from one ark to another.'

Reports about the state of things outside tended to vary, and had long ago taken on the timbre of myth. The Rats themselves were either pitied or feared, depending on how recently one of their factions had attacked the community you lived in. They were the rejects, the ones who'd been branded as worthless to every community on the planet. And I could easily end up being one of them.

'Aren't you curious? I mean, if you could sneak out there and just take a look around for a few hours, wouldn't you do it?'

Eden shifted until her leg was pressed up against mine, and I was pulled sharply from my thoughts of Rats and rejection. Her bare thighs pulled taut the fabric of her tunic. Eden smirked as she followed my eyeline, and I realised I hadn't answered her question.

'The only outside we'll ever see will be on another planet, probably years from now.'

'Wow, you really do need shaking out of this funk. Do you play TAG?' Eden's face lit up.

I shook my head. I'd never heard of it before.

'This is going to be fun!' she said, taking my hand and dragging me to my feet.

As the door to the pod closed above my head, I had to suppress my panic at being in such a confined space. There was nothing quite as fun as a dark, padded cylinder with concealed nervex tech prickling at my skin as the sensors probed my body. Except for every other thing ever invented.

She's not going to be impressed if you freak out, I told myself, having realised what 'TAG' stood for. *Tunnel Adventure Game* ... shit.

The door opened again, and Eden reached in and handed me a VR helmet. 'Almost forgot,' she said, still grinning. 'I've added a few *custom* settings. I'll tell you the rules once you're plugged in.'

Before I could ask her what she meant, the door snapped shut. I lay back and put the helmet on. Immediately, the inside of the visor lit up, a spectrum of colours flashing in front of my eyes as it configured to my bio-settings. Faint electrical pulses tingled through my nerve endings, starting at my head, then spreading like a wave down my arms and torso, through my groin and legs, all the way down to my feet.

I'd used these kinds of simulators before, but I could already tell that Eden had made some kind of modification to the sensory settings. Just as the last few sparks of electricity passed through my toes, her voice came through the speaker built into the helmet. With my implant's sensitivity, it sounded like Eden was whispering right in my ear. I shivered, closing my eyes.

'Are you ready?' she asked, and my eyelids snapped open again.

'I'm not sure what I'm meant to do,' I admitted.

'Track me through the tunnels. If you catch me, you tag me. First to three wins. It's straightforward, really,' she said, then added, 'but you'll never catch me.'

I laughed at her confidence in that.

'All right, I'm ready.'

'Then … go!'

Immediately the visor image changed to an underground tunnel. I could even smell and feel my surroundings – the sandy floor of the tunnel under my now bare feet, the cold, dank smell of the stagnant air, tinged with smoke from the dim lamps burning at intervals along the tunnel walls.

As I was about to set off running, I felt something like a gale force wind run through my body.

'Tag!' Eden yelled, running ahead almost in a blur. I took a deep breath and went after her.

I was already a strong runner, but in the game every movement was exaggerated by whatever creative settings Eden had applied. I moved like I had jets in my heels. Every sense was heightened, the wind running icy fingers through my hair as I ran, and I could hear my heartbeat thumping like a bass drum inside me. The sound pulled me along as though it was outside my body, but connected by some powerful cable to my chest. I ran faster, following the thud of my heartbeat. But it wasn't my heartbeat, it was the sound of her footsteps in the gloom up ahead. I was catching up.

Eden came into view as the tunnel opened up into a large, round cavern. I chanced a glance and saw that it reached up about ten metres. It was perforated by dozens of dark openings, probably leading to further maze-like tunnel networks. I focused ahead, seeing Eden no more than an arm's length away, and ploughed right through her.

The feeling of *tagging* someone was different from being tagged. My skin tingled as I ran through her, the sensation exciting every cell in my body with adrenaline. Almost without meaning to, I leapt, landing easily in one of the upper-storey tunnel entrances. Exhilarated, I stopped and checked to see if she was following.

Eden was crouched on the floor of the cavern, her head down with one hand on her chest like she was winded. I jumped down and hurried over, worried that I'd hurt her. Just as I was about to reach out, Eden's head flicked upwards. Grinning, she sprang. The whole length of her body passed through my chest, focusing the blow more than the first time. It felt like I'd been hit by a wrecking ball.

'That's two to me!' she called out from somewhere above my head, and I looked up in time to see her disappear into a tunnel on one of the upper levels. I breathed in a lungful of air, suppressed the urge to vomit, and followed.

I leapt to a tunnel running parallel to the one Eden had taken. Sprinting at full speed, I watched to see if her form flashed by at any of the regular intersections between my tunnel and hers. Soon, I began to catch glimpses of her. I slowed to make sure I timed it right. Once I'd put enough distance between us, I veered sharply, crashing through her sideways at the intersection.

'Two!' I called, feeling some satisfaction as I heard Eden shriek with surprise behind me. Adrenaline once more flooded my system, spreading from my toes to my scalp. Not really keeping track of where I was going, I ran on, turning left or right at intervals to give Eden a chance to catch up.

I heard her footsteps chasing after me, getting louder as she closed the gap. I glanced behind me as I rounded a corner. She was nowhere in sight. *Not yet.*

As I faced straight ahead, I realised my mistake. It was

confirmed almost instantly by Eden's laughter bouncing off the tunnel walls.

Dead end.

I stopped, putting my back to the hard rock behind me. Eden slowed to a walk. I thought about making a dart through her, but something about her smile made me want to wait and see what she was planning.

'Hold out your hand,' she said. I turned my palm to face her as I scowled in mock surrender. Eden slowly, carefully, placed her hand so that it was no more than a centimetre from mine. Immediately I felt my skin pulling towards hers. I peered at the space between our palms, seeing the snapping sparks of the electrical charge as it fought to close the gap.

I must have closed my eyes for an instant, because when I opened them, her face was right in front of mine. Her breath felt warm against my lips.

'Tag,' Eden whispered, closing the tiny distance until our mouths became a shower of white-hot sparks.

The scene dissolved, and I was once more aware of the pod's tight confinement. Removing the helmet, I looked up to see the door opening. Eden's face, framed by extremely mussed-up hair, came into view.

'That was fun,' she said, her eyes focused on my mouth. I pretended not to notice as I climbed up through the hatch.

In the normal lighting of the anteroom, I saw that we

were both dripping with sweat. My hair was matted around my face and neck, my shirt soaked through.

'I need a shower,' I said, and looked up to find Eden staring at my chest. 'Want to join me?'

She bit her lip and blushed. I swore silently, wondering if I'd completely misread her interest. Maybe it wasn't *me* she liked. Maybe it was just the novelty of meeting someone – anyone – she hadn't known her whole life.

'Not today, Coulter,' she said at last. 'But I will claim my prize before I take off.'

'Prize?' I studied my feet, trying to remember whether she'd mentioned a prize in her rules. I was startled when her fingers brushed against my lips.

'Show me how a bad boy kisses a girl,' Eden said. Her voice whispered through me like a touch, purging that seed of doubt from my brain just as effectively as the doors got rid of all my other unwanted crap.

I grinned. *This* I could do.

I ran my hand up the warm skin of her arm, watching her eyes follow the movement. A trail of goosebumps rose at my touch. She didn't look away from my fingers until they reached the smooth line of her jaw, tilting her head to where it was at the perfect angle. Then her eyes locked with mine, pupils wide with the same excitement I felt. I couldn't stop the smile playing across my lips as I touched them to hers, couldn't help the way my body reacted to her.

I leaned back against the wall, angling my hips away as I pulled Eden forward to straddle my leg. She gasped, and I used the moment to deepen the kiss, loving how she responded when I slid my tongue against hers, almost losing myself when her hands trembled against my chest.

I eased away, trailing kisses from her mouth to her throat before releasing her.

'Like that, you mean?' I asked, amused at the way Eden's fingers traced the path my lips had kissed along her skin.

She nodded mutely. 'Did I do something wrong?'

'N-no,' she stuttered. 'But I think I did.'

I frowned. 'What do you mean?'

Her expression morphed into a cheeky grin. 'Now I know what that feels like, I'm not going to be able to think about anything else.'

Oh, there were a few *more* things I'd be thinking about, but judging by her reaction to my shower remark earlier, I was going to have to take things slowly with Eden. This would be a definite first for me.

I straightened up to my full height, nodding. 'Shall we go, then?'

Eden moved towards the door with an odd look on her face, until she felt my hand slide into hers. Her smile came back with added wattage.

CHAPTER SEVEN

Sector 24

Noah moved slowly as his eyes adjusted to the darkness. Having woken to find the house empty, he had gone outside and found the others nearby, cast in stark relief by the light of a large fire.

Tinny-sounding music played from a device on Beth's wrist. As he drew nearer, Noah could tell that Beth and Saul, at least, were drunk. Michael stared straight ahead, the firelight casting no reflection in his eyes.

Beth waved a bottle at Noah as he sat next to her.

'Here's our boy! Have a drink.' She winced for a second – whether because she was in pain or the drink tasted foul, Noah couldn't tell. Either way, the moment passed and she jumped to her feet and started singing along to the music coming from her wrist device, spilling some of the drink over Noah as she handed it to him.

He sniffed the neck of the bottle. Whatever was in there smelled noxious, so he tried not to breathe in as he took a mouthful.

You might not want to do that, an oddly hoarse voice said inside his head – too late. The liquid burned his throat like acid, inducing a vigorous bout of vomiting. Saul clapped him roughly on the back until Noah held up a hand, signalling he had finished. He used the edge of his hand to flick some dust and rubble from the ground to cover the mess, then shimmied away from it, closer to the fire. Beth continued her dance, oblivious.

Noah sat quietly watching as she moved, darkly silhouetted between him and the fire. As her arms moved above her head, the light of the fire glanced over a black mark on her wrist. It looked a lot like the one on Noah's own wrist.

A movement in Noah's peripheral vision tore his gaze from her. A cockroach scuttled across the freezing ground a few centimetres from the edge of the fire. The light reflected off its back, like the flames were a part of it. The insect stopped dead for a moment, then hurried away from the heat towards where Saul sat.

'What orders you got for this one, Mike?' Saul asked, kicking up the dirt with a sharp jerk of his boot and sending the cockroach sailing into the fire. The insect hissed for an instant before the flames destroyed it.

'Unfortunately, the information I have about Noah isn't complete,' Michael said, frowning. 'My first task is to check out his serial number at a med facility to see what we can find out about his background. I will take him there tomorrow, if you can do without the roach.'

Saul considered a moment. 'Maybe I'll come with you. I want to see why the programme's got you so confused about him – and don't tell me y'aren't, 'cause I can tell.'

Michael sighed. 'As I've told you many times now, this isn't a programme. This is real – it's *life*.'

Saul got to his feet, grabbed the bottle from where Noah had discarded it, and took a deep mouthful from it. 'Some fucking life,' he shot back, and strode off into the night.

The song Beth had been dancing to ended suddenly, and she sank back into her spot at the edge of the fire.

'Did he take my bottle?' she asked. Both Michael and Noah nodded. 'Asshole.' She paused before nudging Noah with her boot. 'I'm going to bed. You coming?' Beth winced again, and it definitely looked like a flash of pain this time.

'I only just woke up.'

Beth laughed and shook her head. 'Forget about it. I've got a headache anyway,' she said, then strode inside, leaving Noah and Michael to sit listening to the crackle of the fire.

The following morning, Noah sat on the bench as the doctor scanned his retina. On close inspection, the doctor looked like Michael – both were short and broad, with thick arms and legs. Their faces were also very much alike, with a wide nose and mouth, small deep-set eyes, and an angular jaw and cheekbones. Still, it wasn't immediately obvious how similar they were. There was warmth in Michael's blue eyes and jet-black hair; the doctor, on the other hand, had very dark brown eyes, and hair so blond it was almost white. Standing side by side, they could have been negatives of each other. *Must be different models*, Noah thought.

'The data on Noah lists his parents' names. They each have a military serial extension. His parents may have been drafted in the early period of the conflict.' The doctor addressed Michael rather than Noah. 'I have no information as to their whereabouts. You will need to check the military records for that.'

The doctor handed Michael a data pad, then abruptly left the room, leaving Michael and Noah alone.

'Isn't there any more information about his parents? About why they haven't come looking for him?' Beth asked from her seat in the corner of the room, making Noah jump. She had been quiet for so long, he had thought she'd fallen asleep.

Michael studied the data pad, frowning as though displeased. 'It does list an address here in Sector 24, near one of the military bases. It may be worth going there to see if we can find out anything else.'

Noah was silent for a moment. 'Do I really want to find out more about them? To find them, if they're alive?'

Michael looked puzzled.

'I mean, they just left me here.' Noah shrugged. 'Either they're dead, or they've forgotten me, so why waste my time?'

Michael studied him for a second. 'Having a family is not something you should take for granted,' he said, his voice low. 'And I wouldn't be too quick to judge them, either. There are some communities far from here that haven't been touched by the war. It is possible your parents managed to get into one of them, and haven't been able to come back here.'

'So why not take me with them?'

'They may well have tried, but it's not always so easy. Once you are in a place like this,' he pointed to a window, gesturing towards the barren landscape outside, 'it can be difficult to find your way out. The people who live in the gated communities don't let in many from outside. They have to protect themselves, keep diseases out, so people can't just come and go as they please.' He held Noah's eye. 'But it's *something*, you know, to be safe. To have people who care about you. If I were you, I would want to find my family.'

Noah took a second to consider. 'So, what next?'

'We should try the address that's listed for your parents; see if they're there or if anyone knows where they are now. If that doesn't provide the answers we're looking for, we can access more information at one of the military bases, now that we know they are military personnel.'

Military personnel. Something about that didn't sit right with Noah.

The three headed out of the medical facility, back to where the roach sat waiting for them. Before they reached the vehicle, Noah ground to a halt.

'Why are you helping me like this? I mean, I'm grateful to you for getting me away from the enemy, and for helping me find out about my family, but I have to ask: what's in it for you?'

Michael shrugged, a smile in his brown eyes as he gave Noah a friendly push towards the vehicle.

'That's what I'm here for,' he said.

It wasn't until Noah was inside the roach that the thought occurred to him. *Weren't his eyes brown a moment ago?* Now, they had changed back to a piercing blue – the same blue that some part of Noah knew the sky should be.

Michael knew there was something wrong even before the roach trundled up to the building. This was the address, he was sure of it. But where there should have been an old colonial-style house, there now stood two blackened walls, the bitten-off chunks the bombs had left littering the ground around them.

'This isn't right.'

Noah shifted his weight from foot to foot, looking lost in the dust. 'Can you tell if they were in there when it was bombed?'

Michael had known they wouldn't find Noah's parents here, had been certain they would have moved on when the area became a target for the enemy. Most people had. But there should have been *something*.

'Michael?'

'They weren't here,' he said, his confident tone hiding his doubt. Michael did not like this feeling, this uncertainty. He needed to contact his superiors.

'What's he going to do now?' Beth asked, swinging her legs out to jump down from the roach.

'Like I said yesterday, we will travel to the military base in the north of the sector,' Michael said. 'We will access their databases. I am sure we'll find out something there … I'm sure we will.'

All three jumped at the unmistakable sound of jet engines overhead. Two distinct whistles followed, the inevitable roar of the explosions so close that Beth and Noah almost didn't hear Michael's yell.

'Back in the roach!' he barked, angry that he had allowed himself to become so distracted that he hadn't heard the enemy's approach.

Noah leapt up through the hatch, turning to offer Beth his hand. When she stared at it, frozen, Noah wrapped his arm around her waist instead and hauled her inside the vehicle. They were both jostled backwards onto one of the bunks as Michael hurried past to the driver's seat, Beth finally finding her voice and spitting curses at Noah.

The roach lurched and groaned as Michael kicked it into drive. Still Noah held Beth against him on the bunk.

'Let go of me!'

'Shhh.'

'Don't shush me, I'll…'

'Shhh.'

Beth couldn't say whether it was the hand stroking her hair down the length of her spine, or the steady beat of his heart next to her ear, but something inside her clicked. It was no brilliant epiphany, no sudden remembrance. But something had subtly, undeniably, shifted. She lay still in Noah's arms, breathing evenly as bombs exploded around them and only the boy holding her kept Beth from being thrown across the roach's interior.

Noah lay with her hugged tightly against his chest. His eyes were fixed on the grey square of daylight at the back of the roach, on the grim landscape fading away as they stormed over the terrain. Even as his hand smoothed over Beth's hair, soothing her until he was almost certain she slept, Noah tried to imagine what kind of landscape his parents might be seeing at that precise moment.

They skidded to an inelegant halt in front of the farmhouse. The headlights settled upon the dishevelled figure of Saul as he sat drinking from a metal canteen on the porch steps, his eyes glazed. Michael jumped down from the roach and strode over to him.

'I've told you, you shouldn't drink that stuff. It will cause internal damage.'

Saul waved a hand at him dismissively. 'Mike, you say all kindsa crap like that. You tell me what to do, and I do it, but I'm still stuck here in this shithole…' he paused to take a drink from the canteen, '…with you, you lifeless piece of crap, and that frigid cow over there.' He waved the canister in Beth's direction as she climbed down from the cabin of the roach. 'And now this … this *boy* turns up with a whole new set of rules, and I have to start from scratch!'

'What do you mean, new set of rules?' Noah asked him. The older man didn't answer, just got to his feet and staggered over.

'Come on,' he slurred, shoving Noah roughly. Noah took a step back, not sure how to react. 'Come on, you little shit, have a go! You know you want to.' Saul shoved him again, and Noah almost fell. Michael intervened.

'Saul, what are you doing?'

'Shut up!' he shouted, then focused on Noah. 'Come on, just one little swing.'

'You want me to hit you?' Noah asked, warily.

'Yes!' Saul hissed, then waited.

'Why?'

'To see what happens!' Saul was still shouting.

'Saul, I'm not going to hit you.'

Saul studied the ground for a minute, then ran his hand

down his face. When he looked up, he shot Noah a flat smile before striking out with his fist, catching Noah's jaw and knocking him to the ground.

But it was Saul who yelped with pain. Michael stepped forward, laying a restraining hand on Saul's shoulder as he clutched his head.

'Get out of here, Saul. Go and sober up,' Michael directed. Saul glared at him for a moment, then swayed towards the roach, snatching the ignition key from Beth's hand as he passed. Beth hurried over to help Noah up.

'See you when the programme turns me the hell around, I guess!' Saul cried, waving the bottle through the roach's open hatch.

He went careering down the track in the direction the others had just come from. As the dust settled in Saul's wake, Beth went back into the silent darkness of the house while Michael strode around the back.

Noah stood alone, feeling the shadows close around him. The punch to the jaw had hurt, but it was Saul's attitude that had unsettled him the most. He looked around, taking in the dusty, shadowy expanse surrounding the house. None of it familiar, none of it … right. But how could he trust his own feelings when he had no memories to give them context? Was this what had driven Saul to his insane belief that his life, the world around him – none of it was real?

Finding no answers in the falling blanket of night,

Noah followed Beth inside and found her sitting on the floor by the hearth. He sank down next to her, watching her back move as she built up the fire.

Beth spoke without looking up. 'Did Michael tell you about Noah? The one who was here before?' Even from her back, Noah got the sense that she was frowning. 'You're a lot like him. Weird how I never noticed it before.'

'Who was he?' Noah said.

'He stayed here for a while.' She finished piling up the flammable items in the fireplace – old broken furniture, cloth that had been worn beyond further use – and leaned back on her haunches. 'He'd been in some kind of accident, almost completely lost his sight. He was here with Michael and Saul when I arrived, right after my memory crapped out.'

'How long ago was that?'

Beth shrugged. 'I don't know, a few weeks … months, maybe. It's hard to track time here. There's not much to keep you busy, except looking for food and things to burn. And thinking. Always thinking.'

'Can't you remember anything from before you got sick?' Noah asked.

'No,' she answered flatly. 'The first thing I remember is seeing Michael. He took me to the med facility you went to today, and Dr Raphael told me that I was a survivor of an enemy attack not far from here. The only survivor.'

'What about your family…?' Noah let the question trail

off into silence as he saw her body tense. *Only survivor.* Her words rang through his head. 'So you didn't even know your name?' Noah asked, trying to steer the conversation a safer way.

Beth shook her head and held up her right wrist. 'I didn't need to – it's written right here. BETH2082-2-22-24. Looks like a load of little ducks lined up, don't you think?' She smiled thinly. 'And it just figures my name would mean *house of God*. I can't think of any place less godly, can you?' She smiled grimly. 'How about you? Nothing coming back to you yet?'

'No, nothing.' Noah watched the fire as it fought to bring some heat into the room. 'What about Saul? What's his story?'

Beth shook her head. 'I don't know. It's hard to say. He's burned off his serial number, so I don't even know if Saul is his real name. You've heard him, he has some weird-ass ideas.'

Noah laughed. 'I don't really get what he's talking about most of the time.'

'Yeah, he's a bit sketchy sometimes. I think he's … he's just not very happy with his life.' Beth looked stern and shifted in her seat. *'My life is no kind of life … this is a conspiracy, and you're all in on it!'* She shook her fist in the air and they both laughed at her exaggerated impression.

'What happened to the other Noah?' Noah asked.

Beth shrugged again. 'I don't really know. He just

disappeared one night. Michael says he moved on someplace else, but I was surprised he didn't say goodbye to me if he was leaving.'

'He didn't tell Saul why he was leaving?'

'Not that he ever said. They didn't really get along – I think Noah was a little scared of him.'

'Why?' Noah asked, intrigued.

Beth looked up sharply, as though realising she had said something she shouldn't have. 'I guess Saul is a scary guy.' She shrugged. 'Not like Noah. He was just the most accident-prone person I've ever met.'

'How so?'

Beth looked at him for a moment, scrutinising this new Noah, perhaps looking for the same vulnerability. 'It was weird. The worst things happened to him, like he couldn't walk out of the door without nearly getting crushed by a falling tree. One time, he just walked by the roach, and I swear it powered up all by itself and one of the legs kicked him a clear three metres in the air.'

Noah laughed at the image she had conjured. 'What, and nobody was inside it?'

Beth shook her head and smiled. 'Not that I could see. Michael and Saul were inside the house, and I was standing right next to Noah.' She held her hands out towards the growing fire, examining her chewed fingernails. 'So what happened to your arm? Do you know?'

Noah moved to cover the red weal self-consciously, shaking his head. 'Maybe the enemy did it when I was in their camp or something. I can't remember.'

'Probably for the best. So, do you think you'll stick around here for a while? We could use an extra pair of hands to help fix this place up and gather supplies.' She looked away as she spoke. 'There are worse places you could be, you know. Worse even than being in the middle of a war. It can make things clear; make people look at who they really are. Heroes and cowards, good and evil – it all comes out when you're facing what we live with every day.'

Noah paused, thinking back to what Michael had said to him at the med facility. 'Michael thinks I should try to find my parents. They may have fought in the war.'

Beth mulled this over. 'Well, that's something you need to decide for yourself. It's hard to say what's important when each day brings the possibility of losing what life we've managed to salvage. I'm looking for answers just as much as you are, Noah. Trying to figure out what's important.'

Noah sighed. 'I suppose so. It's just … I thought maybe learning about my parents would make things click into place, but it didn't.'

He studied Beth as she built up the fire a little higher, watched her for what felt like a long time.

CHAPTER EIGHT

Alteria Community

With no lessons scheduled and my work placement not due to start for two more days, I was most definitely bored. I went back to my quarters and placed a call to Angela. *One last binge*, I told myself, *then I'll clean up*. I requested a secure channel and waited for the connection.

'Citizen not found,' the computer told me. I tried again, without success. I didn't want to call her at work, but decided to take a look around the Chem Facility to see if there was any sign of her there.

I wound my way through the corridors to the labs, managing to avoid the more crowded areas of the community. When I got there, I checked the register to see whether she was due to work a shift that day. Her name didn't appear anywhere on the roster. *Strange*, I thought. It had only been a week since I'd seen Angela, and it seemed unlikely that she would have left Alteria so suddenly. Left with no other option, I went back to my quarters and placed a call to a guy called Sam – another of my contacts in the lab. Maybe he would know what was going on, and more importantly, he could get me some Pi.

Sam answered after a few seconds, looking very unhappy to see me.

'Hey, Sam…'

'Mason, I'll meet you at the Rec in five.'

Before I had a chance to say another word, he ended the call and the screen faded to black.

Sam was waiting for me when I entered the Rec. As soon as I caught his eye he disappeared into the storage closet, and I waited a couple of minutes before following him.

As I emerged into the dingy room hidden beneath the Rec, I could see that Sam was agitated. His eyes moved furtively around the room in the subdued lighting, taking in the writhing forms of the few Pi-heads who were tripping at this time of the day.

There was some smooth dub playing that rolled around the walls, a heavy flood of sound that I could feel in my chest. Resisting the urge to switch off my implant, I joined Sam at his corner table.

'Angela's gone,' he said, and I waited for him to continue. 'She was taken by Security last night, erased from the Citizen list.'

'Why?'

He gave me a look that told me not to be so dense. She must have been caught dealing, which although technically against community protocol, was usually only a wrist-slapping offence. I knew this from personal experience.

'Protocols are tightening up here. Have been for the past few months, ever since they started letting in people like…' His voice trailed off, but I knew he meant people like *me*. Outsiders. 'Look, something's going on in the lower levels, and security has gone off-chart.'

I couldn't tell whether he was spitting out his words like bullets because of the competing noise level, or because he was stressing out.

'So where is she?' I asked.

He looked at me impatiently. 'Mason, I'm only here to warn you – keep yourself clean, all right? Tell your girl, too.'

I gathered that meant Pi was off the menu for a while. 'Sure, Sam.'

'And do me a favour,' he added as he rose to leave, 'don't contact me again. Nothing personal, but I don't need them looking into my business if you screw up.'

Hard *not* to take that personally, but I nodded. Sam returned the parting salute and left through the crawlspace.

I wasn't sure what to make of it all, but *something* was going on within the community if they'd only recently changed protocol about letting in outsiders. *Why now? And why all the extra security?*

Then I remembered that Alteria was seizing Rats. I had

no idea what they did with them afterwards – didn't care, really – but perhaps it made sense they'd want more security with Rats around the place.

Eden let herself into my quarters that night as I lay reading. I quickly flicked on my implant as she threw herself down on the bed next to me.

'I have been working since daybreak … without any time out, and my feet … are killing me.' She punctuated the last sentence with shaky intakes of breath as she kicked off her slippers and closed her eyes.

I laughed at her drama, my mood immediately lifting. I wondered if I had the same effect on her, or whether she was the one creating this … whatever it was, between us.

She yawned, rolling her head towards me and opening one eye. I caught her checking me over, realising I was only wearing jeans.

'Is it all right if I crash here tonight?' she asked. 'I mean, you know, just to hang out.'

'Of course,' I replied.

'Don't suppose you've got anything to perk me up a bit? I'm out.'

I shook my head. 'Pi's a no-go for a while.'

She closed her eye again, letting her head roll to the side in feigned death. I knew exactly how she felt.

'Why would you say such a thing?' she gasped, her eyes still closed.

I told her about my meeting with Sam. I explained

about Angela being removed from the community – to who knew where – and Sam's anxiety about going the same way if his activities as a dealer became known.

Eden looked far less concerned than I had expected her to, although with her eyes closed, it would have been difficult to tell whether she was particularly worried.

'Well, it makes sense, I guess, with everything that's going on downstairs,' she said, matter-of-factly.

'What's going on downstairs? You mean the Rats?'

'The Rats?' She opened her eyes. 'Oh ... no. It's not that. I listened in on one of Dad's security briefings, and apparently they've cleared and sealed all the levels in the lower half of the ark. You need top-level clearance just to go down there. It's all being kept off the public grid for now, but of course they'll let us know what's going on when the time is right.'

I felt my face set in a frown. 'What makes you think that?'

Eden leaned up on one elbow, tilting her head as she looked at me. 'I don't know *exactly* what they're doing down there,' she said, 'but nobody in Alteria would be involved with anything that went against the pursuit of knowledge and truth. Especially not my dad.'

'Look, I know you guys are really big on the whole knowledge-is-godliness kick, but that doesn't mean that someone couldn't be acting shifty,' I said.

Eden looked at me flatly.

'You're being ridiculous. Do you really think anyone would risk being taken to Level One?'

'Level One?' That section would be way down in the bowels of the ark – somewhere I hadn't been tempted to explore as the sound compression below the waterline knocked me sick. But now Eden had me intrigued enough that I forgot we'd been kind of having an argument. 'What's down there?'

She looked puzzled, as though she was surprised I didn't know, then guilty. 'Mason, you mustn't tell anyone this. I'm not really supposed to know, either. There's a rehab facility down there. Alteria takes in some of the criminals and deviants who've been outcast from the other communities – for a fee, of course – and fixes them.'

'Fixes them *how*?'

'Intensive rehabilitation. It's designed to purge bad behaviour, then release the person with a clean slate. Alterians don't believe anyone is beyond redemption.'

A slight curving of her lips let me know she was talking about me.

'There's no way Lyle's putting me in rehab…'

Eden looked horrified. 'Oh, of course not. You'd have to do something pretty terrible to be sent there. And people always come out so … different. I'd never want that to happen to you. My brother spent a week in there when he was younger. He was always a bit of a creep, but he got so bad I had to tell my parents. They sent him to get better, but he was way worse when he came out. That's why it scares me so much.'

'Wait – so that's what they do with the Rats they bring in? Fix them, then just … let them go?'

Eden nodded. 'Catch, cure, release. The ones who are brought in from the wastes, like the Rats from a few nights ago, will either have to apply for entry to another community, or stay here if they have nowhere else to go. I'm really just guessing about that, though. I've never actually seen a Rat wandering around Alteria.'

I let that sink in for a moment.

'I guess the Citizens go back to the communities they came from, if that ark has paid for them to be treated,' she added.

'Have you never used your magic card to go down there? To see what they're doing with all those extra levels?' I asked her, nodding towards the stolen access card lying on the bed between us. 'I mean, it's not as if they can be filling the whole space with Rats, right?'

Eden shook her head. 'The security down there is so tight you need a biometric ID scan to get past the doors. Anything below Level Sixteen is off-limits.'

'Hasn't your father ever hinted at what he's doing down there?'

'He said it was just being emptied for storage. But it's obvious what they must be doing, don't you think?' She gave me a pointed look.

'Uh, not really.'

'I bet they're working on something to do with the launch. We must be getting ready to leave for New Earth.'

As sceptical as I was, my heart still sped at the idea. But no community would ever build a transport vessel *inside* the domed structure; it just didn't make sense. All the other communities had a Suit Staff – the hazmat-suit-wearing arseholes who had the unfortunate task of building the external hull of their spacecraft before the real engineers moved in to work inside it in safety. I hadn't seen any of that going on at Alteria, but that didn't mean it wasn't. The ark was huge compared to most others I'd seen, and could easily have been hiding a spacecraft behind its back.

Eden perked up. 'You can always try to have a poke around there when you start work at the water purification facility. There's no way they could relocate that during the renovations, so you'll have to go past the restricted areas to get down to it.'

Ugh. My work placement.

I'd been trying not to think about it. The sound of the shields would be a nightmare down in the water facility.

In other communities, my placements had included work as a lab assistant, sports coach, waste systems technician (when I'd short-sightedly pissed off the placement coordinator), and a minion in the community archives. As a rule, the coordinator would allow you a couple of months to settle in before assigning you a placement. They did this in consultation with your personal counsellor – in theory, so that you could be assigned an occupation you'd be suited to, although I'd never seen any evidence of that. In Alteria, though, I'd already been assigned shifts at the water purification facility, and allowed only a couple of weeks' grace to settle in.

'Now be quiet,' Eden said. She rolled onto her side next to me, laying her palm flat against my stomach. Before long, her breathing took on the steady rhythm of sleep, and I lay there, listening to it. The sound was relaxing. I couldn't even remember the last time I'd thought that.

Careful not to wake her, I let my hand rest at the nape of Eden's neck, tucking her in closer to me. Her black hair flashed green as my vox's screen lit up. *Midnight*. I'd made it another day without getting kicked out. I reached over and turned off the display.

Before tonight, I hadn't given much thought to why Alteria had so much tech compared to other communities I'd lived in, or how they'd been able to afford it – though that seemed obvious now, if they were being paid to take in the gutter element and rehabilitate them. But Parisia, where I'd spent my early teens, had probably been the most primitive, technologically speaking. The ark had been mostly unshielded, the rust-ridden hull staining the sea around it a murky brown. It was vulnerable, as far as the Rats were concerned, but being so run-down also meant it wasn't exactly a prime target. Parisia was the butthole community. Just a glimpse inside the gates was usually enough to discourage travellers from staying long. Especially if the radiation hadn't damaged their sense of smell – the funk of decay didn't exactly scream *welcome*.

But Alteria was nothing like Parisia. All their tech wasn't just to keep everything so damned squeaky clean – it was to keep the criminals hidden away from their pure society, their dirty little money-making secret. I needed to see this battery farm of freaks for myself, and find out what the hell the Alterians were doing on the other sub levels that made it so high-security.

All I had to do was get a little lost on my way to work.

I entered the lift and instructed it to go down to the water purification facility, way down on Level Zero. I held my breath without thinking as the doors closed, listening for the change in shield harmonics that would tell me I'd gone below sea level. When the ugly, grating sound like chewing aluminium kicked in, I only made it three seconds before tapping my implant off and breathing again.

I'd been given a brand-new security pass with clearance to enter these areas of the community, but only at designated times, my whereabouts being carefully and constantly monitored. I'd tried to go to the newly designated storage section *by mistake*, but had been pleasantly informed by the lift's automated response unit that I didn't have clearance for entry to those levels. I'd have to find some other, sneakier way in.

The lift doors swooshed open at a gate room where I announced my presence through an intercom. I'd forgotten to switch on my implant, so I wasn't sure if there was any vocal response, but the gate did eventually swoosh open.

I entered a corridor, the way lit only by a dull amber glow.

The water technicians were somewhere between the engineers and the chem workers within the community class system. This meant that they were *fairly* well rewarded, with quarters allocated to them in the more desirable higher levels and plenty of credits to get whatever food and other comforts they wanted. But this was to compensate for the shabby working conditions – no light, no windows, and very little company.

A door opened ahead of me. Just as I reached it, the doorway was filled with the form of a burly man, at least a head taller than me and twice as wide. His sudden proximity forced me to take a step back, creating a gap for him to thrust a hand towards me.

He said something from beneath a moustache so bushy I couldn't read his lips. The moustache was pitch black – a strange contrast to his white halo of curly hair – and stretched across from one ear, under his nose and cheekbones, and landed firmly next to his other ear.

I assumed the words I'd missed were some sort of Alterian greeting, and reeled off one of the nonsense phrases I'd memorised. The man's name tag told me he was *Frank Astos*. I took his offered hand and he shook mine with vigour, his broad grin extending almost as wide as his moustache. I touched the spot next to my ear, trying to hide my flinch as the noise rushed back in. It was a trapped roar, the water outside the shields making the buzz a million times worse than it was above the sea line. Frank looked at me quizzically, but didn't comment.

'What you might not have realised,' Frank said a little while later as he led me on a tour of his domain, 'is that down here, we also generate around twenty per cent of Alteria's power. We draw it from tidal floats connected to the hull.'

I had not realised that.

'And,' he went on, his eyes sparkling as his enthusiasm grew, 'we are the first line of defence against these critters.'

We had come to a vast water tank, much larger and deeper than the swimming pools in the leisure facility, and filled with water that looked black in the low lighting. As I watched, a dark shape briefly broke the surface. It created a wave that rippled across the tank and spilled over the edge, then drained away through the grille flooring. It made me want to pee, though I really didn't need to.

'What is that?' I asked, intrigued as much as I was uneasy.

'*That* is Monique.' He took a step closer to the tank, tilting his head as he peered through the clear side. 'I named her after my first wife.' His booming laugh reverberated around the walls.

Almost like she was responding to the sound, Monique raised a black tentacle out of the water and hooked it over the edge of the tank, only a metre or so from where Frank stood. He jumped, then laughed again as he slapped the glass with his palm and the tentacle withdrew into the dark depths of the water.

'Squid,' he clarified eventually, 'don't normally come anywhere near the surface, but they're drawn to the electrical current in the outer shielding of the ark. The shields are set to shut down any section where a squid is detected nearby – can't go zapping one of His marvellous creatures, of course.' Frank rolled his eyes in a way that led me to think he wasn't entirely on board with the whole Alterian philosophy. 'But that just means the soft-headed beasts start humping the hull and get tangled up in the pumps. On top of that they cluster together sometimes, like they're hungry and they think if they all charge at once they'll be able to crack open the hull. They've not done much more than blow a few circuits so far, but they do keep us on our toes.' He chuckled, but I found the image of giant hungry squid a bit too horrifying to join in. 'Anyway, the ones that get tangled are brought in to recover until we can turn off the pumps and give them a chance to swim out of range before we start them up again.'

'How long has Monique been here?' I asked, not sure whether to be impressed by Frank's fearlessness in standing so close to the tank or just concerned for his sanity. Something about him, maybe his huge laugh or his buoyant demeanour, reminded me of my dad. He didn't really look like him – my dad had been fair, like me, and lean. Still, there was something there, and it made me like Frank instantly.

He smoothed one side of his moustache as he considered. 'Well, she got tangled last time we started up the pumps on the eastern side, which was nine days ago. But Monique's stayed with us a few times before – I think she likes it in here.'

'And when will she be released?' I asked.

'Now that's where you're lucky, young Mason. You get to set her free today.' Frank whistled as he walked back to the main section.

Not feeling all that lucky, I followed him out of the room, keeping as far away from the tank as possible.

Well, this should be interesting, I thought as the door swooshed closed behind me, and something that sounded very much like a half-metre thick tentacle slapped against the other side of it.

CHAPTER NINE

Alteria Community

I dressed in my best suit, even putting on a tie and combing my hair. *Not bad*, I thought, checking myself in the mirror. Then I loosened my tie and the top button of my shirt. *No need to go overboard.*

I looked at my watch; it was time. I went to call for her, waiting a few seconds until she opened the door and smiled. Her platinum hair was swept up, and she wore her favourite swishy green dress.

'You look nice,' I said, kissing Ari on the cheek.

'Thanks, little brother,' she laughed. 'You're looking pretty dapper yourself. Hang on.' Ariadne reached up to straighten my tie and refasten my top button, just like my mother would have. 'There, that's perfect.'

'Shall we go?' I offered her my arm and she laced her fingers over the crook of my elbow, like we were some centuries-old gentlefolk.

We walked to the lift and rode it to the top level, exiting at the arboretum.

'We don't have to keep doing this, you know. I don't blame you for what happened, Mase.'

I didn't respond, but felt my smile slip.

We followed the circular pedestrian path that skirted the arboretum, watching the sun as it lowered its weight into the ocean for another night. Finding a bench, we stopped and sat in silence, waiting for the day to end.

We did this every year on the anniversary of our father's death. I didn't look at Ari, knowing she would be wearing the same expression: sad around the eyes, with a forced smile on her lips for my benefit.

I thought back to the last time I saw him, as I tended to on this day, and every other day of the year.

Shut up in the cubby, a few weeks after my daring theft of the Pi, I came face to face with the man I'd stolen it from.

Usually packed tight like a sweaty sardine tin, the cubby was empty except for me, him, and a woman who seemed to be stacked in the corner – unconscious and topless, vomit drying over her naked breasts like makeshift clothing.

The man's face was no more than a few centimetres from my own, but I couldn't tear my eyes from the woman. I blinked as a spray of spit hit my cheek, and realised he'd been speaking to me. Whatever he said, he didn't bother repeating it. He clenched his fists in the front of my shirt and started shaking me.

'What's the matter, you deaf or something?' Something in

my expression must have confirmed it, as he laughed. 'Little Rat, eh? No matter. Where's my stuff, space cadet?'

'What stuff?' I asked, feeling my voice cracking in my suddenly parched throat. 'And I'm not a Rat, I just – '

'You can't have used it all,' he said, cutting me off, 'otherwise you'd be cracked by now. Where have you hidden it?' He looked at me levelly, his eyes shifting from my left eye to my right, making it hard for me to focus. I squirmed, trying to shoulder my way past him so I could at least get to my feet. He pinned me down with one hand laid heavily against my chest.

'Have you got it with you now?' Even as he asked, he started patting me down, not showing any regard for my golden 'no man touch' rule.

'Hey!'

'Look.' He had lost what little patience he had, and I sensed I'd better make some kind of move to extricate myself from there – quickly. 'Just give it back, and I promise not to break any bones when I beat you. What do you say?'

'I say screw you.' Smart mouth, even at thirteen. He pulled back a fist. 'Okay, okay. It's in my room. I'll bring it to you.' I hadn't yet made up my mind whether I was lying about the last part, but it stopped him mid-swing.

'I'm coming with you,' he said.

'That's not a good idea,' I said. 'My dad might be home.'

He smiled thinly. 'So that means he's probably not. Come on.'

Standing back, he let me get to my feet. He followed me all

the way back up to my quarters, one hand gripping the back of my shirt so I couldn't bolt.

I tried to think of a way to lose him. No sparkling ideas materialised, and we arrived at my door in an unnecessarily short time, me cursing under my breath. I'd just activated the door when I saw my father emerging from the bathroom, a towel wrapped around his waist and another over his shoulders.

I struggled not to break out my happy dance. I'd been sure Dad would be out at work.

Dad headed straight for his room without spotting me in the open doorway, but he was there – within shouting distance if I needed him. More importantly, the guy behind me had seen him, too. I took one step forward, shooting the arsehole a smirk as I saw safety ahead, then felt it quickly dissolve as the iron hand on my shoulder pulled me back to face him.

'You're going nowhere, you little shit.'

'Well, I can't get it while he's here,' I reasoned. 'He'll start asking questions.'

The door locking panel flashed, alerting me that I'd left it open. I edged backwards, hoping I could move far enough into the room that the door would shut automatically. But he pulled me roughly back into the corridor, and the door closed – with me on the wrong side of it.

'Get rid of him,' he said, his words difficult to read through his gritted teeth. He screwed up one side of my collar in his fist, half choking me.

'No.' Suddenly cocky at knowing my father was a few feet

away, I decided I'd had enough of this guy and his acid breath. 'How about you get lost, and I won't hand in your stash to Security and tell them it fell out of your pocket.'

He stopped, then let out a bark of a laugh that was not so much a sign of humour as it was threatening. 'Nobody would believe you just found it.'

'Maybe not.' I was growing braver, or more reckless, by the second. 'But even if they don't, they'll still test you, and I'm sure your blood won't come up completely clean. I'm just a kid, I'll get a slap on the wrist. You, on the other hand, will get a few months' brig-time.' That was probably true – he'd be in far more shit than I would if he got caught with contraband.

He said nothing for a moment, and I eyed the door panel, gauging whether I could shove him off me and get inside before he could give me a beating.

After a few seconds, the man released me. I hit the panel and backed inside.

'See you later, space cadet,' he said, his mouth twisted into a snarl.

'Fuck off,' I said as the door closed, just in time to see his face turn purple with rage.

'Who was that at the door?' my father asked, appearing in front of me in his bathrobe, a wet towel still hanging around his neck.

'Nobody,' I shrugged, wandering past him into my room, my thoughts already moving on to more urgent matters – drugs, sex and homework.

As I locked the door and sat on my bed, wondering how to combine these most important pastimes to best effect, I was unaware of the man still standing in the corridor just outside our quarters. I had no idea that he'd punched the unit next to our door in anger, shattering the cover and exposing the security panel inside. I didn't know he would look at the panel, see the CleanSweep mechanism, and come up with a way to get rid of the drugs, leaving him free to get even with me at his leisure.

And what neither he nor I knew was that in shattering the panel cover, he'd disconnected one small circuit connected to the CleanSweep – one so innocuous-looking that you might not realise its importance if you weren't familiar with the intricate workings of the system. It controlled some of the simple functions people took for granted, like not allowing the sweep to remove the fabric from furniture, absorb the soil from potted plants – or purge living human matter.

As I lay vegetating in my room, the sweep passed through the lounge, stripping it of everything – all the carpets and furnishings; Ari's favourite geranium in the corner; my scuffed boots, thrown to one side as I walked in the door earlier that day. It continued through to the wet room, gathering up the residue from my father's shower, absorbing the washcloth he had left on the edge of the bath. The sweep continued its circular path around our quarters, combing next through my dad's room. It removed the hairbrush on the dresser, all the clothes hanging neatly in the wardrobe. Then it moved on to my father, who lay napping on the bed as he disintegrated into molecules.

The sensor detected the bio matter entering the CleanSweep filters and shut down the sweep immediately. I remained in my room, oblivious to anything bad having happened until strangers appeared in my doorway a few minutes later, grim expressions on their faces. I looked up from my book, and immediately assumed they'd come about the drugs.

'I haven't done anything,' I said, naively letting them know that I had. It was only when I saw Ariadne between them that I knew something much worse had happened.

The look in her red-rimmed eyes said everything as Ari broke the news. Dad was dead. I knew it without needing to be told. Ari shook her head firmly, knowing exactly what I was thinking without me having to say a word, denying what we both knew: it was my fault.

I glanced at my sister, still sitting with that strange, sad smile on her face. I wondered what her last memory of my father was, how they'd left things. I also knew that was something I would never ask her. After all she'd given up to keep us together – climbing the ranks in engineering so that she'd earn enough credits to keep us both inside an ark, having to look after a kid brother who caused her nothing but trouble, intentionally or not – I had no right to ask her for anything.

But I remembered the last conversation I'd seen them

have. It was the morning before Dad's accident. Ari had been doing that annoying thing where she spoke without moving her lips properly, making it hard for me to follow. But Dad never did that, so I caught on pretty fast to what they were arguing about: me, as usual. Ari was already working as an engineer then, and one of her co-workers had offered to design a device that would tap directly into my auditory nerve – and be undetectable to scans, of course.

Dad, always cautious, thought the risk of being caught was too high.

Ari said he was denying me something that would make my life better.

Dad argued that all our lives would be a million times worse if we were cast out into the wastes.

They went on and on, talking in circles they thought I couldn't follow from the other side of the breakfast table. Or maybe they'd both just forgotten I was there, because neither of them said anything when I left to go and get high.

'Do you remember when Mum and Dad taught you to waltz?' Ari asked, breaking the near-silence of the arboretum.

I laughed at the memory of the three of us dancing in an awkward sandwich, me balanced on Dad's feet between him and our mother, my face on a level with her waist. I must only have been six or seven, because I'd still been able to hear the music. I couldn't remember the tune now. I couldn't remember the sounds of my parents' voices, either. But the memory of listening for that beat was like crystal.

'I kept slipping off Dad's feet,' I said. I had so many happy memories of my parents, of the four of us together, but I rarely opened the lid on that particular box of tricks. There were too many painful memories snapping at the heels of the good ones.

The sun slid below the horizon, closing another year.

'Shall we go to dinner?' Ariadne asked, rising to her feet.

On our way out of the arboretum I paused in the doorway, savouring the feeling of being purged. Tiny prickles like static ran through me. I let the sweep pass through me over and over while I remained in that in-between space.

It's going to take a lot more than some fancy doors to purge all of my dark spots, I thought. I stepped out into the corridor, immediately feeling like myself again.

After years of sleeping in silence, the high, trilling bleep coming from somewhere near my head made me jolt upright so fast my head spun.

I opened my eyes in the darkness, saw Eden's sleeping profile in bed next to me, and felt a little of the tension draining from my body. The incoming call light flashed on my wall monitor. Red then dark, red then dark. I shimmied down the bed, and Eden stretched into my vacated space almost immediately. In a whisper, I activated the monitor. Eli grinned back at me.

'Not so funny now, is it?' he greeted me. I looked at the time display in the corner of the screen. It was almost four in the morning.

'What's up?' I whispered, loathing the sharp feel of the sound in my head. It was always worse when I'd just woken up.

He squinted, trying to peer past me into the darkness. 'Why are you whispering? Have you got someone there with you, you dog?'

I smirked in reply, and he laughed. Feeling Eden stir behind me, I looked back at her sleeping form tangled in the bedsheets. I'd sent her a message the night before, asking her to come over after her tour shift. After dredging up all those old memories of Dad and the man I'd stolen from, I'd known I wouldn't be able to sleep without her. And I *had* slept. Maybe it was being with someone who didn't know what I'd done. Or maybe it was because Eden came without question, knowing I just needed her there. We hadn't even talked. She'd just fallen asleep with her head against my shoulder, still wearing her beige tunic and slippers. Eli cleared his throat. 'I'm calling about Dallan, really.'

'How is he doing?' I asked.

'I thought you might be able to tell me that, actually.'

'What?' I squinted through half-asleep eyes. 'Why would I be able to tell you?'

He exhaled through his nose, disappointed. 'Some of the guys from the lab were talking earlier. They said he's been shipped out to Alteria.'

'Really? When?'

'A few days after I spoke to you last.'

I worked out how much time had passed since then. 'That was three weeks ago. If he'd been here all that time, I'm sure I would have seen him.'

'Oh. Right.' Eli seemed bored, now that I had come up short of the information he wanted. 'So, is that the girl?'

'I sure hope so.' Eden's voice startled me, her head almost resting on my shoulder. 'Hi, I'm Eden.' She smiled at Eli.

'Mason, you weirdo, why are you still here talking to me when there are so many *other* things you could be doing?' Eli said.

'*Eli.*' I gave him a *shut your face* look.

Eden laughed, surprisingly unfazed. 'Nice to meet you, Eli.' She scooted back up the bed, pulling on my hand to go with her.

'Look, feel free to leave this thing on if you want to…' Eli's voice called through the monitor.

'Goodnight, Eli,' I said as I deactivated the screen and turned my attention to kissing Eden senseless.

CHAPTER TEN

Sector 24

Noah opened his eyes, blinking as they adjusted to the dying light of the fire. Beth was sitting near him on the floor, lost in thought. Or so it seemed.

'Can't sleep?' she asked in a low whisper so that she wouldn't wake Saul, asleep in his makeshift bed in the corner.

Noah nodded. His dreams left him feeling drained when he woke, but he still couldn't remember them, and always felt hollow when he awoke to find himself here, in this wasteland. *Sleeping on the rock-hard floor doesn't help*, he thought to himself.

'Do you want to share my bed?' she asked, as though she had heard what he was thinking.

Noah couldn't hide his grin. 'Are you asking me to have sex with you?'

'Noah!'

Saul stirred in his corner, grumbling to himself as he rolled away from the noise. Beth put a hand to her mouth to muffle her laughter.

Noah continued in a whisper. 'Wasn't that what you meant the first night I was here? By the bonfire?'

Still working hard to keep a straight face, she whispered back, 'Yes, sorry. I was a bit drunk, and I wasn't thinking straight. But I did mean *sleep* just now, nothing else.'

He thought for a moment. 'What if I don't want to sleep?'

She raised an eyebrow. 'Are you trying to make something happen here?'

'I think I am,' he said, smiling crookedly. 'Apparently I'm not doing very well.'

In his corner of the parlour, Saul watched Beth smile and whisper to Noah, how he touched her shoulder in the hollow of her collarbone with his fingers.

Saul felt jealousy prickle inside him. He looked at his own hand, unconsciously outstretched in front of him, and closed it around the glowing shapes of Beth and Noah in the firelight, crushing them in his fist.

He weighed his options. He could kill Noah, put things back to the way they were before he arrived, and Beth need never know. Almost involuntarily, Saul began acting out the murder in his head. The boy wasn't that strong, and Saul was sure he could overpower him. He imagined approaching him in the dark, putting his hands around the boy's throat, squeezing until there was no more breath, no more life.

But how would going back to the way it was before be better? Saul thought. He knew that Beth would retreat again, the way she had when the first Noah left.

His eyes wandered to the darkened window overlooking the backyard. He couldn't see much beyond the thick grime covering the glass, but there was very little out there now, anyway. An old wood store, with barely any timber left inside. The charred ruin of a neighbouring house, left to burn to ash with nobody to douse the flames. Apart from that, nothing interrupted the expanse of dust surrounding them on all sides. Only dust and dirt – and death.

I could leave.

The thought occurred to Saul for the thousandth time. A knot twisted in his guts as usual, and he ignored it.

Saul thought back to the first few months he had spent here, just him and that flaccid android. Saul had tried to leave a dozen times, only to find himself wandering half-starved and filthy, the clustered towns he knew to be within walking distance inexplicably beyond his reach. He inevitably found that he had somehow stumbled onto the path back to this place, this house. And Michael would be here, waiting without judgement or question. Saul knew he could not really leave until he was *meant* to leave. What he hadn't yet managed to figure out was how to earn his escape.

When Beth stood and made her way to her room, Saul closed his eyes again and feigned sleep. Through his closed eyelids, the fire still cast shadows as his mind picked over what he had just seen. His final thought before he sank into a dreamless sleep was that he wouldn't allow them to leave this place together, to leave him here alone.

Not this time, he thought. *If anyone's getting out of here, it's going to be me.*

While his charges huddled over a breakfast of cold beans the next day, Michael stood at the head of the table. He pretended to focus on re-labelling their latest haul of rusted tins, scanning the contents of each one before marking them with neat, precise letters. But across the table, he sensed something had changed. He saw it in the way Beth's pupils dilated as she listened to Noah, how his cheeks flushed when she laughed and her fingers brushed against his on the table-top. There was an attraction there, and he had yet to establish Noah's status.

I should intervene – make sure it does not become something more.

But that might undermine Beth's trust. That, he knew, would steer her *away* from her exit trigger. Michael could not allow that to happen.

Yet he had also noted Saul's increased agitation – the way his spoon clanked against the tin as he jabbed at the beans Michael had given him. Saul's eyes, usually quick to observe all that went on around him, were now fixed on the centre of Noah's forehead.

Saul had only a short time left to make his transition before he was reset. If the attraction between Noah and Beth was going to prove to be a setback for Saul, then Michael would have no choice but to intervene. Saul *had* to be Michael's priority.

Humans do whatever they want, Michael thought, *as long as it's the wrong thing.*

Although Michael could never ask him directly, he had often wondered whether Saul was even vaguely aware that his own actions had stranded him here, in this place. He had not progressed as Michael had hoped. Instead he took every opportunity to derail Michael's efforts to help him. Since they first met, Saul had fought like a corkscrew in quicksand – twisting desperately as he tried to free himself, not realising that he only dug himself in deeper.

At least in the early days he had some hope of redemption, Michael mused, then immediately rebuked himself. *Nobody is ever truly hopeless … except people like me.*

Michael activated his remote interface to the government network. Once he had a connection, he uploaded his latest report and asked for further instruction.

Error, the reply read. *Unable to verify subject. Programme not recognised. Separate from other charges immediately.*

Michael didn't understand. He had never received a command like this before, and no answer came to his requests for clarification. With a sigh that was more human than android, Michael debated how to get Noah away from the others. However he did it, at least one of his charges would be left unsupervised, and that went against Michael's core directive.

I will just have to make sure Noah is not left to fend for himself for long.

He put in the request for Noah to be reassigned and waited a few moments for the response.

Negative.

Cursing his superiors for their habitual obliqueness, Michael analysed the possible courses of action.

'When you are finished,' he said at last, summoning the attention of all three humans, 'we will head out to look for Noah's family.'

'What's the point?' Saul snapped, slamming his beans down on the table and sending a spray of bright orange juice over the edge of the tin. 'They're probably dead anyway.' With that, he left the room. Seconds later, the front door banged shut, rattling the battered walls of the house.

The silence that followed was shortly punctuated by Noah's laughter.

'Wow,' he said, and Beth started laughing with him.

Yes, Michael thought. *The sooner I deal with the Noah problem, the better.*

Beth drove the roach as Michael directed. Noah watched through the grimy window as the scenery rushed past, unchanging and unrelenting. The grey light of late morning settled like another layer of dust on top of the chaotic aftermath around them.

Noah saw the shattered buildings, some partly intact and supporting traces of life, others deathly shells. The buildings with people living in them looked almost as dilapidated as the empty ones, riddled with the last few survivors who consumed them.

Why do people stay here? he wondered.

Where else could they go? the voice in his head asked in reply. Weirdly, the voice sounded nothing like his own, but had a scratchy quality, like its owner needed to cough.

Great. Now I'm hearing strange voices in my head. Phlegmy ones.

Noah caught sight of a pale face at the window and jerked away before realising there was nobody outside. 'Scared of your own reflection,' he muttered. The face in the window moved its lips in perfect synchronicity.

The roach screeched to a halt next to a square fortress of a building. They parked a few metres from a huge metal door which appeared to be the only way in or out.

Beth climbed out of the driver's seat and came over to where Noah sat in the rear. She smiled, seeing that he had been sleeping.

'You ready?' she asked, nodding towards the airlock. Noah looked through it and saw Michael already waiting for them near the entrance. He pulled himself to his feet and followed her outside.

As they reached Michael, the android banged loudly on the door. It was only a moment before a voice responded through an intercom panel next to it.

'Identify yourself,' it said. The panel lit up with a red light, and Michael pulled back his right sleeve to hold his wrist up to it. The light promptly changed to green. A mechanism snapped and clicked, allowing the door to open slowly. Michael turned to Beth and Noah, halting them as they went to follow him inside.

'Wait here a moment,' he said. 'I need to make sure it's safe.'

Noah watched Michael enter, and the large door shut behind him with a clang. Beth sat on the ground with her back against the grey cement of the wall.

'This is a military facility?' Noah asked. Beth nodded. 'So why would it not be safe?'

She shrugged. 'Michael probably just wants to check it out.'

'Why?'

Beth looked up at him, and he saw something he hadn't noticed before behind her expression. Something … lost.

'He always has a reason,' she said.

'Noah.' Michael's voice roused the boy from where he lay sleeping at the gate. 'They want to see you.'

'Who does?'

'Come inside,' he snapped, then held up a restraining hand as Beth moved to get to her feet also. 'Just Noah.'

'I'll wait here for you,' she assured Noah as he shot her a questioning look.

Noah followed Michael into the building, and the heavy door shut behind them. They were met inside by two military-looking men, both in battered uniforms. Neither said a word, but one turned and led them further into the facility. Noah noticed that the other had taken up position at the rear of the party, effectively hemming him and Michael in.

They were taken up a flight of stairs, lit only by one dust-covered skylight. As they neared the top of the staircase, Noah saw a door ahead of them with a security lock next to it. The officer leading the way pulled a key card from his breast pocket and held it to the sensor. The panel flashed green, and the door opened.

'Hang on a minute.' Noah stopped before reaching the top stair. 'Have you really traced my family, or am I in some kind of trouble?'

Michael stopped next to him. 'It's nothing to worry about, Noah. They've located your father, and will take you to meet him. But first they need to carry out some tests.'

'What kind of tests?' he asked, looking from one soldier to the other, then back to Michael.

The soldier behind him spoke for the first time. 'We need to confirm you are who you say you are.' He urged Noah forward with the butt of his gun.

'Michael…'

Noah looked to the android for reassurance. Instead, he found Michael already descending the stairs. 'I hope things turn out all right for you, Noah,' he called back over his shoulder, then was gone.

With that, Noah found himself alone with two armed strangers.

Outside, Beth chewed her fingernails as she waited, ignoring the dull pounding of the migraine that never seemed to be far away. After only a few minutes, she heard the bolts inside the door activate, and it swung inwards. Michael emerged alone.

'Where's Noah?' she asked, looking over Michael's shoulder to see if he was following. But the door closed with a final-sounding thud.

Michael smiled. 'It's great news. His father is a general stationed in a community in the southernmost part of the sector. He has agreed to meet Noah at the nearest military base, and they're sending a transport out there this evening.'

'Just like that?' Beth asked.

'His father was overjoyed when he heard that Noah had survived. He had been told that the entire facility where Noah had been based with his mother was destroyed in the bombing, otherwise he would have returned for him.'

As he spoke, Michael headed back towards the roach so that Beth had to follow to hear him.

'Hang on, Michael!' The android kept walking. 'This is all very sudden – isn't Noah even going to say goodbye?' Beth's voice broke, and Michael stopped.

'Aren't you happy that Noah found his family? You should be pleased for him.'

Beth looked at her feet, feeling the sting of his words. 'Of course I'm happy for him. I just wasn't expecting him to leave so quickly.'

Michael was smiling again when she met his eyes. 'He's going somewhere better. We all want that.'

He guided her into the roach and started the engine. Michael waited for Beth to take her usual seat next to the controls, but instead she slumped down onto the bench in the rear section.

'You drive,' she said, lying with her face turned away from him. 'I'm tired.'

Michael watched her for a moment, saw the shaky intake of breath and the arm raised to cover her eyes. He took the driver's seat and set a course back to the house.

Saul sat in darkness, listening to the rain rattling like stones against the upstairs floorboards, the rotten and battered roof providing little protection against the elements.

He took a mouthful from the bottle in his hand, well used by now to the acrid taste. The bottle caught the narrow beam of light breaking through a gap in the shutters, and the cockroach floating inside mocked him in dead silence. Saul threw it into the fireplace, sending shards of glass and evil-smelling liquid spraying back across half the room. He thought about setting a match to it, but was distracted by the sound of the roach outside, growling its approach above the noise of the rain.

Footsteps made their way onto the porch, one set heavy and sure, the other light but weary. Saul couldn't hear them talking as they came in, and he made no effort to announce his presence. Both Michael and Beth had been soaked on the short walk to the house, and Beth went over to the fireplace, crouching to light the fire. Then she stopped.

'What's this?' Beth peered into the darkness, trying to make out the strange gritty texture of the floor under her boots.

'Dropped my bottle,' Saul said, watching Beth jump as she noticed him sitting not more than a metre from her.

'For crying out loud!' She rose and strode out of the room, slamming the door behind her.

Michael started sweeping the broken glass into the hearth with the edge of his boot.

'At least it will burn,' he said.

Carefully, methodically, Michael built up the fire in the grate and set light to it, stepping back as he did so in case the fire coursed out across the floor. Once he was satisfied that it would stay put, he took the chair opposite Saul.

'You should try and make things a bit easier for her,' Michael said.

'Why's that?'

'She's upset about Noah leaving.'

'He's been gone ages now,' Saul countered, thinking of the young man who had been so badly burned.

'No, I mean the other … the *new* Noah.'

Saul let this sink in, allowed the rage to surface and show itself in his eyes before he stood and gripped Michael around the throat, shoving him backwards out of the chair.

'Are you kidding me? He's been here two seconds, and already he gets to leave? I've been here years … years!' He went to lift the android by the collar of his shirt, but Michael did not move. His solid weight was too heavy to lift, so instead Saul straddled the android on the floor and started beating his face and chest with his fists.

'Stop it,' Michael said levelly. The beating continued unfettered. 'Saul, if you don't stop, I will be forced to subdue you.'

Michael sat up, sending Saul sprawling backwards onto the glass-covered floorboards. Rising easily to his feet, Michael grabbed the front of Saul's shirt with both hands.

'Are you done?' Michael said. Saul pulled back his lips in a snarl, then spat in Michael's face.

Michael drew his head back, then brought it sharply down against Saul's temple. The man went limp in his grip, out cold. Michael let him drop back to the floor, then leaned down to use Saul's sleeve to wipe the spittle from his cheek.

'Dirty,' he said, sneering down at Saul's unconscious form. At that, he strode out to the kitchen and started scrubbing his face.

CHAPTER ELEVEN

Alteria Community

The following afternoon I opened my door to find guards waiting for me.

'Mason Coulter?' one of them asked, his tone as crisp as his mocha-coloured uniform. I didn't get a chance to respond before the other one – a big bastard with a waxy sheen to his bald head – grabbed hold of me. I didn't struggle. Yet.

'What's this about?' *Or, more specifically, what did you catch me doing this time?* I didn't voice the last part. Just as well, because my voice was suddenly embarrassingly high and choked-sounding.

The big bastard answered. 'Just come with us. We're not interested in what you've got to say, so just save it for when you get there.'

'I'd better call my sister…'

The smaller guard shook his head, but neither of them said anything. Not really seeing many options, I went with them. We walked – or rather, I was dragged – past several

Alterians who gave me The Look with their wide eyes, ushering children to stand behind them like I was some kind of bogeyman. One even pointed and hissed, 'His mind knows only darkness! His kind must be purged!'

I showed him my teeth, and he skittered away.

A calm fell over me which would have felt strange had I not gotten used to the feeling over the years. It wasn't really calm, though. Just a weary sense of inevitability. Something bad was about to happen, and it was probably my own fault, but I still wasn't going to like it.

We were only a few corridors away when I realised where the guards were taking me. 'Seriously? Lyle's office?'

The smaller guard grunted an affirmative. Something in my posture must have changed, because the big bastard tightened his grip on my arm.

As the door opened, Lyle looked up from his desk monitor and smiled in greeting. I glared at him as he waved the guards away.

'What the hell's going on?'

Lyle raised his eyebrows. 'What? Oh, the guards? Standard procedure, I'm afraid. You've been late to our last three counselling sessions.'

There was a long moment of silence, during which I calculated exactly how many ways I could kill Lyle using only the phallic-looking dolphin sculpture on his desk.

'You couldn't have just sent me a reminder?'

Lyle gave me the smile again. 'The guards *were* a

reminder. One I am sure you will not soon forget. It's quite a trek through the community to get here from your quarters, isn't it?'

Words could not do justice to how much I *hated* this guy. What made it worse was that I knew I was stuck with him, had to play nice until the arsehole signed off my Citizen card application. Staying on Lyle's good side – or at least staying off his shit list – had to be my priority.

But now that I was apparently *not* in any serious trouble, I was impatient to go back to work, to see if Frank could shed some light on what was going on in the storage levels. I had made a concerted effort not to appear *too* interested in what was going on in the levels above 'Deep Blue', as Frank affectionately called the water purification facility, but he had broached the subject a couple of times himself – only stopping short as he seemed to realise he was straying into dodgy territory. But if I kept my mouth shut and let Frank talk, I was pretty sure I'd have the information I wanted before long.

'So, shall we begin?' Lyle said.

I was actually aching with pent-up anger as I took my seat across from him.

Lyle started talking and I nodded and filled the gaps with *yes* or *no* where I was supposed to. But I'd noticed something different about his office, and I – always in favour of a diversion from Lyle's bullshit – started wondering about the new white cube sitting in the corner.

Lyle stopped talking and studied the data pad on his desk. I had learned that was a sure sign he was about to broach a subject which excited him.

'Mason, I don't like to use the word *complaint*, but I have had a … *concern* … raised, about your conduct with one of your classmates.' He checked the pad again as though he'd forgotten Eden's name. I knew that he had to mean Eden as I didn't particularly hang around with anyone else in my class.

'Oh?' I leaned back in my seat and waited for the train wreck. 'What kind of *concern*?'

Shifting in his seat, he licked his lips before answering. 'A concerned Citizen has raised a query about the amount of time you and Eden spend alone in your quarters.'

'It has an excellent view,' I said, immediately regretting the flippant remark. I could tell from his expression that he thought I was trying to conceal something, and as much as I enjoyed winding him up, I didn't want to take any chances if Eden was in the line of fire. 'We're friends,' I tried again.

'I don't doubt that.' Lyle went for the co-conspirator approach, leaning forward in a way that was meant to invite me to confide in him. 'But what do you do while you're alone together?'

'I read a lot. Eden likes to paint. Sometimes we talk. That kind of thing.' *All very pleasant and chaste.*

This was all true. It was also not the *whole* truth, and

Lyle knew it. He tapped on the edge of his desk with stiff fingers, but was otherwise silent.

'You're very interested in Eden,' I remarked, not meaning anything by it until his expression told me I'd struck a nerve.

'I'm interested in *you* at present, Mason.' Lyle's face flushed. 'As I'm interested in everyone I counsel,' he added clumsily.

'Do you counsel Eden too?'

The glint in his eyes was pure anger now, and I had no idea how I'd caused it. That didn't mean I wasn't enjoying it, though. The tendons in his neck were pulled tight as bowstrings, which I had to assume was what kept him from answering the question. I fought to keep my face neutral, trying very hard to remember that I needed this arsehole to authorise my Citizen application. So I gave him an out – grudgingly.

'So someone would have a problem with Eden and me being more than friends?'

'*Unclean* activity is forbidden in Alteria, as you know. Especially between those who have not undertaken a holy union.' He shifted again in his seat, like he was trying to rediscover the exact arse-position he'd had before I dislodged him from his perch. 'It would certainly be wise to spend more time out of your quarters, with others in the community. And of course, you should pay close attention to morning Lessons.'

His patronising tone bugged me. I stayed silent until

I'd calmed down enough to respond without punching him. 'I will certainly do that.'

'Excellent.' Lyle was back to looking pleased with himself, and I retreated to my thoughts of sadism for a few quiet moments. Then I noticed his eyes darting to the box in the corner too, as though he didn't want me to see the movement. 'Sh-shall we continue where we left off at the last session?'

'Remind me.' My tone was even, my brain now entirely focused on the damn box.

'What are your plans for the future?' he prompted. I thought it over, taking longer than Lyle judged to be a reasonable amount of time. 'You must have some idea what you would like to do with your life.'

'I haven't decided yet.' This was half-true.

'How are you enjoying your work placement?'

'It's good. Interesting,' I said, with uncommon sincerity.

'And you don't mind the conditions on the lower levels?'

'The restricted sections, you mean?'

He frowned. I had obviously taken the question the wrong way and was sure I was about to regret it.

'The isolation,' he corrected. 'And the lack of light in the underwater sections. Some find that … claustrophobic.'

I shook my head, not trusting myself to speak without revealing more than I wanted to. The sounds around me seemed amplified as my heart raced, and I had to grip the armrests of the chair to stop myself reaching up to deactivate my implant.

130

Do the notes tell him about my claustrophobia? I'd already had the implant fitted when I started therapy, so I knew my record wouldn't give *that* away. But as I thought back, one of the counsellors in Parisia had commented that he'd noticed I didn't like tight spaces...

'Have you worked in the underwater sections in other communities?' He looked at his data pad, checking my previous assignment list, I assumed.

'No,' I said, although he continued checking. *But I have spent time there.* Without meaning to, I thought back to Parisia, retreating into the dark space in my head again.

The man's face flashed before me. I stared into his dark eyes, filled with hate as they led him away after my father's death. He had been stripped of his Citizen status – an outcast now. No other community would take him in, so if he wasn't killed by the radiation before he could find shelter, he would spend the rest of his short life as a Rat.

I didn't care. He deserved it. And I wanted to watch as Security shoved him through the airlock.

Ari had tried to pull me away, back to our quarters, but then I'd seen that he was saying something, his thin lips snarling around the words.

'Be seeing you, space cadet.'

'So, you would consider that line of work?' Lyle's voice dragged me back to the present. I didn't even try to work out what he had been saying prior to the question.

'Sure,' I said. 'Why not?'

Lyle splayed his hands on his desk, so I knew he was excited about whatever was coming next. 'Now, I have something … interesting planned.'

'Interesting how?'

His eyes flickered back to the box in the corner. It was at this point that I noticed something about the one-metre cube: there was a hole in the top of it, perhaps the diameter of my finger.

Air hole, my brain supplied. *He's going to lock you in a box.*

I'd heard about this kind of 'immersion therapy' before. It basically amounted to forcing you to face what terrified you most, over and over again until it didn't scare you anymore. Either that, or you stroked out.

Bile rose in my throat. I knew I needed to get out of there before he said the words, before he knew he'd hit on something he could torture me with. I focused all my thoughts on that burning feeling rising in me. The churning in my stomach, the sweat beading at the back of my neck.

'It says in the notes that you also have an issue with…'

His sentence was cut short as I vomited quite spectacularly across his desk. The sight of him skittering backwards to avoid the sluice now pouring over the edge of his desk was probably the funniest thing I had seen since I arrived in Alteria, but I managed not to laugh. I wiped my mouth on my sleeve and stood up with a sort of *job done* finesse. 'Sorry, must have been something I ate.'

I opened the door and slipped out, hearing him activate the CleanSweep in his office in an almost pained whimper.

I was in such a rush to get out of there that I bumped into one of the Alterians as I left Lyle's office. The woman squeaked, and I ducked past her, muttering something along the lines of, 'Sorry, it was … uh, God in Light … and stuff.'

The woman squeaked again – this time in outrage – but within seconds I'd rounded the corner and was gone.

Eden and I lay on a patch of grass in the arboretum, looking at the stars through the domed roof. There were only the two of us up there so late at night. The plants seemed to swell in the darkness, filling the entire space, hiding us away.

We had some snack food with us – hardly a picnic, but the necessities of stomach-filling: chocolate, crisps and what the Alterians passed off as coke. All good clean fun. I'd loaded some music onto my vox, real low-vibe stuff that wouldn't grate on me too much. We lay for a while not saying much, just listening to the music and loading up on sugar.

'This is romantic,' Eden said, her voice sticky with chocolate.

'Romantic?' I laughed.

'Romantic,' she drawled, rolling onto her side and curling into me.

'I suppose you're right.'

We lay there for a while until I thought she had fallen asleep. I was just considering whether I could carry her to the lift without waking her when she spoke.

'Lyle told me someone complained about us.'

I hesitated before answering her. 'He told me that, too. I assumed it was your father, to be honest.'

She shook her head against my ribcage. 'Dad wouldn't do that. He's strict, but not a complete tyrant. Whenever he's upset with me, he yells and grounds me or something, but he wouldn't talk about it to Lyle. It's just not his style.'

It crossed my mind that maybe he hadn't had to deal with Eden sneaking out to sleep in a guy's quarters before. Even if we hadn't actually been doing anything – well, not *much* – as Chief of Security, he'd have no problem locating her using the ark's sensors and drawing his own conclusions. But either way, I figured Eden knew her dad well enough to know how he'd react.

Eden seemed to follow my train of thought. 'Don't you think he'd have searched my room for the security card if he knew I'd been using it to spend nights with you? He thinks we're friends, that's all.'

'Friends?'

Eden didn't answer. 'But who else would complain about us?' I asked. There weren't many people I knew at Alteria, and of those, I couldn't think of one who would raise an objection to my relationship with Eden.

I sensed Eden hesitating. 'How about your sister?'

I dismissed the idea almost immediately. 'She doesn't know about us.'

'She doesn't?' I couldn't tell whether Eden sounded surprised or insulted.

'We don't talk about that kind of thing much. Or about anything, really.'

'Oh,' she said, and was silent again for a moment. 'Could it just be Lyle making it up? He talks about you a lot.'

'He does? Why?'

'He's fascinated by you. I can kind of understand that.' When I looked at Eden, she was grinning. 'Do you fancy going for a dance in the Rec? All this sugar has got me wired.'

'I don't dance,' I said, quickly.

'Well, come and watch me, then.'

We stood outside the unusually silent Rec, peering beyond the barrier blocking off the entrance.

A notice on the door stated that it had been closed for refurbishment, but when we asked a couple of kids who were hanging around nearby, they said it was being turned into more storage.

'For them to fill up with God stuff while we have squat to do,' one of them added, looking up at me from his seven-year-old frame and getting a sharp rib-dig from one of his friends.

Eden sighed as we headed away from the Rec. 'This place is getting seriously low.'

'Shall we steal a sub and get the hell out of here?' I asked, wearing my serious face.

'I think that would be for the best.' She chewed on a fingernail absently. I moved to swipe her hand from her mouth, but she – not as absent as I'd thought – ducked out of my way, still chewing the nail. 'Get your own,' she said.

I made a dive for her and she spun deftly out of my reach, setting off at a pace down the corridor. I could catch her easily if I wanted to, so I hung back, watching her wavy black hair swinging as she ran.

Turning a corner, Eden sprinted ahead and disappeared into a lift. I took the one next to it, watching the monitor inside to see which level hers stopped at.

When I emerged, the change in the shield's harmonic frequency told me I was near sea level. It took me a few seconds to recognise that I was near the gateway where I'd first entered Alteria more than a month ago.

I didn't hear her until she had her arms wrapped around my neck from behind, her legs gripping me around the waist and her quick, shallow breath in my ear. I very nearly fell backwards on top of her, but managed not to stagger too much.

'Excuse me,' I said to my recently acquired limpet. 'Can I help you with something?'

'Yes, I'm thinking of stealing one of these subs.' She

gestured vaguely towards the entrance to the launch bay, sliding off my back. 'I wondered whether you could take me for a test drive?'

'Sorry, Eden,' I said, fighting the urge to do whatever she wanted. 'I can't afford any more strikes if I want to get my Citizen card.'

Instead of looking at me like I was a loser, she just arched an eyebrow. 'And you're just telling me this now?'

'It never came up.'

'Funny thing is,' she said, breaking into a grin, 'I'm on my last strike, too. One more and it's off to rehab I go.'

'What did you do?' I hadn't meant to sound incredulous, but I did. She laughed.

'Nothing major. But it doesn't take a lot when your parents are completely anal. Well, and one of them is the Chief of Security.' She started counting off on her fingers. 'I got caught out after curfew once, and had a reprimand for stealing paint…'

'*Paint?*'

'Well, I didn't exactly steal it. I woke up in the middle of the night with an urge to paint, but I'd run out of the kind I needed. I went up to the supply area, but it was shut – as you'd expect – so I just took the paint and left a note.'

'That's not exactly stealing,' I said, although even as I did so I could imagine how someone – let's say Lyle – might twist the facts. 'But you were willing to risk this anyway?' I nodded towards the launch bay door.

'Nah,' she shook her head, 'I knew you were too chicken to go. And anyway, you'd never let them put me in rehab.'

'Wouldn't I?'

She looked at me seriously. 'Nobody ever comes out of there quite the same as they went in. It changes them. I'd never want anyone to do that to *you*.' The look faded. 'And you wouldn't let them take me, either – not if you want another shot at showing me that *bad boy kiss* thing. You know, I think I've forgotten it already…'

'Right!' I made a lunge for her, allowing her just enough time to turn on her heel and run screeching back into the lift. This time, I was fast enough to catch her.

CHAPTER TWELVE

Alteria Community

Frank's heavy footsteps rattled the floor plating next to my head, and he waited while I crawled out from under the control panel. Then he handed me a large pail.

'Monique's back,' he said, the broad grin splitting his face in two as usual. 'And I reckon she's hungry.'

I took the pail, which I now saw was full of decomposing fish. I groaned.

'I get all the fun jobs.'

Frank laughed as I headed to the tank room, then called after me.

'Be careful, Mason. They let off an electric charge sometimes, and you don't want to be in the way if she does. It might fritz your implant.'

That stopped me dead in my tracks. 'My what?'

'It's nothing to worry about, just keep your distance.'

'But – but what did you mean … how did you know about my implant?' My pulse thrummed through my skin, my words tripping out in a rush.

Shut up, shut up, shut up!

'Oh, I can tell when you switch it off,' he said, like it was no big thing. 'You stare at my mouth when I'm talking.'

'That's because you've usually got food in your moustache.'

Frank responded with his deep belly laugh, but I didn't think it was funny. He knew about me, knew enough to get me kicked out of Alteria. Then what would I do? What would Ari do? She'd already told me there was nowhere else we could go. I'd messed everything up for both of us – again.

Shit.

The stink of the rotting fish seemed to be getting stronger and stronger, somehow. A dozen lifeless eyes stared up at me from the pail, and I had to swallow hard to keep from retching.

When I looked up, the grin fell from Frank's face. 'Hey, you don't need to worry about hiding your deafness down here, boy. Makes no difference to me. You're too healthy to have spent much time out there in the wastelands, and too young to have had anything to do with the attack on Cardis, so I know you're no Rat. I don't need to know the particulars of how you came by your implant, or what happened to make you need it. Just keep it hidden from Lyle if you can. He'd most likely make a fuss about it, could make trouble for you if he wanted. Whoa there, easy now…'

140

My breath was coming out in sharp stabs, making my chest ache. Frank took the pail from my hand, giving me a reassuring shoulder-pat. I shrugged him off.

'Stop … talking to me … like I'm one of your pet squid.'

I focused on slowing my breaths, inhaling through my nose in spite of the stench. Gradually my heart stopped trying to assault my other internal organs.

'You okay now?' Frank said.

I nodded.

'Good.' He handed me back the bucket of fish and trundled back towards his office.

I wandered through the cramped corridors to the room where Monique's tank sat. The water was black, which Frank had told me was caused by Monique trying to camouflage herself by colouring the water with her ink, although I had a feeling it was just because squid are innately evil. Looking at the water now, I thought I saw something glowing inside the tank – just for a second. I kept watching, waiting for it to appear again, but after a few minutes there was still nothing.

I must have imagined it.

Keeping close to the wall farthest from the clear side of the tank, I looked at the heavy pail in my hands, wondering how I could get the fish from there to the tank without moving any closer to it myself. I took a few experimental half-swings with the bucket, gauging whether I could launch the fish clear of the pail and into the tank from where I stood. I thought so, but it would have to be a good swing. I squared myself, and started to build momentum with the pail.

In the final instant before the launching shot, my left foot slipped on the wet metal floor. Both my feet flew out towards the tank as my body jerked backwards, and I could only watch as the pail flew from my hands in what seemed like slow motion. It sailed through an impressive arc, then landed with a heavy splash in Monique's tank.

I scrambled to my feet, a sharp pain shooting from the back of my ankle up to my knee. Hobbling backwards, I braced my back against the wall and watched for movement in the tank. The surface of the water was still moving, occasionally sloshing over the sides, but the inky blackness was impenetrable. I waited a moment, seeing whether there would be any immediate repercussions of my poorly coordinated attempt to feed the bloody squid. Nothing happened.

I didn't dare move closer. After testing my leg, I limped out to find Frank.

He was in his office, feet crossed one over the other on the edge of his desk. He made half a move to get to his feet when I walked in without knocking, but his huge size made rapid movement impossible. Instead he froze, as though hoping I might not see him if he kept very still.

Frank held something in his right hand. He pulled it under the desk when he saw me looking.

'Frank, what have you got there?' I asked, as casually as I could.

The usually verbose water technician was silent while he considered his response. Finally he sighed and brought his hand out from under the desk. In it he held something that looked an awful lot like his *other* hand. The hand which I now realised was missing from the end of his left sleeve.

The prosthesis rocked a little where he set it on the desktop.

'Meet Old Lefty,' Frank said. 'Or I should say *New* Lefty. Old Lefty got a bit stuck when I was fixing the hydraulic float system a few years ago. I opted for a working prosthesis – it seemed less messy than getting them to clone a replacement.'

'Okaaaaay,' I said. It looked like a bloody good prosthesis – not something he'd had to botch together in secret. 'Good to know the people here aren't complete dicks about this kind of stuff.'

Frank nodded slowly. 'It's not the same for you, though, is it?'

He was right – it wasn't. Frank's hand didn't connect him to a massacre. They wouldn't point at him and scream terrorist.

'Maybe if I manage to stick around long enough to prove myself useful to the community, they might give me a chance to explain,' I said with a shrug. It had never worked that way anywhere else, and there was really no reason why Alteria should be any different. People only ever mentioned Cardis in whispers, like saying it out loud would bring Rats raining down on them. I doubted even Alteria would say those particular Rats were redeemable.

'Are you all right?' Frank said, reaching for his prosthesis, and I wondered what my face was doing to make him look so concerned. But just then a small silver container fell out of a hollow in his wrist. Frank grabbed it before it could slide off the edge of the desk, but not before I got a good look at it. It was just like the one Angela had given me to hide my Pi from the sensors.

'Damn.' Frank pursed his lips beneath his moustache, then sagged back in his chair with a sigh. 'I guess that wasn't such a great hiding place after all.'

Frank reattached his left hand with a snap, then opened the container to reveal a dozen or so little black pellets rolling around inside.

'What are they?' I asked, peering closer.

'Ink capsules,' he said. 'Monique's ink has certain side effects when you ingest it.'

'What do you mean?'

'Well,' he continued, looking off to the side in a way that looked half-shifty, and half-amused. 'I accidentally released some of her ink into the main drinking water line. Turns out it's an hallucinogenic. It had everyone in Alteria tripping for a couple of hours.'

I laughed, imagining the stuffy Alterians baked on squid ink. 'Is it anything like Pi?' He gave me a funny look. 'I dabble,' I explained with a shrug. There wasn't really much point lying to Frank now. He already had enough dirt on me to get me tossed out into the wastelands if he really wanted to.

'It's like Pi, but not as mellow. The hallucinations get a little freaky sometimes … you have to be careful not to take too much.'

'What did they do after you released it into the water supply?' I was surprised he had managed to avoid a spell in rehab for doing something like that.

'Not a lot. My record is otherwise stellar, and nobody else wants to take over down here, so what were they going to do?' He shrugged and plucked one of the capsules from the container. 'Here, have one to try. But whatever you do, don't go into Monique's room when you've taken that stuff – it makes you smell like food to her, for some reason.'

I hesitated, suddenly remembering why I had come in to see him in the first place. 'Can I take a rain check on that? I had a little bit of an accident feeding Monique just now … I lost my grip on the pail and it went in there with the fish.'

Frank raised his eyebrows and grinned at the same time, creating a very strange series of furrows and lines on his face. Then his eyebrows dropped again, following his train of thought.

145

'It's no danger to Monique, obviously…' he began.

'Obviously,' I agreed, although I hadn't actually known this.

'But last time this happened, she chewed it into small pieces and they clogged up some of the filters. We'd better go and take a look, just in case. She's not due for release for another three days, and we can't leave her water unfiltered all that time.'

Frank slipped the capsule container into the pocket of his overalls, and we headed to Monique's room.

I watched in disbelief as Frank opened the hatch and gestured for me to go inside. I stood still, my eyes darting from the small, dark opening to Frank's friendly – but increasingly impatient – face. After a few seconds, he squeezed his gigantic frame through the opening, then disappeared.

'You coming?' His voice boomed from a few metres inside the hatch. I knew I was going to have to follow – after all, I was the one who'd thrown the bloody bucket into the squid's tank.

For an hour we'd watched the monitors in his office. They'd showed an infrared image of the huge beast as she rolled and shredded the metal bucket, enthusiastically seeking out the fishy contents. We could just make out the metal fragments as they rolled merrily along the bottom of the tank, got swallowed by the filters, and were sent clanking into the system.

So now we were both crammed inside a strangely hot, dark crawlspace which led who knew where (well, actually I presumed that Frank did) to go and sort out my mess. I followed him, trying to concentrate on something other than the cramped confines of the tunnel and Frank's enormous buttocks. He shuffled along in front of me, looking not unlike a grazing hippo.

'Frank,' I said, deciding it was more important to distract myself from the claustrophobic conditions than his backside, 'your arse is huge.'

There was a metallic thud as he banged his head against the ceiling of the crawlspace, followed by his echoing laugh.

'I offered to let you go first,' he called back to me, his voice muffled by his own impressive girth. 'Didn't realise you would actually enjoy the view from back there.'

We continued without further conversation for a few minutes until Frank stopped suddenly. As I caught up with him, I saw that the space had opened up a little at a vertical intersection in the crawlspace. With some difficulty, Frank manoeuvred himself upright. He waited for me to clamber to my feet next to him and directed me up the ladder.

'As long as you've had enough of the show,' he added, laughing again and shaking his head at me. I gripped a rung, then hesitated.

'Where do all these tunnels go, Frank?'

He narrowed his eyes, trying to guess why I was asking. 'They run along the outer edge of the ark and in between the levels. Why?'

I decided not to lie, which felt weird. 'I was wondering if I would be able to get into the restricted levels to have a look around.'

'Why?' he asked again, although he didn't seem particularly surprised.

'I want to see what's up there.'

'Well, I can tell you that real easy,' he said. 'I know they've been installing equipment into the storage levels – thousands of bio-cylinders, VR tech, bio monitors, IV feeds, and a whole mess of other stuff. They're expanding the rehab facility.'

Frank told me everything was installed across the fifteen levels which had been cleared, each level having the capacity to hold more than a thousand inmates.

'Fifteen thousand,' I said, with a low whistle. 'Hang on, that's twice the residential capacity here, isn't it?'

'Yup. But they don't exactly need roaming space while they're plugged into the machines. They have a cylinder each, hooked up to whatever programme they've been given for their treatment, a feeding tube and not much else. It's not exactly meant to be *roomy*.'

'Wait, a *cylinder*?'

So far I'd been picturing Dallan sitting around in group therapy, sharing secrets and braiding hair – not floating inside a tube, hooked up to a VR programme. I suppressed a shudder. After seeing how Alteria used expensive purge technology as a human laundry service, I really shouldn't have been surprised they'd take a tech-heavy approach to rehab.

'I need to see it,' I said, half hoping I'd be able to find Dallan, and half hoping I wouldn't.

Frank thought about it, then nodded. 'I don't suppose it'd do any harm. I know you're not going to go shouting about it, anyhow. But we'd better clean out these filters first.'

I saluted my agreement and moved on up the ladder.

The seemingly endless row of cylinders looked like some kind of human battery farm. The inside of each cylinder was lit up eerily with a dull blue glow, the naked inhabitants appearing lifeless inside their liquid confinement. I walked along the row, looking at their faces. Most had their eyes closed, so that you could sort of imagine they were sleeping. Others stared blankly. It was hard to believe they were sentient. Alive, even.

Every once in a while I'd spot a Rat. It was easy to tell them apart from the others. Their bodies were slower to heal after years of radiation exposure, lesions and other markers of disease scarring their sallow skin. The ones who'd been out there the longest were also hairless, all their follicles deadened and useless. That was how I'd have looked by now, if Dad hadn't managed to con our way back inside an ark after Cardis.

Frank walked ahead, moving relatively stealthily for him. He seemed even more unnerved than I was.

'Come on, Mason,' he whispered. 'We'd better get out of here before someone comes in and catches us.'

But I was already heading over to a computer station. Frank came to stand next to me, still surveying the room.

'What are you doing?' he asked me as I typed quickly, scanning the results on the monitor.

'Checking the inmate manifest. My friend, Dallan – he's listed here. It says he's in 24N.' I cross-referenced this information with the location grid and found his pod two levels up, almost directly above where we stood. 'But why do you think there are so many? Alteria can't need the money *that* badly…'

'Money?' Frank laughed. 'No, lad. It's not the money.'

I looked at him over my shoulder. 'What then?'

'Think about it: a community, about to set off and stake a claim on a new world, with all the tech they could possibly want but one distinct shortage…?'

I mulled it over, my eyes roving over the rows upon rows of glass cases. 'People,' I said. 'They needed more people.'

'Not just any people, though,' he said. 'People who won't be missed, and who don't have Citizen rights. People they can *control*.'

My stomach turned over. 'You're talking about slaves,' I

said. Frank didn't answer, just looked at me with a deep frown on his face. 'Let's get out of here.'

I wiped my computer search from the log and stalked back to the crawlspace hatch. Frank hurried after me, seeming happy to be leaving. He was *less* happy when I finally convinced him to come with me up another two levels to find Dallan's cylinder. Having seen the layout on the monitor, it didn't take us long to locate it once we'd broken in two levels up. *24N* was clearly marked on the cylinder casing.

We stood looking at him, saying nothing. The weird blue glow made us both look ill as it lit our faces through the glass.

Dallan's eyes, unlike the other inmates', were covered by a medical visor – the kind used to heal damaged tissue. His hands were covered with gloves that did the same. Until then, I'd somehow managed not to digest what Eli told me Dallan had done – probably on purpose. It was eerie looking at the pale skin, the light hair so like my own. With his eyes covered, I could almost have been looking into a mirror. A really frightening mirror. Was this where I'd end up if the Alterians found out about my implant? I was trying to decide whether it was better or worse than being outcast to live as a Rat when Dallan's arm shot out. His knuckles struck the inside of the cylinder with a muted clack. I stumbled away from him, my back meeting the casing of another pod behind me.

'Can he see us?' I whispered, but Frank shook his head.

'They're just muscle spasms.' He put a hand on my shoulder. 'How long has your friend been in there?'

'Just over three weeks,' I said. Dallan was totally still now, floating in front of us like some creepy science experiment. This was worse than being exiled, I decided. 'How long do you think it'll be before they let him out?'

Frank shook his head. 'I don't know, Mason. I really don't know.'

CHAPTER THIRTEEN

Alteria Community

I switched off my implant, not wanting the angry shouts to come crashing in on me as I ran to Engineering. I was stopped by some burly security guy whose oversized teeth made it hard to read what he was saying. Shoving me back the way I'd come made it a little more obvious, but I tried to force my way past him until we ended up grappling on the floor. He'd just managed to pin me against the suede-like carpeting when I saw Ari's feet appear next to my face. They looked pissed off.

Whatever she said to Burly Security Guy got him off my back – literally – and Ari helped me to my feet with only the mildest look of irritation. That is, until he was out of sight. Ari poked the side of my head to activate my implant – which she knew I hated – then dragged me around a corner and started yelling at me. Well, yelling in whispers.

'Damn it, Mason! You know better than to come up here and make a scene, especially when you're obviously off your face on … what is it this time? Pi? Or have you found some new chemical to eat away at your brain? You promised you were going to try to keep it together. I didn't think I needed to spell out exactly how hard it was to get us in here, how much I had to grovel and beg for them to let us in the bloody door, but apparently I was wrong…'

'I haven't taken anything,' I said, matching her tone. 'And I wasn't trying to cause trouble just now, but we really, *really* need to get out of this place. Like, *now*.'

Her eyes narrowed. 'What's happened?' The switch in Ari's mood was sudden and complete. She wasn't angry with me anymore, she'd gone into protection-mode.

I couldn't feel anything but grateful for my sister right then. Any time she'd thought someone was giving me a hard time when I was growing up, Ari'd been there to stick up for me. Whether it was because of my deafness or whatever trouble I'd gotten into, my sister – little Ariadne with the blonde pouf of hair – would always show up with her sleeves rolled back, ready for a fight.

I didn't want her to fight for me this time, though. I just needed her to believe me.

I told her what I'd seen down in the restricted levels, including finding Dallan's pod, and Frank's theory about the Alterians using non-Citizens as slaves on the new world.

'There were just so *many* of them, Ari! They even have *Rats* down there. If Alteria doesn't manage to get their shit together and build a ship in the next few years, what

154

are they going to do with all those criminals? There isn't room for them all here if they let them out, and nowhere else will take them, and *I* don't want to end up in a tube like that, or worse still, a slave…'

Ariadne put her hand on my shoulder, stopping the flow of words I couldn't seem to stem on my own. 'Hang on a minute, Mase. What Frank said was just his opinion, and not based on any kind of evidence, as far as I can tell. You said that you knew Alteria was taking in *some* criminals and offering rehabilitation for a fee – well, there weren't *many* Rats, were there? So that means the rest have come from one of the other communities, who must be paying that fee. So if they've paid for someone to be rehabilitated, wouldn't it make sense that they're going to let that person back in once they have a clean bill of mental health?' I nodded mutely. 'Well, the fact that Alteria is taking in *more* now doesn't mean that the purpose of the rehab unit has changed. This community needs money just like any other – how else will they pay for the materials and labour to build a ship? And throwing in a freebie rehabilitation whenever they bring in a few Rats is probably just part of the whole Alterian enlightenment agenda – showing compassion for the enemy, you know?'

Ari stopped talking, seeing that her point was hitting home. She pulled her mouth into a tight smile and squeezed my arm.

'You're right,' I said, 'of course you're right.' I let out a long breath and relaxed against the wall, my head lolling back to meet the fuzzy coating with a snap of static.

'Now I'd better get back to work,' Ari said with a final squeeze-and-release. 'Are you sure you're okay?'

I nodded, feeling like an arse for making such a scene. Even if I wasn't entirely convinced that the Alterians' motives for taking in all those crims were good, at least Ari'd given me a reasonable alternative. I would try to give them the benefit of the doubt. For now, at least.

Back in my quarters, I sat with my NightReader on in the dark, the weird blue light of the visor eerily appropriate for what I was searching. I trawled through file after file of very important, very *dull*, information before I found what I wanted: the spec for the rehab technology that had been brought to Alteria. I was surprised I was able to access the files at first, until I noticed that everything I read was being logged and reported back to my student counsellor. But by then it was too late to block the report.

I can always tell Lyle I'm thinking of going into biotech programming as a future career, I thought, and couldn't help snorting. There was no way anyone would let me be in control of someone else's rehabilitation.

What I knew about this kind of VR technology was pretty sketchy, so it took me a while to get my head around the spec for the latest developments. Looking at the design of the hardware, it seemed that it was only a small step away from the stasis technology Eli was working on, except the rehab pods didn't stop the occupants from ageing. They did, however, slow down metabolism and vital signs until they were *practically* zero.

Clever, really, I admitted, as uncomfortable as I felt about it all. At least the hardware made sense to me. It was something tangible, with parts and function.

I moved on to the section which described the programming, picking up the scraps I could even half understand.

…multifaceted android simulations, programmed with every rehabilitative technique currently used by the counselling profession, I read. *…combining 99.99% accuracy of social interaction with three-dimensional personalityscaping. Subjects will feel completely at ease, whilst at the same time being completely unaware of the programme itself… Time perception warping ensures rehabilitation is achieved in minimum real-time.*

I removed the headset, unable to make much sense of it all. Wherever Dallan was, and whatever he was seeing right now, it didn't sound like something I'd want any part of. I decided I'd have to ask Eli to translate if I was ever going to understand what it was all about.

But Dallan will probably be long out of rehab before I wrap my head around it, I thought. *I hope.*

In Deep Blue the next morning, Monique was giving me extremely unfriendly vibes after the whole pail-tossing incident. I did my best to avoid the tank, but as Frank had me checking his recalibrations on the filters, I had little choice but to skulk around the edges of the tank room, pretending I didn't have my eyes glued to the viscous shape moving through the ink-blackened water.

Frank had informed me that this year marked his twenty-fifth as a mole, working down in the depths of Alteria to make sure the ungrateful bastards didn't choke on their own piss. Maybe Frank hadn't phrased it that way, but I knew that was what he meant. I could tell from his cheerful demeanour that being away from the general population for ninety per cent of the time had not upset him one little bit. If that didn't say something about the folk that lived in the upper levels, I didn't know what did.

'Mason, when you're done checking the calibrations, I need you to lower the water temp in Monique's tank, get her ready for release tomorrow.'

I jumped at the sound of Frank's voice before I realised he was speaking to me through the vox strapped to my wrist. The device gave his voice a tinny, squeezed sound I didn't like. I tentatively tapped the vox to reverse the broadcast.

'How much should I lower it?'

I moved over to the temperature dials on the far side of the tank, my wrist hovering in the vicinity of my ear so I could hear Frank without his deep bass tone knocking me sick. Three dials faced me, all set at different levels, and none of them labelled.

'Four degrees should do it.'

I peered at the dials again in case I was missing something obvious. 'Frank, which one of these three controls the water temperature?'

There was a pause before Frank answered. 'You're not next to the dials right now, are you? I told you not to talk too near the tank, the vibrations…'

I tapped my wrist, cutting him off. 'No, Frank, you didn't. So which…'

Something sharp and hard wrapped around my forearm, and I screamed as the tentacle tossed me across the room. I slid over the grille flooring, my arm hugged to my chest as I rolled and skidded to a stop against the door.

Frank's pounding footsteps sounded from the corridor. I managed to shimmy out of the way before I could be hit by the door as well. His massive head appeared first, hair stuck out all over the place like he'd run through a gale to reach me. His deep-set eyes zeroed in on my bad arm. I clutched it against my body as something hot and wet seeped through the sleeve of my overalls. I didn't dare look.

'Damn, boy! Monique got you.' He bent down to help me up, taking all of my weight so that I almost left the ground when I stood. 'Let's get you to the infirmary.'

I felt my face set in a horrified expression. 'No! They'll

put me in one of those tubes!' The image of all those deathly still faces flashed before my eyes. What if they put me in there, and I woke up a slave on a new world? I wasn't a Citizen yet, none of the criminals had that to protect them… *What if…*

Frank shook his head, like he could tell what I was thinking. 'I'll make sure they don't, lad. Now let's get you up.'

The urge to cling to the grille flooring like a cat subsided a little at Frank's assured tone. Plus, my arm hurt like hell. I stopped struggling and let him help me through the door. 'Frank?' He turned his wild-haired head to look at me. 'I fucking hate that squid.'

The infirmary was right next to a cafeteria on Level 20. I made a mental note never to eat at that cafeteria.

Frank went in ahead of me to speak to the receptionist, but what started out as a hushed conversation soon rose to a level where it could be heard by the diners next door.

'Get the doctor out here now!' Frank bellowed, his gut wedged threateningly on the reception counter. The receptionist, who up to that point had been sitting with a waspish look on her face, skittered out through a door behind her.

'What's the problem?' I asked, trying not to sound too whiny. My arm really hurt. The skin about an inch below my elbow had been shredded all the way around, presumably from the evil hooky-claws on Monique's tentacle. But at least she hadn't taken it right off, which she easily could have. Or dragged me into her tank. I shuddered at the thought.

Frank gave me a smile that didn't reach higher than his moustache.

'No problem, boy. Just a misunderstanding with the receptionist.'

He was saved from any more bland lies as a middle-aged woman in a thoroughly pressed beige tunic strode in, the receptionist cowering behind her.

'What is the problem here, Astos?'

She said it a lot more shittily than I had a moment ago, and Frank bristled. 'The boy is injured, and your receptionist seemed to think you wouldn't treat him.'

The woman whispered something to the doctor, who nodded. 'We are under no obligation to treat Mr Coulter as he has no Citizen card. He needs to go to the rehabilitation chambers. You know this.'

'There's no way in hell I'm…' I started, but was cut off as Frank's palm slammed down on the counter.

'Dammit, Serena!'

The doctor looked unmoved by the outburst. '*He* is unclean. Our resources are for those seeking enlightenment in His Wisdom, not stray dogs who are taken in from the wild only to urinate all over the furniture.'

I was grudgingly impressed with her insult, but Frank

wasn't deterred. 'You're being ridiculous! It's not your place to judge Mason, even if he does piss on the furniture…'

'I really don't,' I interjected, earning a scathing look from all present – even the receptionist.

'Aren't you forgetting that "nobody is beyond redemption"?' Frank continued, obviously quoting one of the Alterian tenets. 'And haven't you taken a vow to treat *any* person in need of medical assistance?'

The doctor reached behind the reception counter and grabbed a white cylinder. She tossed it to Frank. 'There. That'll seal the wound and deal with the pain.'

Frank sighed, and I knew he'd lost the battle. Opening the cylinder, he sprayed some clear fluid all over the wound. Honestly, that shit was sent straight from heaven. The burning pain stopped instantly, and within a couple of seconds I could see the skin start to knit back together, leaving me with an angry red stripe that was definitely going to scar. But at that moment, I couldn't have cared less.

'Thank you,' I said to both Frank and the doctor, who huffed back into her office. The now unshielded receptionist looked torn between taking her seat at the counter again or scurrying after the doctor. 'Come on, Frank. Let's get out of here.'

Frank ushered me back out into the hallway, where Alterians on their way into the cafeteria for lunch stopped and gawped at the outsider before hurrying away. The infirmary door had removed the blood that had congealed on my overalls and skin during the encounter, so at least that wouldn't put them off their food. Because I was very concerned about that, of course.

'I'm sorry about her,' Frank said, deliberately putting himself between me and the gawkers as we headed back in the direction of the lifts. 'Serena has always been a bit holier-than-thou.'

'Not the best quality to have in a doctor.'

Frank snorted. 'Not the best quality to have in a wife, either.'

The lift pinged as the doors opened. '*What?*'

'Yeah, she was my second wife.' The doors closed behind us, but I almost didn't notice the change in vibrations until Frank guffawed inside the moving metal box. 'If I ever have a pet sea-viper, I've got a name ready for her.'

I laughed with him as we headed back down to Deep Blue, trying not to stare at the new scar on my arm.

CHAPTER FOURTEEN

Sector 24

Noah sat in the dark, listening to the freezing rain hitting the roof. From feeling his way around the walls of the room, he guessed he was in some kind of cell. It was a couple of metres square, at most. Apart from the door he had come in by, he could feel no other opening or possible means of escape. The door itself was solid, with several bolts and hinges keeping it firmly in place.

He listened for any sounds coming from outside the cell. Noah thought he could make out muffled voices passing the door from time to time, but when he called out, he received no reply.

Noah turned over the last few days in his head, wondering whether he had done something to warrant this treatment. He hadn't done anything to make Michael turn on him. Noah rubbed the sore spot on his arm where the soldiers had taken his blood – to confirm his identity, he assumed.

What part had Beth played in all this? If she'd been

involved, Michael wouldn't have lied to her before they entered the base. *At least that's something,* he thought. *Even if I never see her again, I know someone cared about me.*

He felt an unexpected weight in his chest, as though he had swallowed something that had lodged itself deep in his oesophagus. Not for the first time that week, he found himself struggling to catch his breath.

Calm down, the rasp in his head told him. Feeling chastised, if only by his own thoughts, he swiped his palm roughly down the length of his face. Gradually, his breathing evened out. Noah stood and stretched, feeling the pleasant pull of his muscles.

'What do I do now?' he said aloud in the dark.

Reach higher, the voice said. Again, that scraped-raw voice which sounded oddly familiar. Noah knew there was nothing normal about hearing voices in his head, but reasoned that he had nothing to lose by listening to it.

Edging forward until he felt his breath bounce back off the cool stone of the cell wall, he reached up as far as he could, feeling along the rough surface. He had almost completed his circuit of the room when he looked straight up, and saw a thin strip of light shining through the wall directly above him. He stretched up onto his toes. Feeling with his fingers, he could just about tell that it was a window, boarded shut. The lowest board had warped inwards, battered by the rain.

Noah reached as far as he could, and managed to work

165

his fingers between the board and the window frame. Pulling back on it, he tried to wiggle the board loose, but it wouldn't give.

He resumed his blind search of the cell, now focusing on the floor to see if anything there could be used to pry the board free. His search produced nothing useful, just an old food-encrusted plate, a screwed-up piece of paper and a broken shoelace. Noah checked his own clothing, not expecting much, but when he reached the belt at his waist he realised he might have the makings of an escape.

Carefully, so that he wouldn't misplace them in the dark, Noah removed his boots and laid them directly beneath the window. He stepped forward onto the steel toes, giving himself an extra few centimetres of height. It wasn't much, but it was enough to give him a little more leverage against the boards. Balancing so he wouldn't upset his precarious platform, Noah unbuckled his belt and snaked it out of the loops of his trousers. He worked his fingers once more under the board, edging them as far as they would go into the crack, then pulling to make it as wide as possible. Noah slid his belt into the higher part of the gap so that the buckle was left poking out, the tail wrapped around the width of the board. Then he took an even length of the belt in each hand, braced his foot against the wall for leverage, and pulled.

At first, the board moved only a little, groaning as though it had been woken up after a deep sleep. Apart from this and the rain, Noah could hear no other sound outside the cell. He leaned further back, adding more weight.

With only a creak of warning, the board split, sending Noah flying backwards against the opposite wall. He stood there, winded for a moment. As he caught his breath, Noah looked up, seeing the wide strip of grey light coming from the evening sky.

He picked up the broken board, then tested it against his knee. It felt strong enough. Working up a sweat, he used it to pry the others loose one by one, the rain streaming into his eyes through the window. Once the hole was large enough for him to fit through, he put his boots back on.

Allowing himself the smallest run-up, Noah leapt as high as he could, planting both hands firmly on the window ledge. He hung there for a moment, then pulled himself up to the ledge. He looked down.

The sheer face of the building stretched out below him, with not a foothold to be found.

Look up, the voice directed. He did.

'Now you're talking!'

He reached up to catch the first rung of the fire escape ladder, the angry mark on his arm illuminated for a second as though he had been lashed by the lightning tearing the sky overhead. Noah hauled himself up, climbing steadily until he was over the top of the wall and onto the roof.

Beth lay staring at the ceiling. A damp patch had gradually been growing over the months since she had arrived. In the half-light, it almost looked like the shadowy outline of her own body, suspended in the air, unmoving.

Michael appeared in the doorway. He stood in silence for a moment, perhaps wondering whether she was asleep.

'Are you all right?' he asked finally.

'I'm fine,' she said, her tone flat.

'I'm sorry if I upset you.'

'You didn't,' she replied. *I don't know why I'm feeling like this.*

'All right then.' Michael took a step back, then stopped. 'I'm going out for a while. Saul's upstairs in the back room … I'd stay out of his way if I were you. We had a bit of a run-in earlier, and I imagine he will not be very happy when he wakes.'

Beth shifted to a half-seated position, leaning back on her elbows.

'When he wakes?'

'Yes.' Michael didn't elaborate. He turned to leave.

'Did you hurt him?' Beth asked, surprised. Michael paused, his back still to her.

'Not really. The only one interested in hurting Saul is Saul.' With that, he strode out of the room. Beth heard the front door close a few seconds later.

She listened for signs of movement from upstairs. Nothing. Rolling off the bed and onto her feet, Beth made her way quietly through the parlour and stopped at the foot of the stairs. She listened again. Still nothing.

Creeping up the stairs, she hugged the edge nearest the wall, keeping her weight off the middle of the boards. As she neared the top step, Beth could see the door to the back room between the upper floor banisters. The door was open, but she could see nothing beyond the threshold. Faintly, she heard Saul's breathing, steady as ever. Now that she had made sure he was alive, she debated whether she could just leave him there and go back downstairs. Beth scolded herself for being a coward.

It's only Saul.

She strode across the landing and knocked lightly on the frame of the open door. Saul sat leaning against the wall, the light of the hallway hitting his profile and making Beth catch her breath.

'Oh, it's you,' was all he said, then went back to staring into the darkness.

'Are you all right, Saul?' He flinched when she said his name. Beth crouched next to him, warily. 'I'm sure Michael didn't mean to hurt you.'

'You don't understand,' Saul continued in his peculiar monotone, rising to his feet. 'You know nothing.' He faced her, now clearly visible in the light spilling through the doorway.

'What don't I know?' Beth backed away, feeling the stair railing hit the small of her back. Her voice caught in her throat when she saw his face. Dozens of tiny cuts marked one side of his face where he had fallen on the broken glass, but it was Saul's expression that caused Beth to stop short. He looked at her with eyes glittering with rage.

'I remember.' He took a step towards her, closing the gap between them to less than a metre. 'And all it took was a sharp knock to the head.' He tapped his temple, his eyes widening. Saul was now within reach of her. He stared, assessing her like she was a piece of meat he couldn't decide whether to eat or bury.

'What are you doing?' Her voice betrayed her nerves. Beth edged away, trying to create enough space to escape. But Saul moved closer, blocking her escape. His hand closed on her hip, crowding her against his body.

'I can help you remember, too,' he said. 'I bet you don't remember what it feels like to be with a real man…'

'Let go of me!' Beth shoved against his chest as forcefully as she could, only managing to put a small gap between them, but it was enough. She vaulted herself over the stair rail behind her, landing halfway down the stairs. Beth paused for only a fraction of a second when she saw Saul following her.

'Come back here, you little bitch!'

Beth bolted for the front door and yanked it open, the rain hitting her face like icy needles. Snatching the roach's keys from a hook by the door, Beth ran out into the night. She kept going, flying towards the roach, even as she heard Saul closing the gap between them.

CHAPTER FIFTEEN

Alteria Community

My door swooshed open to reveal Eden sitting next to the window in my quarters, painting on an old-fashioned canvas block. She swiftly threw a sheet over it as I walked in.

'Do you want me to come back later?' I asked, smiling. My arm no longer hurt, thanks to the doctor's marvellous medicine, but I covered it with my shirt so Eden wouldn't see the mark.

She smiled back. 'No, I'd rather look at you than a canvas, seeing as you're here and all.'

'Well,' I said, schooling my face into a serious expression, 'I'm only here to escort you back to your quarters.'

Eden frowned. 'You want me to leave?'

'Only if you want to get changed. I'm taking you out.'

She immediately perked up again.

'Where are we going? The arboretum?'

I shook my head. 'Stop asking questions. Come on, all will be revealed soon enough.'

I took her hand, twirling her to her feet, and she laughed in a twinkly sort of way.

'What should…' I cut off the question by kissing her, then shushed her with mock severity. Eden put her finger to her lips, signalling that she wouldn't ask any more questions.

'Good,' I said, my lips grazing the finger which barred her mouth. I took her hand, moving it so I had better access. Eden's lips parted for me, a slight hitch in her breath as I pulled her tight against my body and kissed her the way she loved to be kissed. She smiled against my mouth, sliding her hands down to grab my arse.

'If we let this go any further we'll never make it out of my quarters,' I muttered. 'Although I'm really struggling to remember why that's so important.'

Eden laughed, disentangling herself. I waited outside her quarters while she changed. Going out to eat wasn't something I did often – it was, in fact, more of an annual event which I did for my sister's sake. I'd learned to hate eating around others before I got my implant, when every glance my way made me wonder if I was chewing noisily or making weird sounds when I swallowed. That discomfort was hard to shake, even now. Ari understood, but neither of us was willing to be the one to suggest breaking the tradition.

Eden had probably been to this particular restaurant hundreds of times, but it was as spontaneous a gesture as

I was able to make within the confines of our goldfish bowl. What was different tonight, though, and probably due to the sudden closure of the Rec, was that a large section of the restaurant had been cleared to create a dance floor. I saw her take note of it as we walked to our reserved table.

'Well, Mason,' she said, appraising the whole room as we took our seats at opposite sides of the table, 'I think you're up to something.'

'Up to something?'

She nodded. 'I think it's only fair to tell you that it won't work.'

'What's not going to work?'

'Your plan to seduce me,' she said, matter-of-factly. 'I'm unseduceable.'

'*Unseduceable?*' I laughed as I mimicked her odd word, then straightened my face. 'Well then,' I said, rising to leave, 'I'd better not waste my time.'

Eden put her hand on mine as my fingertips lingered on the table's edge, but her smile told me that she hadn't bought my act for a second. Some people at surrounding tables had, though, and were openly staring at us.

'But I didn't say that you shouldn't try. It shows character, you know – to try something even if you know you won't succeed.'

I took my seat again, grinning as I summoned the menu on the table monitor and turned it towards her.

'And it shows wisdom to admit when something once declared impossible is now entirely probable,' I said.

Eden stopped midway through her sip of water and laughed, almost choking as she did so. 'Did you seriously just use faith rhetoric to get me to admit I want to have sex with you?' She looked at the tables around us and winced. Her voice was considerably lower when she continued. 'I suppose it would show good grace to admit … there is some truth in that.' Her eyes wandered over me as she bit her lip, stifling a grin. I probably looked more than a little smug.

Eden made her selection from the on-screen menu and waited for me to decide. I chose something inoffensive-sounding, and pushed the menu away.

'I remember the first time I saw you,' she said after a while.

'In the room beneath the Rec?' I thought back to the night I'd stood watching her, making my covert transaction with Angela, feeling almost hypnotised as she moved in the weird light.

'No, it was before that.'

I frowned. I was sure that I would have remembered if I'd seen her before that night – even without the peculiar setting, the sight of her stirred those unmistakable pulling sensations in my chest. And elsewhere, obviously.

'Where?' I asked.

'When you first came in from quarantine.'

I tried to picture her there that day, to find Eden somewhere in one of my memories.

'You didn't see me, but I was picking up a tour group as you came in the airlock,' Eden explained. 'I noticed *you* right away.'

'Why?'

'Well, I loved your shoulders,' she said, her eyes following their lines. 'You looked like an athlete – strong, but not too bulky. I could tell what your hands would feel like without touching them…'

'I knew you only wanted me for my body.'

Eden smiled, nodding once as though in partial agreement. 'But it was actually the look on your face as you were coming through the airlock that made me decide to talk to you.'

'What look?'

'Like you were a caged animal. Like you would rather be anywhere else, as long as it wasn't here.' She sipped her drink as I took this in. In truth, this wasn't the first time I'd been called an animal. 'You still look like that,' she added, 'most of the time.'

'Sorry,' I said, not sure whether this was something I was actually sorry for.

She shook her head. 'You look the way I feel.'

'I thought you loved it here?' I said.

'Oh, I do. I mean, I love my people, but living inside an ark … there has to be more, doesn't there? I can't wait until we arrive on New Earth, and we can really start to live, to build something new instead of just scraping an existence on a planet that can't support us any longer.'

I had the feeling that she'd started this conversation knowing my particular reason for taking her out this evening. But of course, that couldn't be true.

'Eden, there's something I wanted to tell you…'

'You mean…?' she discreetly touched a finger to her ear. I blanched.

'No … wait, you know?' I checked the nearby tables to see if anyone was suddenly paying us an unwarranted amount of attention. They weren't.

But how had she known I was deaf, and for how long? Had I suddenly become really sloppy about hiding it? Who else had spotted it, besides Frank? I kept these panicked thoughts to myself.

Eden smiled reassuringly.

'I've known since the day we played TAG.'

'But you know I'm not…' *a Rat*. I left those words unsaid. 'Eden, I'll tell you about it, and how it happened. I want to tell you.' I was shocked to realise that was true. Even with Dallan and Eli back in Parisia, I'd waited until I really couldn't avoid telling them before getting into the whole Cardis massacre story. But I wanted to talk to Eden about it, to answer her questions and not have to hide my deafness from her.

Eden waited like she knew exactly what was running

through my mind, and what conclusion I'd draw before I even admitted to myself that I trusted her. Cared about her, more than I ever meant to. More than was smart.

'When we're alone.' She nodded. 'Is that … is that why it's hard for you, living inside an ark like this?'

I cleared my throat, trying to rattle away the sudden tightness. The memory of Cardis didn't exactly make it easier living in an ark, and neither did the constant threat of the Rats. It wasn't even that I still struggled with the noise always pounding inside my skull. I searched for the right words to explain the feeling I'd always lived with – the need. 'I find confinement … uncomfortable. Tight spaces especially. It's partly the constant noise, but that's not the whole reason. I just feel like I have to *get out* sometimes, and I never can while we're stuck here. Well, unless I get exiled.'

'Isn't that something you could work through in therapy?'

'Or I could just find a way out.' I swallowed back the nerves now trying to strangle me. *This* was it – what I'd brought her here to ask. 'That's why I'll have to leave as soon as a community announces it has a vessel ready to launch for the new planet – I need to be on it. I can't hang around Alteria for the next decade while it gets ready to launch, and … well, I'd really like you to come with me.'

'Huh,' she said. I watched her emotions flit across her face, as wild and hard to capture as a flock of starlings. I'd seen a video of starlings once, from back before they became extinct. 'Mason, I can't leave with you. I've lived here my whole life, and I know you don't *get* our faith, but we are all about learning about the cosmos and everything in His creation, and using that to help us become better people. Sure, we don't always agree on everything, and I know we're far from perfect, but I won't turn my back on my beliefs. On *them*. If we're the first people to land on New Earth, we can start to set things up so that when the others arrive, we won't make the same mistakes we made here.'

She'd gotten more and more animated as she continued. It still floored me that she could believe in something so strongly. I'd never been able to do that.

'But I still don't think this is going to be an issue for you and me,' she said. I'd been staring at her, and her smile was a little sheepish. 'Alteria will be the first to launch.'

I debated telling Eden what Frank and I had seen, the thousands and thousands of people in storage just waiting to be shipped off as slaves to the Alterians on the new world, if Frank's theory was right. But as I watched Eden sipping her drink and smiling as she caught my eye, I knew I couldn't. I had no evidence. And I didn't want to ruin everything by upsetting Eden. I'd seen a shittier side of Alteria. I didn't want her to see it too.

The waiter arrived then, letting me avoid having to say anything. I looked at the meal on my plate, and imagined the feel of it in my stomach – a churning mess. Eden was already attacking her burger. The relish was smeared across one side of her face, but she didn't seem to feel it.

'What's wrong?' she asked, her mouth still full. I must have grimaced, because she ran her hand across her face apologetically – not getting rid of the mess entirely, but spreading it a little more thinly across a larger area.

'You have relish on your ... everywhere,' I laughed.

I caught hold of her chin. Very deliberately, I rubbed away the relish stains with my thumb. Eden held still for it, although I could hear mutters of disgust from the next table. This was not the kind of scene the Alterians were used to seeing in a public place. We were both laughing now, and drawing far too many staring eyes. I let my hand drop.

'They'll kick us out if we don't behave ourselves,' Eden whispered. As she had already finished her burger, she watched me pick at my own food until everyone went back to their own conversations, their own business.

'You don't like that much, do you?' Eden said after a while. I wrinkled my nose and shrugged. 'I thought you brought me here to dance, anyway?' She nodded towards the makeshift dance floor, where a small number of couples were moving awkwardly together – close, but not touching.

'My parents taught me how to dance,' I said as we walked over to join them. Eden leaned into me, my hand resting naturally at the small of her back. I ignored the stares zeroing in on us. 'I used to be quite good at it. But I had to focus on practical things, things that would help me go undetected, and make me a useful commodity when the launch happened.'

I cringed at how cold and clinical I sounded. We were leaning so close together, Eden's face was against my chest, so I couldn't see her reaction.

'I wish I'd known that you could dance sooner. I feel like I've wasted a lot of opportunities.' She sighed melodramatically. 'As we're sharing secrets, I have one for you. Despite my aversion to tomatoes, I have magical green fingers,' she said. 'I am going to be a botanist on New Earth.'

'I thought you were going to be an artist?' I said.

Eden lifted her head just so she could roll her eyes at me. 'I told you – that's only one of the things I'm going to do with my life.'

'Fair enough.' I tucked her head back against my chest and whispered into her hair. 'I really hope I get to walk on a beach with you someday.'

'You will. I…'

The song cut off abruptly, and the floor disappeared from under us.

CHAPTER SIXTEEN

Alteria Community

We were plunged into darkness and thrown into the air as the structure shuddered. The floor made a violent re-entry as it slammed against my back, and Eden delivered a second blow as she landed on top of me.

We both lay still, winded. Around us, the other Alterians in the restaurant seemed to be doing the same. A few bangs and thuds echoed in the dark, but nobody spoke. Then a voice boomed through the space, hissing and crackling with background static.

'Well howdy, folks of ... let's see, what did they say this one was called? Alteria? Alteria, right?' The man – whoever he was – sounded like he was speaking to someone away from the microphone he was using to broadcast through the ark's PA system. 'All righty. This is your friendly heads-up that my colleagues and I have breached your shields – kudos on keeping us out so long, by the way; that's some decent tech you've got going on there – but now we're claiming this fancy ark for ourselves.

As we aren't complete savages, despite what you might've heard, we'll give you … oh, let's say five minutes to get to your escape pods – '

The broadcast cut off with a loud snap, and I tightened my arms around Eden instinctively. The lights came back on. But they didn't reach their full brightness, which meant they were now running on a back-up power supply – emergency power levels.

Eden lifted her head and braced her hands on the floor either side of my torso, taking most of her weight off me.

'Are you okay?' I asked, studying her face for any sign of pain. She nodded.

'Soft landing. You?'

'I'm fine,' I said after checking myself over. Before I could say anything else though, another voice filled the room. This one lacked the background static that had made me want to reach inside my skull and scratch my implant right out of my head.

'Good people of Alteria, this is your Chief of Security speaking. Please do not be alarmed at the intrusive broadcast you just heard – the outsiders did manage to affect one small section of our defences, but the threat is being neutralised as we speak. For the moment, please remain where you are. If anyone is in need of medical assistance, help will be with you momentarily. I will provide an update as soon as we have dealt with this … inconvenience. God be with you.'

Eden sighed against me. 'Thank God, my dad's got it under control,' she said.

All around us, people were shakily getting to their feet, beginning to right tables and chairs, dusting off their tunics.

Eden's vox started beeping on her wrist. I automatically looked for my own, and realised I'd switched it to silent mode. Seven missed comms glared at me from the display.

'Eden?' Frank's voice boomed from the device as Eden answered the call.

'Hello?' she replied, sounding confused. Maybe she didn't know Frank, what with him being a mole.

'Frank?' I interjected.

He sounded instantly relieved, but still hoarse, as though he was exerting himself. 'Mason, I hoped you'd be with Eden. I couldn't get you on your vox. Where are you?'

'Sorry, I had it on silent. I'm in a restaurant on Level 16.'

He paused. 'Good, you should be able to make it. Can you come down to Deep Blue? We've got a big problem – several, actually...'

'What's going on? It felt like the Rats set off a bomb under us or something.'

'Sorry, Mason, it's a longer story than I have time to tell you right now. I know Security just issued a *stay calm* mandate, but things are a little more serious than they made out. If we don't get the power back within the hour, Alteria goes into lockdown.'

Lockdown.

The prospect of being trapped as the bulkheads separating the levels slid and locked into place was pretty much my worst nightmare.

'I'll be right there, Frank.' I looked at Eden, saw the worry she was trying to hide. 'Will you be all right getting back to your quarters?' She nodded. 'I'll come and find you as soon as I've sorted out this problem with Frank.'

I was about to tap the vox again when his voice stopped me. 'You won't be able to get down here in the lift,' he rasped. 'The power's not back up yet. You'll have to use the crawlspace.'

Okay, maybe *this* was my worst nightmare.

'Frank, please tell me you're joking.'

I heard a low chuckle over the line. 'Don't worry, kiddo,' he said. 'It's only sixteen levels down. Hurry, though.' He said this last part seriously. I was going to have to move very quickly to get down to Deep Blue before the lockdown trapped me somewhere in the crawlspace between a couple of emergency bulkheads. 'And keep your damn vox on in case I need to reach you.'

I felt the room spin a little and worried that whatever had impacted the ark was starting again. Or had fritzed my implant. Then I realised it was just me freaking out.

Thanks for that, Frank, I thought, helping Eden up before I stepped out into the darkened corridor.

'Mason,' she called after me. I paused in the doorway, noticing that the purge system was also offline.

'Don't go. I'm sure Frank will be able to handle it.' I understood without her having to say it. The climb down in the crawlspace would be difficult for anyone, even without the clock ticking. But for someone not too comfortable with small spaces … well.

'I'll be fine,' I said, disappearing into the darkness.

I looked down into the confines of the crawlspace, following the beam of the torch as it disappeared down the steel shaft. Closing the cover of the emergency store, I slipped the wrist strap of the torch over my hand and took hold of the ladder.

I left the hatch of the crawlspace open. The longer I could convince myself that I was in no danger of being trapped, the less likely I was to freak out. I made my way down the ladder, marking my progress against the time on my vox. I figured I had about forty-five minutes before I'd be trapped in the crawlspace, and it was taking me just under two minutes to climb down one level. Plenty of time to get down to Deep Blue. Whether it'd be enough for me and Frank to stop the lockdown altogether was another thing.

I picked up the pace and did my best to ignore the horrifying feeling that I was lowering myself into my own personal hell.

I'd been making good time, with only two more levels to go, when my heart dropped into my stomach. There was a sound of rushing water coming from below me in the tunnel. I looked down, following the beam of light from the torch strapped to my wrist.

A salty-smelling spray rushed into the crawlspace a few metres down the shaft. The hole looked about the size of my thumbnail, but the fact that the seawater was coming in at all told me that the electric shielding around this section had failed. At any moment, this part of the tunnel could collapse like a tin can. I was right at the outer edge of the ark, maybe next to where the Rats had managed to break through the outer shielding. They might be right outside for all I knew, sitting in their subs, waiting for Alteria to show some sign of weakness. I didn't know how they'd managed to breach the shields, but they had. My mouth grew spitty, and I fought the urge to throw up.

Because I'd been trying to move quickly and ignoring the sickening thickness of the sound bouncing around me, I hadn't noticed the air temperature creeping up. But now that I stood still, I could feel that the heat outside my body was a lot stronger than it should be. One at a time, I took my hands off the ladder and wiped them dry against my clothes.

I forced myself down the ladder to see how deep the water had become. As if to spur me on, a loud groan echoed down the tunnel. The weight of the water outside was threatening to crush this section, and me with it.

The torch had a distance gauge built into it. It was normally used to find hull breaches by bouncing sound waves off the tunnel walls and pinpointing the site of any weakness, but I saw that it wouldn't work through water. *Shit.*

I looked at my vox again. Twenty-five minutes until lockdown.

I climbed down until I reached the flooded section. Trying to make out the bottom of the tunnel in the torchlight, I saw nothing but dark water. I pointed the torch upwards and activated the distance gauge. I hoped that it would recognise the hatch on the level above as the nearest 'weak spot' in the tunnel walls, so that I could work out roughly how deep the water was below me, then dive down and open the hatch to get into Deep Blue. Whether this would make the hull collapse more quickly, I wasn't sure, but it looked like my best option. If I tried to get into the level above – the first of the restricted levels, where the rehab pods were – I'd be trapped in the antechamber, where the high security meant it would already be in lockdown.

The reading showed that the water was just over six metres deep. I looked again at the torch and made yet another horrible discovery – it wasn't waterproof.

I now had just over twenty-two minutes to dive down six metres in pitch blackness, open the access hatch at the bottom of the tunnel, and then figure out whatever Frank wanted me to figure out to stop the whole ark going into lockdown.

Perfect.

I took a deep breath but couldn't let it out again, couldn't move a muscle. My lungs were stretched to capacity, my heart thumping in my chest, and I knew that I was about to die.

But it was hardly the first time this had happened.

As I'd been taught, I started making a list of all the decisions which had been made, the actions carried out, to get me to this particular point. Then I ran through them in reverse.

1) I decided to climb this far down the ladder instead of getting out through the hatch on the level above.

2) I decided to carry on going, even when I knew that there was a leak in the tunnel.

3) I picked up the torch without checking to see if it was waterproof.

4) Some arsehole – probably in control of ordering stationery supplies – decided to go for the cheap option, and bought a non-waterproof torch to use in the underwater sections of the crawlspace. Nice one.

My breathing became a little easier, the moment passed.

I let the torch drop into the water. It was useless to me now. The light went out almost instantly, leaving me blind as I carried on down the ladder. Cold blanched my skin as I lowered myself into the water. It crept higher, swallowing me. Before I ducked my head under, I switched off my implant, sucked in a couple of lungfuls of air, and held my breath.

I used the ladder to pull myself along quickly, feeling the

pressure increasing in my lungs. I exhaled some of my air, which felt better in my chest, but didn't relieve the tight band that was wrapped around my head, and getting tighter. It took around thirty seconds for my feet to touch the floor of the tunnel. Keeping hold of the ladder with one hand, I faced the wall where I knew the access hatch would be.

I hooked my heels under the bottom rung of the ladder and knelt on the tunnel floor, keeping my hands free to turn the lever that would open the hatch. Feeling along the wall, I found the shape of the lever.

It wouldn't move.

The burning in my chest was like acid as I forced my weight against the lever. The last of my air bubbled around my face. This was it. I was going to die. For real now. I was…

The lever turned.

The hatch flew outwards, releasing a torrent of water into the antechamber of the lowest level, and I went sprawling in the dissipating tide. I gasped in huge breaths of air and pulled myself to a sitting position against the wall. Shoving the hatch shut behind me so the water wouldn't keep leaking out as it refilled the crawlspace, I looked across the antechamber to the opposite wall, where someone – presumably Frank – had scrawled, in what looked suspiciously like squid ink, '*Welcome to Deep Blue.*'

I shook my head and dragged myself to my feet, soggy and sore, then staggered to the entrance of the facility.

CHAPTER SEVENTEEN

Alteria Community

I hurried through to the control room, leaving a wet trail behind me. Looking at the wreckage, it was as if a typhoon had blown through. I turned on my implant and listened. Nothing.

'Frank?'

Seeing no sign of him, I was about to head for his office when I heard something heavy slap against the metal flooring. I froze, imagining in a moment of panic that Monique had somehow managed to find her way into the control room. The control room – a dry cube full of electric consoles and not too much else that would interest a squid, besides myself. I almost laughed. Then, as I turned towards the source of the slapping sound, I saw him.

'Frank!'

He lay on the floor in a corner of the room, pinned by a heavy electrical unit – one of the instrument panels we used to control the community's water flux. It was like it had been torn up from the floor and thrown at him. *The shockwave must have been ten times as strong down here as it was in the restaurant,* I thought.

I ran over to him. His face had turned purple under the unit's weight. I grabbed one edge and braced my foot against the wall behind Frank for leverage. Then I pulled.

I'd known it was going to be heavy, but not *how* heavy. Blood rushed inside my head, my knuckles turning white with the effort. Still, it only moved a few centimetres. Shaking as I struggled to maintain my grip, I shouted to Frank through gritted teeth.

'Can you move?'

I heard him grunt and shift as he tried to free himself, but he was still wedged in. My grasp on the unit slipped, giving me just enough time to hiss at Frank to move before it fell back to its original position. He'd used the extra few centimetres to move farther into the corner, so that not all the unit's weight was resting on him.

'Thanks, kiddo,' I heard him call wearily from behind the hulking metal panel.

I leaned forward, trying to catch my breath, and became aware of a noise in the room besides the pulse still pounding inside my skull.

'Frank,' I said between gasps, 'what's that noise?'

'It's the countdown for the lockdown sequence,' he wheezed.

'How … long?'

'About three minutes, give or take.'

'Oh,' I said. I had no idea whether that meant it was too late to stop the lockdown now, but freeing Frank was my priority. 'Frank, have you got a jack or something I can use to get this thing off you?'

'There's a jimmy in my office that might do it. But first, I need you to stop the lockdown…'

'One thing at a time, Frank.' I was already heading for his office.

It looked like the site of an explosion. His desk lay on its side against one wall, tools and data pads strewn everywhere. I started rummaging around the heaps of Frank's stuff, looking frantically for the one piece of junk that would actually be helpful right now. My hand closed around the jimmy and I ran back through to the control room.

'Frank? You still with me, pal?'

His deep, throaty laugh echoed from behind the unit.

'Yeah. Did you think I stepped out for a minute or something?'

'Just checking you didn't croak on me, old man.'

I eased the jimmy into the gap between the angled edge of the unit and the floor. Heaving my entire body weight against it, I managed to create a small space between the corner of the unit and the wall. Gradually, and with much sweating and creaking of metal, the gap grew wider, until finally the unit's own weight forced it back into a standing position. It landed with a hard, metallic thud.

I hurried around the back of it to find Frank peering up at me, his hair slicked down against his head on one side with what looked like oil.

'Little help,' he said, and I saw for the first time that his left leg was bleeding out in a pool in the corner.

'Oh, crap!' I leaned in to support his weight as he threw his huge arm around me, pulling himself up with a loud series of grunts. As soon as he was upright and could see the state of the room, a look of dread settled over him.

'Oh, crap,' he echoed me. 'The control to reset the power for the ark was on that panel.' He pointed with his free hand to where a panel had been fixed to the wall across the room, but now lay twisted and useless on the floor.

'Can't it be done from Engineering? Or somewhere else?'

Frank screwed up one side of his face as he considered. 'Yes, normally Command would do it, but I haven't been able to reach anyone there since the Security broadcast. I spoke with the Engineering section before I called you, though.' His voice boomed louder than the shrill tone of the countdown. 'They said the pulse had fried all their electrics up there, so it might take them too long to be able to restore power. That might be why I can't reach Command, too. We've got better shielding for the equipment down here because of the risk of flooding, so we're the secondary back-up for situations like this.'

'That hasn't done us much good, has it?' I gestured at the ridiculous mess around us. 'What do we do?'

Frank shook his head, then froze as three long, very final-sounding tones sounded. An ominous *bang* followed, reverberating through the walls and floor all around us. With a heavy sigh, Frank shifted his weight from my shoulder and sat against the edge of the unit which had very recently pinned him to the ground.

'Better settle in, kiddo,' he said, rubbing the knee of his injured leg. 'We're here for the duration.'

'How long does lockdown last?'

Frank sighed. 'Unless we can reset the power supply, we'll be here for some time.'

'How long?' Even as I asked, I knew I wouldn't like the answer.

'Hard to say. If we can't restore the power first, we'll be stuck here until the emergency generator fails, and the rest of the shielding goes down.'

'What then?' I had a fair idea what would happen then, but the masochist in me had to be sure.

'Well…' Frank eyed me, clearly considering whether it would be best to lie. Evidently, he decided not to. 'When the remaining shields go down, the water comes in, and so do the Rats.'

'So what the hell happened?' I asked Frank as he leaned back against the wall and allowed himself to slither to a sitting position on the floor, his bandaged leg braced in front of him. I'd fashioned a splint for him out of my wet shirt and two long spanners. It was hardly ideal.

'It was Monique's friends again – but this time they brought the Rats along to the party.' Frank laughed, but I couldn't see what was so funny. I had no idea what he meant about the squid, but I'd seen Alteria handle a Rat attack before, and it had been like their bombs had the yield of a weak sneeze.

'Wait, what? You're saying squid did this?' I said. It took a moment for the pieces to fit together. 'The Rats waited for the squid to attack, didn't they?'

Frank nodded. 'I think they somehow corralled an entire shoal of squid so they'd all head for the hull at once. And when the shields automatically powered down where the squid were clustered, the Rats set their missiles to strike there. I reckon they must've figured out a way to lure more of them up to the surface, too, because we've never had so many take a shine to the ark all in one go. And now the ones that survived the blast are creating even more of a problem.' Frank winced and rubbed his injured leg. 'What do you know about deep-sea squid?'

I shook my head. 'Not a thing. Why?'

He folded his arms. 'Well, Monique is a deep-sea squid from the luciferus family…'

'Lucifer? That sounds about right,' I snorted.

Frank's moustache twitched. I held up my hands in apology and waited for him to continue.

'These squid have only recently been discovered – probably because they normally stay in very deep water – and they're something of a mystery. But something, maybe the shortage of fish, has brought them up much closer to the surface. As you've seen, they can grow to be pretty big. Monique's only a baby.'

My eyebrows shot up. From what I had been able to see, Monique was easily fifteen metres from head to toe. Or tentacle, to be accurate.

'But her species aren't just big. They also luminesce. The scientists thought they were just like other species of deep-sea squid, which have a hormone that causes this bioluminescence in dark water. That was until a couple of years ago when a convoy of eight subs went missing in the waters off the coast of Sector 110. From the wreckage they managed to find – and there wasn't that much left of the subs – they could tell they'd been mangled by squid. Their hulls had been ripped apart like party crackers. It took them a while to realise that squid don't just attack vessels by crushing them. They disable them first by creating a massive electrical surge. Imagine the hit that you got, but times a thousand.' I pulled a face, and he continued. 'Individually, they can send out a charge that would kill a large mammal, but in groups… well,' he waved his hand to indicate the devastation around us, 'the explosives the

Rats used wouldn't have caused all this damage. Most of this was done by the squid. Makes it hard to remember why we don't arm ourselves against God's creatures, doesn't it?' His smile was wry, and I once again got the impression Frank wasn't exactly a believer.

'And the Rats somehow rounded them up to attack communities like Alteria? What the hell were they thinking?'

He shrugged. 'The Rats are desperate. Unless Command is in the same state we are, they'll have hauled in most of the subs by now. But that still leaves us at the mercy of Monique's comrades, and when food's in short supply, a cookie jar like this one starts looking pretty tasty. They've been sending charges through the ark – on a far smaller scale than this, I grant you – for weeks now. Like they were testing the water, so to speak. So far we've only had a few minor glitches with the electrical systems, but I've no idea what a group of squid this size will do if they keep charging the ark.'

I thought about this for a while, not too thrilled with Frank's cookie jar analogy.

'What sort of minor glitches?' I asked.

'A few with our main computer systems, nothing major. At least not yet.'

Then something that he'd said earlier struck me. 'If this has happened before, what did you do last time? I mean, surely you made some kind of plan in case it happened again?'

'It's never been this bad, or anywhere near as many attacking in one go. That's what makes me think the Rats somehow managed to lure more of them to the surface. Last time the squid came calling, Command dealt with it from up there. In theory, if Command are tied up, like they are now, I just have to press that button over there...' he gestured to the destroyed control panel '...and enough power will be restored for the guys in Engineering to fix the rest. Like I said, we're only supposed to be the back-up. Not even that – more like the *back-up* back-up.'

I tried to work out the problem. 'Well, does Command know the button down here is knackered?'

'I tried to get a message to them,' Frank said, frowning. 'They're probably too busy dealing with the Rats to respond.'

'Oh,' I said. 'So, what exactly does that button do? When it's not in pieces, I mean?'

Frank shrugged again. 'I'm the water guy. I know as much about electrics as I need to, but to me that button was just a button.'

I went over to the remains of the control panel and studied the mangled circuits. Electrics weren't exactly my forte either, but it looked like the button had overridden a circuit breaker, diverting enough power from the back-up generator for Engineering to get things up and running again.

I think – maybe..?

I reached into the open wall behind where the control panel had been, following the wires that led from the panel up and out of reach.

'Frank, I don't suppose you were being modest just now, and actually know enough about electrics to find the right wires to connect the circuit and divert the power upstairs?'

I turned to find him making a face that didn't exactly inspire confidence, then looked back at the jumble of wires in my hand. For a second I thought I heard Frank speak, but the voice was too small and feminine to be his. And it was coming from my wrist.

'Uh, Mason?' Eden's voice sounded tense and small through the vox. 'I'm in a bit of a tight spot.'

CHAPTER EIGHTEEN

Sector 24

Michael waited at the threshold, listening. As the front door swung open, he caught sight of Saul sitting halfway up the stairs.

'Are you all right, Saul?' Saul flinched at the sound of his name. 'Where is Beth?'

'She left,' Saul said.

Michael's voice became cold, hard. 'You didn't do anything *bad* to her, did you?' Saul shrugged and shook his head. 'Where did she go?'

Saul looked at him from under his straggly blond hair, his eyes a dark glint in the lamplight. 'I don't know. She took the roach.'

'I'm sorry if I hurt you earlier, but I'm sure you realise that I wouldn't have done it by choice,' Michael said.

Saul laughed, with no hint of humour.

'Yes, you're quite right, Mike. I was out of order, I'm glad you put me back in line.'

Michael studied his charge. Something about Saul was different, but Michael struggled to identify what it was.

'Is your head feeling okay?' Michael asked. Saul nodded.

'All right, then,' Michael said, walking into the house. He paused as he passed the foot of the stairs. Saul looked away, casting his face once more in shadow.

As Michael left him, Saul listened to the sounds the android made as he stalked around the kitchen. His footsteps sounded sure, predictable. Every cupboard door that creaked open closed with a matching creak – no louder, no longer. Systematically, the android tidied up after the humans. After a while, Saul followed Michael and stood in the doorway to the kitchen, watching in silence until Michael stopped what he was doing.

'What did you do with Noah's body?' Saul asked.

Michael froze, but only for a moment. 'Don't you remember? We buried him.' He continued packing items into the cupboards without looking, holding Saul's gaze.

'Yes, I do remember. But last week, when I went out back and dug up the spot where we buried him, he was gone. Where did you move the body?'

Michael shook his head, frowning. 'I didn't move the body anywhere.'

'You're the only one who knew it was there,' Saul said, his voice strangely quiet.

'I don't know what to tell you, Saul.'

'If you didn't move it, then what happened to it?'

Michael didn't answer.

'Maybe Beth moved it. Do you think I should ask her?' Saul said.

Michael stopped what he was doing, but didn't look at Saul as he answered.

'I don't think that's a good idea. She doesn't know what you did to him. It should stay that way.'

'Why shouldn't she know?' Saul asked. 'He was her friend. Doesn't she deserve to know that he's dead?'

'If that was the reason you wanted to tell her, I might agree with you,' Michael answered bluntly. 'But you are only trying to hurt her, and manipulate me.'

Michael moved across the room to where the clean cutlery sat on the drainer. He picked it up in a pile, went back to the drawer, and began systematically sorting it.

'If you just tell me what happened to the body,' Saul continued, 'then I won't need to say anything to Beth. I won't ever mention it again.'

Michael dropped the remaining items of cutlery carelessly into the drawer and slammed it shut.

'I don't know,' he said, his voice still low, but with a very hard edge to it. 'You must have been digging in the wrong place.'

'I'll tell you my theory,' Saul said, now leaning against the door frame, his arms folded across his chest. 'I think that after we buried Noah's body, it disappeared – *poof* –

into nothing. I think his body is gone because he woke up somewhere else.'

Again, Michael said nothing.

'By the way, Beth's not coming back.' Saul threw this last remark in casually. 'She's gone wherever Noah went, I assume.'

Saul saw instantly that Michael had misunderstood his meaning, but had no chance to correct him. Michael crossed to Saul in two quick paces. He grabbed him by the throat, effortlessly lifting Saul's feet clear of the floor. When he spoke, Michael seemed eerily calm, even as Saul spluttered and turned purple above him.

'Ignorant human. Why do you need to undermine – no, *ruin* – everything that's just been handed to you? You are given life, but that's not enough. You screw it up. You are shown kindness by me, by Beth, even by Noah – who had enough troubles of his own – but you decide you don't like him hanging around. And you beat, you *bludgeon*, an already damaged boy to death.' He brought Saul's face closer to his own, lowering his voice further, while Saul's eyes rolled back in their sockets.

'And now Beth. Are you even sorry?' he asked.

'Didn't hurt her … she's fine…' Saul struggled to choke out the words.

But Michael was beyond hearing him. His grip tightened, even though Saul had stopped struggling.

'You are the bane of my existence, Saul. You just. Don't.

Learn.' Michael punctuated this by knocking Saul's head back against the wall, small flakes of plaster showering them both like snow. 'And I would give anything, *anything*, for the chance to live a life beyond … this.' With his free hand, he gestured broadly to the desolate decay surrounding them. 'Why don't you listen, Saul? Why?'

Michael released his grip on Saul and he slumped to the floor, settling awkwardly against the door frame. Michael crouched next to him.

'Saul, you know you can't continue like this, don't you?' Saul's last words repeated in Michael's head. *She's gone wherever Noah went … I didn't hurt her … she's fine.*

'Saul?' He shook the man gently, but Saul's head simply lolled. 'Saul… *Oh.*'

The enormity of what he had done descended on Michael like a rockslide, his fingers finding no pulse in Saul's neck. He moved the body, beginning chest compressions he knew wouldn't work. But he kept trying, kept working Saul's body until it disintegrated beneath his hands.

But instead of the light which normally claimed those ready to leave or begin their lesson again, Saul didn't pass in a wave of light. His corpse collapsed into a swarm of particles like buzzing insects. They swirled about Michael's head before threading their way out of the building through cracks and holes and tears.

Michael remained crouching for a moment, uncertain what he had just seen. What he had just done.

I killed him. The thought formulated slowly. *I need to report this to my superiors. I have no charges now. What ... what will I do?*

Nothing like this had ever happened before. Nothing like this was *meant* to happen. Michael rose to his feet and paced, waiting for a connection. But then he stopped, disconnecting the call.

I have no charges, therefore no purpose. But Beth and Noah are still out there somewhere, and if I can find them and guide them out it will be all right.

It has *to be all right. Otherwise what is the point?*

Michael stepped over the space where Saul's body had been and headed out into the growing darkness. His mechanical body was no match for the roach in terms of speed, but he had no need to stop and refuel, and only one thing driving him. One single, simple purpose. Michael sprinted across the dusty ground, on a direct course for the military base where Noah's father waited for his son.

Beth floored the accelerator, crunching angrily through the gears. She knew roughly where she was going, but the scenery looked different in the grey light of pre-dawn, and it made Beth doubt herself.

She kept replaying the scene with Saul in her head. Each time she varied the ending, imagining Saul meeting with more and more violent consequences. Beth sighed as the true ending snapped back into place every time, and she saw herself flee the house into the night, scared for her life.

She was going to find Noah. Beth had no idea whether he was still at the military base, but she had no choice but to start her search there. She would find him, and ask him if she could go with him – wherever he was going. There was no way she could go back to that house.

The wind had been howling for hours, but now rain beat against the windshield like a warning. A film quickly built up on the glass, thick with dust and polluted rain. Turning on the wipers, Beth craned to peer through the small clear space they made.

The ugly facade of the base loomed into view in the headlights. Beth slammed on the brakes, and the roach skidded to a halt in the slippery mix of rain and dirt.

She peered at the front of the building, but nothing moved out there. Clambering from the roach, she pulled up the hood of her parka and ran to the huge door of the compound. She hammered her fist against it, forgetting for a moment about the panel next to the doorway until a red light flashed. A voice crackled through the speaker.

'Identify yourself.'

Beth held up her wrist to the sensor as she had seen Michael do earlier, but the light did not change to green.

'Identity confirmed. State your enquiry.'

Beth leaned in close, shouting over the sound of the rain.

'I need to find Noah. I brought him here earlier with the android, Michael. Can you tell me if Noah's still here, please?'

The panel was silent, and she wondered whether the person on the other side had been able to hear her over the storm.

'Hello?' she yelled.

'I heard you,' the voice replied, a little testily. 'Noah is no longer at this facility.'

'Where is he?'

'I'm afraid I can't answer that. Noah left of his own accord earlier this evening. We searched the perimeter, but weren't able to locate him.'

'How long ago did he leave?'

There was a hesitation before the voice replied. 'I believe he left shortly after nightfall. I'm sorry I can't be of further help to you.' The voice crackled into silence.

So, Beth thought to herself, *he hasn't gone to find his father. At least not yet.* She couldn't say why, but she felt relieved about that. *And if he'd headed back to the house, surely I would have passed him on my way here ... if I didn't miss him in all this rain.*

Beth got back inside the roach, peeling off her soaked parka. Where was he?

She manoeuvred the roach in a wide arc around the perimeter of the facility. Its headlights reflected off the rain-battered buildings as she searched for any tangible sign of him.

Well, that's tangible all right, Beth snickered to herself. She halted the beam as it settled on the drenched figure sitting with his legs dangling from the ruined fire escape. Noah shielded his eyes with one hand and waved.

Beth moved the roach into position under the fire escape, then waited for the thud of his boots to hit the roof.

A sodden but happy Noah appeared at Beth's shoulder. 'Th-thanks for c-coming back for me.'

He leaned forward and planted a cold, wet kiss on her forehead. Laughing, she batted him away and thrust the roach into gear. They sped off, widening the gap between them and everything that was even slightly familiar.

CHAPTER NINETEEN

Alteria Community

'Damn it!' I turned to Frank once Eden had finished explaining her situation, but he looked as panicked as I felt. 'This is all my fault! If I hadn't told her tight spaces freak me out, she wouldn't have followed me.' I raked my hands back through my hair. 'What the hell do we do?'

Eden had come after me a couple of minutes after I'd entered the crawlspace. She'd made it all the way down into the bottom section of the tunnel before Alteria went into lockdown and the emergency bulkheads slid into place between the levels, trapping Eden between two of them.

There was also the small matter of the leak. It seemed to have picked up speed and, Eden estimated, would completely fill the compartment she was trapped in within ten minutes – if her air supply didn't run out first.

'Come in, Command!' Frank barked into his vox. 'This is Astos in Deep Blue. Come in, we have an emergency down here!' The silence stretched like gum before a voice crackled back through it.

'Sorry for the delay, Astos, but we've been a little busy dealing with those Rats outside the front door, in case you didn't realise. What's your –'

Frank jabbed the controls to cut in. 'There's a civilian trapped in a compromised section of the crawlspace, and our lockdown override button is FUBAR. You need to shut it down from up there so we can release the bulkheads!'

The voice sounded somewhere between smug and annoyed when it responded. 'No problem, Astos. I'll get on that just as soon as the last of the Rat subs has been brought in. Should be clear any second…'

'They've set it to self-destruct! Get it back outside!' A voice in the background shouted over him just as a deep, rolling boom echoed from somewhere above our heads. The grille flooring shook, sending me stumbling against a console. A siren blared through Deep Blue, pulsing so violently I had to squeeze my eyes shut against the sound. It only lasted a few seconds before halting just as abruptly as it started. When I opened my eyes, the floor was no longer shaking.

Frank slapped his vox. 'Command? Command!'

We both jumped as a hiss of static erupted from the device. Then it went dead. Frank tried again, but this time there wasn't even a crackle in response.

'Probably just their communications system acting up,' he said, but I wasn't buying it. 'Don't panic, Mason. I'll try Engineering.'

He kept yelling into his vox, but I wasn't really listening now. Eden was trapped behind a thick sheet of metal, her air supply shrinking by the second.

I gripped the edge of the console. What if I couldn't reach her in time?

My eyesight darkened at the edges, narrowing to a pinpoint that settled on the roiling water inside Monique's tank, visible through the open door. She didn't seem to be any happier with the situation than we were. The water sloshed over the side of the tank as she thrashed about, flickers of light snapping in the depths of the inky water.

I grabbed Frank's wrist – the right one – interrupting his rant at whoever he'd managed to find in Engineering. My knuckles glowed white around Frank's arm as I spoke into the vox. 'If we can send enough power up there, how quickly can you shut off the lockdown?'

'Mason? Is that you?' My sister's voice came out weird and metallic through the device. I'd never been more relieved to hear it.

'Ari!'

'I'm fine, Mase. Are you okay?'

'Yes. Ari, how quickly can you shut it off?'

I could picture the crease forming between her eyes as she calculated. 'Ten minutes, give or take.'

My breath hissed out through my teeth. 'If I can route one burst of power up to Engineering, can you release the lockdown any faster?'

No hesitation this time. 'Yes.'

'Good. You'll have it in about one minute, okay?'

'What are you thinking?' Frank asked as he heaved himself to his feet, unsteady on his splinted leg.

'I'm thinking that if we move fast, we might have a chance to save Eden.' I ran into Frank's office and returned a few seconds later with wire cutters and a coiled length of electrical cable with large crocodile clips at each end. I handed one end to Frank.

'I'm going to attach this to the main power line up to Engineering. Can you take that end into the tank room?'

A broad grin curved his moustache upward. 'Clever boy. Right, I'm on it.'

I went over to the panel as he lumbered off, and started stripping back the plastic coating the main power line. Once that was done, I connected the crocodile clip directly to the bare wire. Now all we needed was power.

'Frank, are you ready?'

'Ready,' he said. Frank stood just beyond the tank room door with Monique's metal food pail in one hand, the crocodile clip attached to it, and a length of the cable coiled in his other hand.

'Throw it now!'

I watched as he shifted his weight to his good leg, swinging the bucket backwards. As he launched it towards the tank, the cable sailed merrily behind it before the pail disappeared into the dark water. The cable snapped taut, catching Frank behind his knees and sending him flying onto his back.

'Shit!'

I ran over to where he lay groaning and knelt next to him, keeping one eye on Monique. Her strange iridescence lit the murk of the water with faint crackles of electricity as she attacked the pail. I thought I could actually *hear* the power buzzing as it pulsed past me through the cable.

I offered Frank my hand to help him to his feet, but he waved me away.

'Need a minute,' he said, his great barrel chest heaving up and down as he caught his breath. He pulled his wrist in front of his face, speaking hoarsely into the device. 'Did you get it?'

'Got it.' Ari let out a relieved sigh. 'Should have the emergency bulkheads out of the way in three or four minutes.'

'Will that be soon enough?' I whispered.

Frank closed the call and placed another. 'Eden?'

'Yes, Frank?' Something about the transmission didn't sound right when she answered. I realised with sinking horror what it was.

'Are you all right? Engineering should be able to override the lockdown in three or four minutes,' Frank said.

Eden didn't answer immediately, so all I could do was listen and hope I'd been mistaken about the sound. 'I guess

I'll just have to be all right until then.' She laughed, a little too shrilly.

'How high is the water?' I asked, trying not to let the panic creep into my voice.

'Oh, not too high,' she said vaguely. 'I'm not worried, Mason. I know you'll have me out of here in no time.'

Her transmission was fuzzy now, confirming what I'd been trying to deny. The reason her voice sounded so odd was that there was absolutely no echo, which could mean only one thing: the vibrations were being dampened. The water had risen more quickly than we'd anticipated. Too quickly.

'Mason, remember what you promised me, about rehab?'

'Look, I'll have you out of there in two minutes. There's no need to be talking about *rehab*.'

'I trust you, Mason. I need to tell you…'

I almost didn't hear the click of her communication device cutting off. I was already running to the access hatch with the jimmy in my hand, knowing that there was no way I'd be able to pry open the hatch with lockdown still in effect, but I had to try. Try *anything*. I started hacking away at the unrelenting hatch, the harsh clang of metal against metal reverberating through my body.

I could just about hear Frank's voice as he hurried my sister through his communication device, and her bleak reply.

'Two more minutes. I'm so sorry.'

CHAPTER TWENTY

Sector 24

The shockwave swept through the sector, capturing everything it passed like a magnet.

There had been other waves before – more frequently, recently – and they were getting worse. It turned an old farmhouse into a burned-out land cruiser, changed the colour of the sky for precisely five-point-two seconds, and drew one dark soul deep into the very fabric of the dust.

On the outskirts of the sector, the roach sat in silence where it had skidded to an ungainly halt. It was completely dark; no external lights, not even the glow of the buttons on the control panel.

Inside, Beth lay against one of the bulkheads. Her eyes were closed, her hair matted across her face. A thin line of blood dripped from the corner of her mouth onto the cold floor of the vehicle.

Noah lay next to her, one arm thrown over his face. He groaned as he rolled onto his stomach, then pushed himself up onto his knees. Surveying the carnage around him, he didn't immediately notice Beth lying next to him. He called out for her, turning too quickly in his panic and stumbling back onto all fours.

Then he saw her. He touched her face, wiping away the line of blood from her chin. Cradling her head in both his hands, he used his thumbs to open her eyelids. Her eyes rolled as she tried to focus.

'You're all right, Beth,' he said gently. 'You're going to be fine.'

As if to lend credence to this last statement, he started tentatively checking the arrangement of her limbs, not sure how to tell if anything was broken. All the lines were straight; no joints had separated. He waited anxiously for her eyes to open of their own accord.

'If you're hurt anywhere, I just need you to let me know.' He paused, uncertain. 'Please Beth, just speak to me…' Noah stroked her hair away from her face and she leaned into his touch. He sighed as Beth's eyelids gradually fluttered open. 'There you are.'

Seeing his worried expression, Beth laughed softly and held her hand to the side of his face.

'So what do you want me to talk about?'

Her eyes fought to maintain their focus, but gradually she was able to concentrate on Noah's face.

He shook his head. 'Tell me something about you,' he said.

Beth's attempt to sit up sent shooting pains through her

head. Through gritted teeth, she said, 'I'll tell you anything you want, as soon as I feel human again.'

Beth breathed in and out slowly, her eyes closed. After a moment, she startled herself awake.

'Don't let me fall asleep. I think I have a concussion.'

Noah frowned. 'What should I do?'

'Just keep me awake. Talk to me. Tell me what happened.'

Put something cold on the bruised area, the voice in his head added, no longer unnerving to Noah, though he knew it shouldn't be there. *Then check that her pupils are the same size.* Noah looked around for something cold to hold against Beth's head, and his eyes settled on a canister of engine coolant. He grabbed it.

'Something hit us, like a bomb went off or something. It knocked out the electrics, and the roach skidded out of control,' Noah said.

'Must have been an enemy attack. Are you all right?' Beth smoothed the skin of his cheek with her palm.

He nodded, leaning forward to check her pupils. 'I'm so sorry,' he said.

She leaned up to meet him, kissing his mouth gently, taking him by surprise. Then he held her face in both his hands, returning the kiss with an urgency he didn't understand. They drew apart, but their gazes stayed locked, searching for something neither could explain. Beth cupped one of Noah's hands against her face, then slowly moved it into the space between them, lacing his fingers with her own. Their hands glowed white on gold in the early morning light.

Beth's eyes fell onto the angry red band spanning Noah's arm. She traced it with one finger of her free hand.

'Does this hurt?'

Noah shook his head. 'No. But I almost feel like I'm starting to remember when it happened … something lashed out at me, like a whip or something. Then … nothing.'

Beth held her arm so that their black ink marks showed side by side across their wrists. 'What about…' Her voice tapered away as she studied Noah's tattoo. They both stared for a moment in mystified silence. 'I think I must be more concussed than I realised,' Beth said, wincing as she tried to focus, 'because it looks like your serial number has changed.'

Noah shook his head. 'It's not the concussion. It *has* changed.'

'But I thought that was tattooed onto you?'

'It is.'

'And isn't it your birthdate? How can that suddenly be different?'

Noah shook his head again. He had no answers, only more questions.

'I wonder when it changed…' Beth sat up slowly, testing to see whether her sore head would object. It didn't.

'It had the other code on there when I was on the fire escape.'

Noah had studied the markings while he waited on the broken metal ladder for his captors to find him again. Sitting there in the rain, he'd had plenty of time to weigh things up.

In the short time he had been with Beth, Saul and Michael, Noah had asked a lot of questions. And he sensed that they had each answered him with varying degrees of honesty. Beth was honest with him – Noah believed that. Yet she didn't have the answers he needed. Even Saul seemed to have been honest with him, in his own way. It was Michael's answers that troubled Noah.

Michael had told him what the code on his wrist meant, and now it had changed. Michael had pushed him to find his family, to leave, even though Michael was the one who had been sent to find Noah in the first place. Why?

'Maybe you're not who Michael thinks you are,' Beth said. 'Maybe it's not your father they've found at the military base.'

'You could be right. But I'd like to find out.'

'So you're still going to find him?' Beth sounded disappointed.

'Not without you. If you don't want to leave, then I'll stick around.'

Beth cast a glance through the windshield where the

roach's tracks led back the way she had come. 'I can't go back to that house.'

'Why?' Noah said. He didn't want to face Michael again – at least not before he had some answers. But that didn't explain Beth's reluctance. 'Did something happen after I left?'

Beth shook her head. 'I just can't.'

'So you're coming with me?'

'It looks that way,' she said. Noah didn't even try to hide his grin.

They had been travelling at a leisurely pace for four days, but even though they didn't push the roach for speed, they could only go so long before they would have to refuel. Food was also becoming an issue.

As they travelled – Beth and Noah taking turns to drive, as it appeared that he almost instinctively knew how to operate the vehicle – the devastation flew by on the periphery. All the places they passed, though probably varied and unique at some point, now wore the same wounded expression. It was the animal that had been kicked too many times.

Beth had followed a route through the uninhabited areas, knowing that running into other people in these desperate places would bring nothing but trouble. But they no longer had a choice. She slowed the vehicle as they came to what had once been a small town. The welcome sign hung crookedly from a charred metal post, and had stated simply *Welcome to Fairfax.* At some proud moment in the town's history, though, someone had graffitied the sign so that it now read *Welcome to hell, muthafukkas.*

Noah pointed to a building looming large ahead of them. It must once have had several floors, but all except the first two had been destroyed. All the windows were boarded over, as though to accommodate the work of art that covered the front of the building.

'What *is* that?' he asked, studying the building's facade.

Against the dark, sooty cement of the outer walls, a brilliant white and red symbol stood out in stark contrast. The rectangle of white paint spanned the entire width of the building, and was almost as high. A diagonal red line ran through it.

Beth shrugged, unimpressed. 'It looks like some kind of warning, I guess.'

Noah continued studying it until a look of understanding spread across his features. 'A warning, yes. I'm guessing androids aren't welcome here.'

Beth looked at the symbol more closely as she pulled the roach to a complete stop next to it, seeing nothing that would lead her to the conclusion Noah had drawn.

'How do you make that out?' she asked, confused. They both clambered out of the roach and stood next to it. Beth instinctively scanned their surroundings for signs of life, but there was no movement in the nearby buildings. The town appeared abandoned.

Noah pointed up at the building, tracing the block outline. 'That's the symbol for an electrical circuit. The line through it means they're barred, I imagine.'

'Ah,' she nodded. 'How do you know that's the symbol for an electrical circuit?'

Noah shook his head. 'I don't know. Must have been in my programming.' He smiled at her crookedly.

'I wonder what else you know about? Try this one.' Beth used her finger to sketch a diagram in the dust covering one of the roach's windows. She drew two strands spiralling around each other, connected at intervals by short horizontal lines. 'What does that mean to you?'

Noah didn't hesitate. 'It's DNA.'

Beth nodded. 'How about this one?' She traced an equation into the grime.

'That's Hooke's Law, about the restoring force in a stretched spring.'

'You're just showing off now,' she said.

'You knew it too!' Noah's laughter stopped short. 'How *do* we know all this stuff? I thought we were supposed to have no memory.'

'No personal memories, about ourselves or our lives before, no. But you might have noticed that I have a fair grasp of language, I know how to eat and dress myself, how to read – which I wouldn't if I had absolutely *no* memory. Seems like we've both kept some basic programming.'

'But don't you think that's a bit odd? That our memory loss is so localised, so specific?' Noah said.

'Different parts of the brain control different functions. It's not that odd, really.'

Noah wasn't convinced. 'I still think it's strange.'

Beth touched the side of his face with her hand, as if to wipe away any doubt. Noah gasped.

'What's wrong?' Beth withdrew her hand, but Noah caught it in his own and put it back against his cheek. His eyebrows drew together as he tried to identify the feeling the contact had triggered.

'I've been wondering about this,' Noah said.

Beth frowned. 'What?'

'I wasn't sure at first, but when you touch my face like this … it feels familiar, like I remember it from a long time ago. How can that be?'

She shook her head. 'You're probably just a bit confused. You've had a lot to take in this past couple of weeks. I'm not surprised your mind is playing tricks on you.'

Noah considered. 'I don't know. You might be right. I mean, I hear a voice in my head sometimes, and I know *that's* not normal.' Beth raised an eyebrow. 'It kind of guides me, tells me what to do when I'm struggling. It sounds like my voice when I talk, but my voice doesn't sound like *my voice* – it's less familiar to me than the touch of your hand.

How can that make any sense?' Noah sighed, the look on her face making him think he'd said too much. 'Maybe I've gone a little crazy, left wandering in the dust too long.'

'Maybe,' Beth agreed. 'Or maybe you're some kind of prophet, sent to guide me out of the wilderness.'

Noah couldn't exactly see himself as any kind of prophet. 'How about you test me some more?'

'Okay,' she said, after chewing her lip thoughtfully. 'Who painted this?' She clapped her hands onto her cheeks, wide-eyed and open-mouthed in anguish. Concern immediately flashed onto Noah's face, but no sign of recognition.

'Edvard Munch, *The Scream*?' she said, but Noah still looked baffled. 'How about this one, then?'

She walked away from the roach, needing a larger surface to work with. Beth drew with her finger on the dusty ground until a scene began to appear: a landscape, as barren as the plains they had crossed so recently. Beth then drew in details, a mountain in the distance, a dead tree with one horizontal branch. Then in what appeared to Noah to be random positions, she drew clocks – old-fashioned ones, twisted out of shape.

'What is it?' he asked as Beth finished her drawing and squinted up at him from her crouched position.

'Salvador Dali, *The Persistence of Time*,' she said, then added with a wry smile, 'sometimes called *The Persistence of Memory*.'

'I'm not doing too well with art,' Noah said.

Beth laughed at his pouting. 'And I was about to test

you with Gustav Klimt's *The Kiss*...' She pushed herself to her feet again and dusted herself off. 'What else should I test you on?'

Noah thought for a moment. 'You choose. I'm only going to suggest something that I *know* I know about, anyway.'

'Okay then ... what about history? When was the First World War?'

'Early twentieth century, 1914 to 1918,' Noah said. 'Is that right?'

'Right on. How about the American Declaration of Independence?'

1776?' Noah wasn't so sure this time. He grinned when Beth nodded. 'Try another subject.'

'I'll think of more questions, but we need to get moving.' She gestured to the darkening sky. 'I want to be back on the road and away from here before nightfall, in case whoever lives here comes back.'

'I don't think anyone *does* live here. And why are you so anxious about being around other people? What do you think they'd do?'

Beth looked uncomfortable. 'I don't know, really. I just find it difficult to trust people. It's probably because of the memory loss.' She shrugged.

'But you trust me,' Noah persisted. She didn't answer. 'You don't?'

'Of course I do – *now*,' Beth drew in a deep breath. 'It's difficult to explain. It's not like a memory, exactly. More like a feeling that I've been, or I'm going to be, betrayed. Does that sound really paranoid?'

'You're asking someone who hears voices in his head,' Noah pointed out. 'But seriously, maybe you're remembering something from before your life here. Maybe that means you'll get your memory back someday.'

'I hope so,' she said, then made a noise which was almost a growl. 'This is so frustrating!'

Noah stopped suddenly. Beth looked around, searching for whatever had made him freeze. Nothing moved in the shadows, but they were lengthening.

Noah turned her face towards his with a light touch under her jaw. He slowly tilted it to the side, her chin raised, as he muttered, 'Hold still a second, I just want to try something.'

Beth held her breath, waiting as though she expected him to kiss her. Noah leaned over her, drawing her to his chest with his arms wrapped around her.

'Close your eyes,' he said. His face was right next to hers now, his lips so close to her ear that he could feel the warmth of her skin against them. 'The Kiss, right?'

'Hmm?' Beth opened her eyes and saw his smile. Then she laughed. 'Oh, yes – you got it.' She punched him playfully on the shoulder and continued heading into the deserted town. Noah caught up with her, taking her hand, and Beth seemed not to notice. It was as though his touch was a secret her skin already knew.

226

CHAPTER TWENTY-ONE

Alteria Community

I sat looking at Lyle, trying unsuccessfully to suppress the image of Eden's face when we had finally managed to get her out of the crawlspace.

Her skin had been so cold, her wet hair clinging to her face. I'd pressed my mouth to hers, forcing air into her lungs under Frank's direction. All over again, I felt my heart like molten rock erupting in my chest as I'd realised, I'd *known*, that she was dead, and nothing I could do would save her.

And then her body had convulsed. A stream of water shuddered from her mouth, and Frank had rolled her over onto her side as she coughed up the rest of the dirty water.

I'd leaned in, brushing the hair from her face, waiting for her hazel eyes to open. They had opened briefly, unable to focus, before rolling back in her head.

I half-listened as Frank called for the emergency medical team to come down to Deep Blue. Eden's breathing had remained shallow, the air wheezing in and out of her as she lay unconscious. Frank, the only one of us not wearing wet clothes, had given up his overalls to keep her warm. I wrapped them around her, glad of Frank's immense proportions. I'd waited, silently stroking her face, just listening to her breathe.

It seemed to take the medical team forever to get down through the crawlspace. They stripped her and put her into a thermal suit, attaching wires from her body to their portable machines before leaving Deep Blue once the lifts were back up. I'd moved to follow, but Frank held me back.

'Let them do their job,' he'd said quietly.

That had been the last time I saw Eden, ten days earlier. Since then, I'd only left my quarters to stalk the corridors outside the infirmary, and to eat when I couldn't avoid it any longer. I'd heard the announcements, the reassurances that the ark structure had been re-fortified, and would no longer be vulnerable to Rats, and blah blah blah… There was no mention of the squid, though, or protecting Alteria from *God's creatures*. They'd learned nothing.

I realised that Lyle was talking to me when he paused for my response.

'Pardon?' My voice came out flat.

'I asked if you are all right.'

'Oh.' I was surprised. 'I'm fine.'

Lyle smiled in a way that looked almost genuine. 'I am pleased to be able to tell you, Mason, that you have officially graduated from mandatory therapy, and are now eligible for full Citizen status.' He paused, as though expecting me to leap from my chair and perform a celebratory dance in the middle of his office. This, what I'd waited so long to hear, floated around my head like a fog. I forced a nod.

Lyle continued, clearly dissatisfied with my reaction.

'Mason,' he said my name again, presumably to draw me to full attention. 'Despite a number of setbacks, you are graduating due to your recent courageous acts in defence of Alteria. You should be very proud. I know your sister is.'

I flinched. Even though I'd seen Ari since the lockdown, I hadn't been able to bring myself to talk about what happened to Eden. As irrational as I knew I was being, I was angry with my sister. I also knew that this was largely because I hadn't been allowed to see Eden, which had nothing at all to do with Ari.

'Sure,' I said. I rose, expecting Lyle to release me from the session, but he just looked startled for a moment, like he expected a repeat of the vomit episode.

'There is something else I would like to talk to you about,' he said, and I sank back down. 'I know that you have been asking to see Eden. I have been authorised to tell you that she is no longer at the infirmary...'

'She's been discharged?' I interrupted him, and he held up his hand.

'As I was saying, she is no longer at the infirmary. She

has been admitted to the rehabilitation programme while she recovers.'

'Rehab?' My head swam.

I trust you, Mason.

But I'd already failed her.

He puckered his lips in what he must have thought was a semblance of sympathy. 'An illegal substance was found on her person by the medical team. This is not the first time Eden has been caught using contraband.'

My brain revolted at the idea. Eden hadn't been able to get any Pi, she'd told me so more than once. So where had she…? The realisation hit me like a headshot. Frank's little box of squid ink, tucked away in the pocket of his overalls – the overalls I'd wrapped around Eden's body to keep her warm.

Oh no.

'How long will she be in rehab?' I managed to form the question finally.

Lyle raised his eyebrows speculatively. 'Well, the physical damage should heal fairly quickly – in around two or three weeks. But the programme is also designed to help Eden work through the emotional issues she is bound to be suffering as a result of the accident. That could take longer, depending on how well she progresses.'

'How do you know she is suffering with *emotional issues*?' I spat the words. 'Shouldn't you wait to speak with her first? Make an assessment based on facts, clinical observation?'

He narrowed his eyes.

'Nobody knows my sister better than I do, and although ordinarily I would not have *insisted* that she entered the rehabilitation programme, the situation has presented an opportunity for Eden to resolve some other longstanding issues as well.'

His sister. Oh shit.

I gripped the arms of my chair, fighting conflicting urges to smack the arsehole in the face or get the hell out of there. *This* was why he'd shown so much interest in me, in whether or not Eden and I were sleeping together? *This* was why Eden had been shoved into the tube like a broken doll?

'What issues?'

My voice sounded like I was chewing glass, but Lyle didn't notice. He shook his head, adopting a smug smile. 'I'm afraid that is privileged information.'

'Which you can't tell me?'

'Which I have no *reason* to tell you.'

No reason. I imagined throttling Lyle, crushing his obnoxious assumption of authority. He picked up a data pad that had been lying on his desk and handed it to me. I stood, taking it without breaking eye contact.

'Congratulations,' he said, sounding so absurdly inappropriate that I looked at the data pad to see what could have caused him to say it. It was confirmation of my Citizen status.

Frank looked worn with guilt as he silently ushered me inside his office.

'I told them the stuff was mine. Lyle didn't want to hear it.'

A wave of relief ran through me at Frank's terse words, even as my hatred of Lyle swelled like a tumour. 'Surely Lyle doesn't get the final say?'

Frank heaved a sigh, his enormous gut rising and falling. 'As her brother and a counsellor, his opinion carries weight. And with the pair of us being lauded for getting the power up again after the attack, the community chiefs thought it would be bad for morale if I got put in the tube right after.'

'Why didn't you tell me sooner? That he's her brother and … I could have … I could have stopped them putting her in there!'

Frank exhaled loudly. 'Mason, there's nothing you could've done. And I had no idea you didn't know Lyle was Eden's brother.' He sighed again, raking his hands back through his hair. 'She *will* be all right.'

The look in his eyes told me he knew how I was feeling even before the tell-tale sheen of moisture blurred my eyes. 'But she wouldn't have been there if it wasn't for me.'

This thought had occurred to me several times during the last ten days, but it still felt like a knife wound to say it aloud.

'I know that,' he said quietly. 'But you didn't know she was going to follow you into the crawlspace.'

'I promised Eden I would keep her out of rehab. She

said that people who go in there come back different, and that terrified her.' I slumped into the chair opposite him. 'Frank, do you know what the programme *is*?'

He lifted his head, nodded once. 'More than likely it's a combination of trauma counselling and aversion therapy – to deal with the other behaviours the counsellor felt she needed help with. I've heard they're high up on Lyle's list of counselling techniques.'

'Aversion therapy?' I was yelling again, concentrating on welding my feet to the floor to stop myself punching something. Until now, my horror had been focused on Eden being put in that tube against her will as though she were some kind of inconvenience. Now I knew how he was probably screwing around with her head, I wanted to beat the living shit out of Lyle.

'I know,' he seemed to answer my thoughts. 'I can't believe her parents agreed to it.'

'Can't they get her out? If we convince them to withdraw their consent?'

He shook his head, subdued. 'I tried. They wouldn't budge – especially her father.' As he was the Chief of Security, he wasn't a likely ally. Especially not if it meant going against his *son's* recommendation. 'But it was pointless anyway. I found out there's no way to get her out once the programme starts. Not until she completes it.'

I hurled my fist at the wall. The thin partition gave way easily, and we both stared at the hole I'd made.

'Sorry about that,' I said. Frank shook his head distractedly.

'She's smart,' he said. 'I'm sure it won't take her long to figure it out.'

'I don't think it's a question of intelligence. If it was that, I wouldn't be worried. But I can't see how you can win when you don't know you've even entered the game. She could be in there a long time.'

There was nothing left for me to say. Eden's brother wanted to torture her for his own sick reasons, and I couldn't do a thing about it. Frank couldn't help her, her parents *wouldn't*, and I had no idea what else I could do. Frank stopped me as I was walking through the door.

'I *am* sorry, Mason. For everything.'

'So am I,' I said, and the door closed behind me.

I hadn't left my room in three days, and the smell was starting to eat at me. Ariadne was being a pain, calling on me at strange hours to bring me food or just to waffle on about nothing. I gathered this was her own peculiar manifestation of guilt, although I didn't say that to her. As angry as I was with Ari for what had happened, I also knew, logically, that I was being a dick. And as all good brothers must, I hid my dickish behaviour as best I could.

I changed my clothes and headed up to the arboretum. I hadn't exactly decided to go for a run. It was just a reflex. Whenever I felt like I was struggling, running usually helped. I started my first circuit, trying just to concentrate on my breathing, enjoying the rough jolt of every pace as my feet made brief contact with the ground.

Un-der-wa-ter, un-der-wa-ter... Without realising I was thinking it, the word in my mind kept pace with the rhythm of my footsteps. I ran faster, angry with myself, and managed to sprint thoughtlessly for a few laps.

When I could feel the burning in my legs almost as fiercely as the burning in my chest, I slowed to a jog. I left the footpath and turned into the middle of the tame jungle. I glanced upwards, following the shape of the clear, domed ceiling through the spaces between the branches above me. When I was exactly underneath the highest point of the dome I stopped, and sank down to lie on the grass.

Overhead, the sky was getting dark. A thick sheet of clouds had built up over Alteria, looking like a worried frown. Rain was coming.

I worked at keeping my mind blank as I waited for the first drops of water to land, but before long her face flashed into my mind. Beautiful and bright, grinning fearlessly, exactly as she'd looked the first time I saw her dancing in the hidden room beneath the Rec. It was like she knew all the secrets the world kept from the rest of us. I tried to hold on to the image, even as I knew her fierce light would fade into my worst memory of her – those few seconds when I'd believed, absolutely, that she was dead.

My heartbeat, still racing from my run, stopped for that instant.

Eden's not dead, I told myself, angry that I couldn't shake off the pain of losing her, even now. *She's just gone for a while.* I tried to claw back that first image, but it hovered in the shadowy parts of my brain, just out of my reach.

The first droplets of rain fell, bouncing off the electric shielding with a bright crackle of sparks before the shield adjusted and the subsequent downpour met with an unremarkable fizzle.

Trapped in one of those liquid cylinders ... the thought made me shudder into the grass. *Is it better or worse, not knowing you're in there?*

On the one hand, I decided it must be better. How could you feel trapped if you couldn't see the cage? But on the flipside, that would make it a thousand times harder to find a way out.

I'd started reading about it obsessively after I found out Eden had been put into rehab, and I knew it meant having your memory purged, even if it was only temporary while they *corrected* your behaviour. You went in a blank slate, cleansed of your sins, but still paying for them.

How can that be fair? I thought. *Having to make up for something you don't even know you've done?* Once you'd passed the tests the programme set for you to check that you had overcome whatever urges or behaviours had landed you in there, you were flushed out – rejoined with your own earlier memories, forced to merge the self you knew with what you experienced in the programme. And from what Eden had told me, the results weren't always good.

I pictured Eden walking around in whatever nightmare Lyle had assigned her, surrounded by Rats and other memory-wiped inmates who she didn't even know were criminals. *Can I really wait and see if she makes it out okay?* I knew the answer before I even asked the question. But it raised a more difficult question: *How can I get her out of there?*

I lay thinking through increasingly elaborate and unworkable schemes, held back because I didn't understand the technology behind the false world Eden was now in. I needed to speak to Eli. Biotech was his area.

He'd be able to help me. He had to.

CHAPTER TWENTY-TWO

Alteria Community

'This had better be bloody important.' Eli glared at me from the darkness of his room, his face changing as he saw my expression. I must have looked a little crazed, the new resolve pasting over the cracks of my desperation. 'Mase, what is it?'

'I need your help.' Now that I'd said this, I wasn't sure how to begin to explain.

'Whatever you need. Are you in trouble?' He looked at me pointedly. 'Is *she* in trouble?'

I shook my head impatiently. 'No, she's not pregnant. She's been sent down to Level One.' Eli looked confused. 'She's in rehab.'

Surprise showed in his eyes. When I'd lived in Parisia, nobody had known exactly *where* people went when they were sent to rehab. It didn't look like that had changed since I'd left.

'What for? What did she do?'

I explained quickly, not trusting myself to control my voice if I went into too many details.

The more I thought about the fact that Lyle was Eden's brother, the more it made sense. She'd told me she had an older brother who'd gone into rehab and come out twisted, and I hadn't even given it a thought at the time. But if Eden had had something to do with Lyle being put in there, I bet sending his little sister into the programme would seem like perfect revenge to him. 'He's a sicko, Eli. He'll justify what he's done by saying it was to *purge her unwanted behaviour*, but it's really just payback.'

Eli's mouth silently formed an 'O', his eyes already narrowed in contemplation. 'You want to break her out.' It was a statement.

'I promised her I wouldn't let them put her in the programme. I have to at least try to get her out of there.'

Eli was already frowning, three steps ahead of me as always.

'If you interrupt the programme before it's concluded, Eden's memories will be wiped from the buffer. All she'd be left with are her memories from the programme. Eden would have no real idea who she was, certainly no memory of you or Alteria or her family...' His voice trailed off, and he looked at me through the monitor, a sympathetic twist to his mouth.

'What about changing the programme?' I asked, searching his eyes for a reaction. He looked uncertain.

'Well, you know I'm more about the hardware ... but to be honest, from what I know about the way the

239

programme is set up, there are built-in safeguards to avoid accidental changes being made. There are probably safeguards to stop anyone tampering with it, too, once the programme's begun. It wouldn't make a lot of sense if the programme changed partway through. The lesson wouldn't reach its logical conclusion.'

'But there is always a logical conclusion?'

'There has to be, otherwise people would be trapped in there forever. There's a safeguard against that, too – a four-year reset.'

I struggled to focus on the correct part of this last statement. My heart had stopped at the 'four-year' part, but my head chased after the word 'reset'.

'What does that mean?' I asked.

'Basically, if the person doesn't complete the programme within four years, the memories they've built up are purged again so they start from the beginning. It's meant to stop people getting too warped in there. But like I said, this isn't my area.' He shrugged, which was definitely *not* reassuring. 'Dallan's the one who would know.'

'Dallan?' As soon as I said it, I knew Eli was right. Not only would Dallan have first-hand experience of rehab, but he was also the best programmer I knew.

'But I can't exactly ask him right now, can I?'

Eli grinned, briefly making me want to hit him. 'Maybe you can. I have it on good authority that his parents left here two days ago for a month-long stay at

Alteria. I'm guessing that either means he's out, or he's about to be.'

'Eli, it's always worth waking you up in the middle of the night.'

He nodded graciously. 'Once you've spoken to Dallan, let me know if there's anything I can do to help. Eli out.'

It was time to go back to work in Deep Blue. Firstly, I wanted to check on Frank, see how he was doing; secondly, I wanted to escape my sister's attention; and thirdly – and most crucially – I needed to get out of my quarters. Waiting for Dallan to appear was making me twitch.

I took the lift down, letting myself into the facility and going straight to the control room.

I thought for a second that I'd taken a wrong turn. I hadn't expected the room to still look like a bombsite, but I had expected there to be some evidence of the attack two weeks earlier. Some lingering debris or twisted fragments of metal, maybe. Instead, huge new panels and monitors hummed with power on every wall and flat surface. The floor, too, was different – now covered in a smooth rubberised layer which squeaked under my slippers as I entered.

Frank sat at one of the new panels, studying the information on the monitor in front of him. Hearing my footsteps, he looked up and moustache-grinned at me.

'Mason, how're you doing?'

'Better, thanks, Frank. How's the leg?'

He looked down, tilting his head to one side as he evaluated it. 'Not too bad. Not so bad that they put me in the tube, anyway,' he grimaced, apparently having intended to avoid the subject.

'Good. And I'm sorry I didn't come back to work sooner.'

Frank waved away my apology. I wandered around the perimeter of the room, examining all the new consoles.

'We got an upgrade,' Frank explained, 'so next time we'll be better prepared.' *Next time?* 'We can get the power up again from down here if we need to. I've had to go on extra training … I suppose you'll have to, as well.'

'I've already got an engineering diploma.'

'This is sparks training,' he countered.

'Okay,' I said, not particularly bothered. 'What would you like me to do?'

Frank hesitated. 'Well, there is a section of the main water feed that needs patching … but you'd have to go through the crawlspace to get to it.' He made a quick qualification. 'It's not urgent or anything, so you don't have to do it right away.'

I laughed. 'I'll be fine, Frank.' Nothing could really be worse than what had happened the last time I crawled into one of those holes. That steadied me, in a weird way. 'Where do you need the patch?'

He brought up a schematic on the monitor in front of him, pointing to the relevant section.

'Here's a patch kit,' he said, reaching into a panel under the console and handing me a small case. I noticed he was putting all his weight on his good leg, like the injury still caused him pain. That explained why he hadn't fixed the water feed himself.

Frank followed me as I went out into the corridor and opened the access hatch leading to the section where the patch was needed.

'Are you sure you're okay doing this?' Frank asked, his voice quiet for a change.

I shrugged and ducked through the hatchway. Pausing for just a fraction of a second, I gauged my breathing, my pulse rate. Quick, but not at freak-out level. I was glad to see the lighting strips were working again. I shuffled on into the semi-darkness.

Frank didn't close the hatch behind me, allowing me the reassurance of an escape route, and stopping the sound from bouncing around too sickeningly. I found the ladder connecting the level to the ones above, climbing steadily until I reached the right section of the water feed. With every step upwards, I felt the hard casing of the patch kit swinging from my belt strap.

I made my way along the horizontal section of the crawlspace so that I was almost directly above where I had entered the hatch five levels below. Opening the wall panel, I examined the feed. My face slipped into a frown. There was nothing wrong with it.

'Frank?' I spoke into my vox.

'Yes?' His voice answered, sounding a little too innocent.

'This section of the feed is fine. It doesn't need a patch.'

'Oh. In that case, come back down.'

'What do you mean? Did you … tell me you didn't just send me up here for a laugh?'

'Sorry, didn't catch that,' he said. I could tell he was lying his arse off.

What is this, his way of getting me back on the horse? He could at least have come up here and damaged the section so that I wouldn't realise. Then I remembered about his injured leg, and knew that he wouldn't have been able to climb up here to sabotage the water feed. *Or maybe he just wanted me out of the way.*

I sighed, making my way back to the ladder to begin the climb down. When I'd descended one level, I stopped. If I'd worked it out right, I was now one wall panel away from where Dallan's rehab pod stood. I hadn't been able to find out about his release yet, and his parents had ignored the messages I sent to their quarters. They remembered me, apparently.

As I'd already wasted this much time on Frank's non-errand, I decided to waste a little time of my own. I crawled along the horizontal section to the nearest access hatch, slowly edging it open until light crept in through the gap. I waited to see if there was any sign of movement nearby. Nothing moved, and there was no sound from beyond the metal hatch. I opened it wider and climbed out onto the grille flooring, pausing while I got my bearings.

Diagonally ahead of me I saw the rear casing of Dallan's pod. I walked around the front of it, peering cautiously between the cylinders in case there were any techs nearby. The level appeared to be abandoned – at least, as far as animated people were concerned. Looking along the rows, I saw that most of the cylinders were now inhabited. I tried not to look at them too closely. I was desperate to see Eden, but not like that.

I forced myself to focus on Dallan's pod. He was still there, exactly as he'd been the last time I visited him. I studied his face – or at least the portion of it not covered with the medical mask – looking for signs of change, of improvement. Dallan looked no better or worse than he had before, just lifeless.

Wake up, I willed him. *While you can still wake up as a free man – as* you.

I lost track of time as I stood staring at him. It could have been minutes or hours, but my attention quickly snapped back to the present when he breathed.

Well, maybe not *breathed*. But he did release a tiny air bubble that floated up through the glowing blue liquid and broke at the surface. Somewhere at the far end of the level, I heard footsteps. I watched a few seconds longer, hoping to see that small sign of life again, but the fast-approaching sound of the techs forced me to retreat.

I couldn't go back through the same hatchway I'd come in by, as I would cross paths with whoever was approaching. Instead I went in the opposite direction. I couldn't hear anyone else nearby, and the footsteps stopped where I'd been standing. I waited, my back against the glass front of one of the cylinders, listening.

'This one's ready to come out,' a man's voice said.

I craned my head, trying to see who had spoken, but I was at the wrong angle to get a clear view. I heard a few snaps, like a hatch being opened or a panel being removed, and then a woman's voice spoke.

'You're right. The reintegration sequence is nearly complete.' There was a pause. 'Three or four minutes.'

'Just as well,' the man answered. 'We need all the empty pods we can get with all the Rats we've taken in lately...'

My heart rate picked up. Unless I'd seriously misunderstood, Dallan was about to be released. He'd been in rehab just under a month and had already managed to find a way out. Hopefully, even if I didn't manage to do something to help Eden, she wouldn't be in there that long.

I waited, hearing a few other low noises I couldn't place. Their footsteps didn't move towards me, though, so I felt fairly certain I was hidden from them for the moment.

The seconds ticked by. Gradually my tension gave way to boredom. I looked along the wall panelling, searching for a nearby hatch into the crawlspace, but saw none in the sections visible between the cylinders. I would have to wait it out.

Waiting – that was what my life would be until Eden came back to me.

If *she comes back to me.*

I closed my eyes. I refused to believe it wouldn't be the same Eden who came out of the pod. Having had nothing to cling to before her, I knew I couldn't let her go.

A countdown beeped from the direction of Dallan's cylinder. As the beeps grew louder, liquid gurgled down into the drains beneath the grille flooring. Finally, there came the hiss of a vacuum seal opening, and a long, final-sounding tone as the countdown reached zero.

I took an involuntary step backwards, banging into the cylinder behind me with a dull thud. I turned around and gawped at the person in the pod I'd been leaning against.

I knew him.

He was older now, maybe in his early thirties, and his face was partly obscured by his long hair and beard. But it was definitely him. I had never known his name – I would never have forgotten it otherwise – but I clearly remembered his snarl as he spoke to me outside our family quarters in Parisia.

'*See you later, space cadet,*' he'd said, mocking me as the door to our apartment shut in his face.

'You,' I said, my breathing too shallow for the word to come out as more than a whisper. The last time I'd seen him, he was being led towards the airlock, about to be outcast to live as a Rat. But although he looked lean, almost frail, floating inside the cylinder, he had no lesions on his skin, and his hair was certainly growing. Was it possible he'd been taken in by some other community before finding his way here?

There was no way he'd been in that tube all these years … was there?

At that moment, I heard the techs moving away, pushing some kind of trolley. I chanced a quick look to make sure Dallan was no longer in his pod. It was empty, the liquid gone.

I couldn't bear to stay any longer. I headed for the hatchway I had entered by and tucked myself into the crawlspace, the hatch clicking shut behind me.

CHAPTER TWENTY-THREE

Alteria Community

I hung around his parents' quarters for the next few days, but didn't catch sight of Dallan. Since witnessing his exit from the programme, I'd spent most of my time pacing back and forth in the featureless corridor, making lists of questions I would ask him as soon as I had the chance. On the fourth day, my perseverance was rewarded.

Dallan shuffled down the corridor, held upright by two techs. He looked more like a prisoner being led to his execution than a free man, purged of his flaws and filled with the Knowledge of His All-Seeing Smugness. A series of emotions flitted over his features as I caught his eye: first recognition, then surprise, and then a guardedness I couldn't explain. He passed me without a word, looking down at his hands. I almost called out after him, but decided it might be better to wait until I could get him alone.

I went back to my quarters to think. I didn't know whether the programme would have made him different from the Dallan I knew. It was difficult to reconcile my memory of him with the shuffling figure I'd seen in the corridor.

My question was soon answered. Either no sound had announced an incoming message or I'd switched off my implant without thinking, but as soon as I woke up the following morning I saw a series of digits flashing on the wall monitor.

A grin spread across my face as I deciphered the code Dallan had used for secret messages when we were kids.

0900 in the arboretum, arsewipe.

Dallan stood leaning against a tree when I arrived, one foot propped against the trunk behind him, his knee bouncing like he was hopped up on something, and his arms crossed. His face gave away no signs of the injuries he'd suffered. His eyes and skin appeared to have healed completely. Dallan raised one blond eyebrow when he saw me.

'You're late.' His voice was hoarse, like it had been when he'd tried huffing solvents as a kid.

I shrugged in apology. 'I didn't get your message until five minutes ago. What's with the croaky voice?'

He scowled. 'Anti-radiation meds. Naturally, I'm allergic.' Then he huffed out a sort of laugh, stepped forward, and threw his arms around me. 'It's good to see you, Mase.'

'You too, Dallan.'

I felt him shaking as we parted. He crossed his arms again, glancing around us as though he expected snipers to be hiding in the bushes.

'It sounds weird, hearing my name,' he said. I must have looked as confused as I felt, because he explained. 'In the programme, you don't have your own name – no identifying marks, so to speak. You don't even look the same, exactly. It's more like how you *imagine* you look when you don't have a mirror. And I've been called Noah for the better part of a year now … at least that's how long it felt like to me.'

Dallan's face creased up on one side in a half-grimace, a muscle in his jaw ticking until he rubbed it self-consciously. 'Sorry about blanking you yesterday, by the way. When I was going through transition therapy downstairs, I heard one of the guards talking about you. I wanted to find out what he was saying, so I didn't let on that I knew you. And my folks aren't too happy for me to see you, either, as you probably guessed.'

'Yeah, I thought so. But what was the guy saying about me?'

'Something about you being a local celebrity,' he smirked. 'Apparently you've just single-handedly saved the whole community from Rats riding on the backs of a swarm of electric squid. It all sounded very exciting.'

'Well, my friend Frank did most of it,' I lied, feeling squirmy.

'Yeah, right. What the hell happened?' Dallan sat down with his back against the tree, waiting for his entertainment. I did my best to spin the yarn for him, and he listened, grinning most of the time, but his face fell when I explained what had happened to Eden.

'So now she's been in the programme for a couple of weeks, and there's no way to say how long she's going to be in there.'

I pulled up an image of her on the tiny screen on my vox, just wanting to see her. Dallan caught my wrist, studying her picture with an odd look on his face.

'What is it?' I said. He lifted his head, and I saw the tic had returned.

'Mase, I've seen your girl before.'

'What do you mean?' I couldn't keep the edge out of my voice, although I knew it was ridiculous. They could never have met – Eden had never left Alteria, and Dallan had never been here before now. And even if they *had* met, Dallan wouldn't have been interested. He didn't swing that way.

'In the programme. My eyesight was messed up until near the end, but I'm certain it was her.'

'You saw her? Is she … was she okay?' My heart thundered so hard I almost missed what Dallan said next.

'She was very quiet at first, like she was in shock or something. I guess that was to do with the drowning. We were living in the same house – me, Michael, Saul and Beth. That was her name. Eden is Beth in the programme.'

'What about Michael and Saul? What are they in for?' I tried to stop my mind leaping to the worst-case scenario.

'Michael's not *in* rehab,' Dallan said, shaking his head. 'He's part of the programme, like a built-in guide or something. There are eight or nine in each sector, and they each get allocated up to three inmates to guide through the programme.' He must have seen the questioning look on my face. Dallan balled his fists, knocking the sides of his head in a way that was kind of freaky. 'It all … it all gets explained, sort of mashed together with your memories as they put them back into your brain. Knowing what the programme is and how it works is the only way having two sets of memories can make any kind of sense.'

'What about Saul?' Dallan's eyes shifted to the side. I recognised the impulse to lie written on his face, so I cut him off. 'He's bad, right? What's he in for? Murder?'

'I don't know what he did.' Dallan spread his hands, the same expression of apology I had used just a few minutes ago. 'You don't get to find out about the other people in there with you, not even when they reintegrate your memories. I know how the programme works, but nothing about the others that they didn't tell me themselves.'

'So why the shifty look?'

Dallan held my eye now, not pleased that I had caught him out.

'He's a killer.'

'I thought you didn't know what he'd done to get put into rehab?'

'I don't,' he stopped me as I was about to interrupt him again, closing his eyes briefly with impatience. 'But I know what he did *in* the programme. He killed me.'

I let out a sharp laugh of surprise. 'What do you mean, *he killed you?*'

He put his hands around his throat, mimicked being strangled. 'I mean he *killed me*. We got into a fight, I lost, and he strangled me. That's how I got out of the programme.'

'You mean you have to *die* to get out of there?' I think my heart stopped when I thought about Eden going through that, even if it wasn't for real.

'No, just me.' My heart began beating cautiously again. Dallan looked uncomfortable. I hadn't yet brought up his reason for being in there, as I'd assumed he would talk about it if he wanted to. 'You know why I got put in there. I was all messed up on Pi, and got it into my head that there wasn't anything worth sticking around for.' He was playing down what he'd done, but I didn't comment. 'So my face and my hands got burned – not a nice sensation, that, by the way – and I had to go in there to heal and to have my head sorted out. Well, it turns out that my *therapy* involved proving that I wanted to live after all, and then seeing what it actually felt like to die so that I wouldn't try anything like that again.' He smiled thinly. 'And I bloody well won't, either.'

'Does that mean the programme works, then? I mean, you feel better?' I said, but I could already tell how he felt from the way his hands shook before he stuffed them back under his armpits.

'It wasn't meant to happen that way … in the programme, I mean. It was meant to be an accident, something quick, but where I'd have enough time to decide to *want* to live, and fight for it. You wouldn't believe some of the things the programme tried to get me with. I fell out of a window and was nearly impaled on a fence, I tripped on the stairs and caught my shirt on the handrail at the top, almost hanging myself … well, you get the idea. It was like the whole world was booby-trapped, out to get me. I've been having these nightmares since I got out, real twisted shit.' He shuddered, then seemed embarrassed by his confession. 'By the way, has anything weird been happening here?'

'Weird how?'

'I don't know, power surges, anything like that?'

I told him about the squid that had been charging the ark like tentacled battering rams. 'Something like that?'

Dallan nodded. 'There were these weird things, like something would just randomly change, or disappear, without explanation. It was pretty surreal at the time, but looking back I think they were glitches with the programme.' He looked unimpressed. 'If *I'd* programmed it, I would have made sure…'

I sensed one of Dallan's epic tangents brewing, so I tried to steer him back on topic. 'So, in the programme, Saul wasn't meant to kill you?'

'No, it doesn't work like that. The real people in there aren't meant to do anything bad, but the programme doesn't stop them, either. Free will and shit. But it's like it keeps a tally of the good stuff and the bad, and you can only get out of there if you can tip the balance in favour of the good. So, I had to keep narrowly avoiding death until I was ready to fight it, and then I'd proved I was ready for the real world again.' Dallan laughed with grim humour. 'So Saul kind of did me a favour.'

'But won't Saul now have the *bad* weighing so heavily against him that he'll never get out?'

'I don't know. But if he can't correct the balance within a certain time, he'll get purged again. His memory will be reset to the point he went into the programme, like a clean slate.'

'The four-year rule,' I said, remembering what Eli had told me.

'But it would feel a lot longer in there.'

I tried to picture it, being trapped in some kind of hellscape while my body floated in a cylinder of goo back in the real world. The image of my father's killer filled my head, the way he'd looked when I found him in the lower levels the day Dallan was released from the programme.

'Dallan, what did Saul look like?'

He flinched at the sharp edge in my voice. 'Kind of scruffy-looking, longish blond hair, really tall. Why?'

'Do you remember that man I stole the Pi from in the cubby at Parisia when we were thirteen? The one who killed my dad?' Realisation swept over his face like a wave. 'I saw him in one of the tubes down in the lower levels.'

'You think Saul's the same guy who killed your dad?' he said. Although he phrased it as a question, I could tell Dallan already believed it. 'Bloody hell.'

I decided it was time for the questions I'd really wanted to ask him all along. 'Dallan, do you know if there's any way to break someone out of the programme? Or help them get out of there sooner?'

Dallan hesitated before answering. 'I take it you know you can't just switch it off?' I nodded. 'So you can't exactly spring someone in the middle of it. But helping them…' his eyes narrowed as he thought about it. 'Maybe, if you sent someone in there with a little bit of *special programming*…'

'I'll go in there,' I said, hoping to speed along his thought processes. 'So tell me, what would I need to do to help her?'

'*You?*' He raised his head, looking a little startled. 'Small spaces aren't exactly your thing, Mase.'

I sighed. 'Maybe not, but there are some things that are more important to me than … well, than myself, I suppose.'

'Like Eden?'

'Like Eden,' I agreed. 'Besides, what if Saul hurts her?'

He nodded. 'You're right. I got out when he killed me because I was ready anyway, and him killing me tied in with my programme. But with Eden… Well, if she dies in there before she's ready to exit the programme, she will have to start again.'

'Shit.' We were both silent for a few moments.

'If I could take a look at the rehab computer system, I could find out exactly what's going on in there. I could see what she needs to do to get out, and figure out what kind of programme to set you up with to help her.'

'And then I could go in there and bring her out?'

'Not exactly. If you go in, the computer will purge your memory, so you won't even recognise her, let alone be able to tell her how to get out. But, with a little bit of creative programming, you might retain a tiny part of your memory – something useful, like recognising her face, a gesture, *something*. Just a simple thing that will draw you to her, make you want to help her, even if you don't understand why. But we'd still need to come up with an exit trigger for *you*.'

'Could that be something more pleasant than dying?' I said.

'Sure. But it has to be something that will have a deep, emotional impact on you.'

'Like what?' I wasn't sure I liked the idea of this.

Dallan thought about it for a moment, then I saw his expression change. He'd come up with something.

'What?'

'It's probably best if I don't tell you. It's not like you'll remember, anyway. Don't worry, though – it's nothing too terrible. Oh, and one other thing – if I tap into the system, I might be able to get messages to you through your implant. I'd be able to speak to you, like a voice inside your head. It would have to be small things, suggestions really, otherwise you'd probably think you were nuts. But maybe it would be enough to give you a steer in the right direction. Would you be okay with that?'

Dallan was one of only three people in the world who I'd talk to openly about my deafness – four, now. He understood it, had seen what it was like and how I'd been treated because of it.

'Yeah,' I said. I'd do whatever it took to give me an edge against a programme I didn't understand. 'So when do I go in?'

Dallan stared at me with wide eyes. 'Hang on a minute – you haven't even thought about *how* you're going to get in there yet.'

'That's easy enough. I'll go and start a fight, light a fire, anything.'

He frowned. 'You'll lose your Citizen card if you do that.'

I was exasperated. 'I don't care.'

259

Dallan looked surprised again. 'You really like her that much?'

'Yes!'

He sighed. 'All right, you can be me. Pretend to be me, I mean. I've already lost my Citizen status. It'll help make sure you get put into the right part of the programme, too, now that I think about it. They're more likely to just hook me back up to the tube I've come out of as it's already set up for my biometry.'

'We'll have to do it quickly, then,' I said, remembering what the two techs had been talking about as Dallan's tube had been counting down to his release. 'They'll put one of the Rats in there if we don't move fast. But how do we make them think I'm you?'

Dallan shrugged. 'If I do something to get put back in rehab, we can switch over before I go into the tube. You'd be going into *my* programme – just with a few modifications to the code.'

I thought about it for a long moment, looking at the angles. 'So, we just need to find out what Eden's exit trigger is, set up the special programming for me, get you put back in rehab, and arrange the switch. Simple.' He gave me a withering look, and I grinned. 'I have absolute faith in you, mate.'

CHAPTER TWENTY-FOUR

Sector 24

Beth watched warily as the darkness began to engulf them, just like the dust had.

'I really think we should get moving,' she muttered.

Noah stood next to her, peering through yet another grimy – and unforthcoming – shop window. They had had very little luck finding fuel or food, and they were going to have to decide very soon whether they made camp here for the night while the roach recharged, or headed on with what little fuel they had left, hoping to find another town nearby. Beth was very firmly in favour of the latter.

'But there must be something we can get from this place. Why don't you go and wait in the roach, and I'll have another look around?' Noah said.

Beth's face screwed up in what he now recognised as her migraine-flinch. Noah had noticed the same look several times during the last few hours of searching. He worried that the accident in the roach had injured her more than she was letting on. Beth didn't complain though.

Odd that the migraines only flare up when we're about to break into one of the buildings, he thought. *Probably a stress thing.*

'You're sure you're okay?'

Beth nodded.

Noah tried the door of the next building along the strip. It was locked, just like the others which hadn't already been looted. He took a step back from the door and kicked it open. Noah went inside, but paused when he realised Beth hadn't moved to follow him.

'What's up?'

She sighed. 'Nothing, really. Just feeling a little jumpy. This place is like a ghost town.'

'I thought you were *hoping* not to see anybody?'

'You just can't please some people, I guess,' she said.

'Even if we did come across some local weirdos, I don't think you'd have a problem dealing with them.' Noah nodded towards the gun holstered at Beth's hip.

'Not just the local ones.' She grinned, then followed him into the shadowy interior of the building.

Inside, it was as dusty and grimy as all the others had been. The windows had mostly been replaced with boards, allowing thin streams of dust to blow into the building on the cold breeze. All the furniture was covered with sheets, left by someone who had probably intended to return, but never had. The thought made her shiver.

Beth followed Noah through the house, watching as he

stooped to check inside cupboards and in the cubby under the stairs for anything they could use. Beth hung back, wary of angering the migraine which was threatening to erupt at any moment.

Suddenly, she felt the tight band ease behind her eyes, melting away like snow in a heatwave. Beth didn't question its sudden disappearance, but she didn't trust that it wouldn't return, either. She followed Noah up the wooden staircase, making him jump as she appeared next to him.

Noah spun around, catching her in his arms and lifting her from the ground, laughing. Beth screeched in surprise. He lowered her back to the ground, still keeping his arms around her.

'If I let you go, you're not going to pull your gun on me, are you?' he said. Beth shook her head, still gasping. 'Come on, then.'

He took her hand and led her through the first doorway to continue the search.

'You know, people don't generally keep fuel or food upstairs.'

'I know that.' Noah scowled at her. 'I thought we might at least find a change of clothes.' He walked across what had once been someone's bedroom and opened an antique-looking wardrobe.

'What's wrong with what I'm wearing?' Beth teased, taking his hand again and twirling under his arm.

'It's filthy,' he answered, laughing.

'We're not going to find anything less filthy in this place. The dust in here is worse than outside.'

Noah pulled out a long garment covered in a white dust bag, contradicting Beth's assertion. He unzipped the bag, slipping the garment free as he discarded the wrapping. They both stared at it for a moment – one in quiet contemplation, the other in mute horror.

'If you think I'm wearing that, you're sadly mistaken,' Beth said.

Noah grinned. 'Go on, try it on. I think it would suit you.'

She backed away from him, but Noah continued to advance, brandishing the yellow-sequined evening gown like a weapon. 'Keep that thing away from me!'

Noah hooked the hanger over her head, then wrapped an arm around her waist to draw her nearer to the wardrobe. He used his free hand to swing the open door towards her. Beth saw a mirror attached to the inside. She squirmed as her reflection came into view, draped in the vile yellow dress. Then her eyes scanned the remaining contents of the wardrobe and she caught her breath. Beth smoothed her hand over her mouth before she spoke to keep her face straight.

'I'll make you a deal,' she said, catching Noah's eye in their reflection in the mirror.

He narrowed his eyes. 'Go on.'

'I'll put this on for you, if you put on an outfit *I* choose.'

'Which outfit?' Noah peered over the top of her head into the wardrobe's interior, but Beth kicked the door shut with a swift movement.

'Do we have a deal, or not?'

Noah shrugged. 'Do your worst.'

She reached into the wardrobe, a look of pure menace on her face, and pulled out the item she had glimpsed. Inside the clear plastic wrapping was a billowy, ruffle-fronted shirt.

'Is that *it*?' Noah asked, unimpressed.

'It goes with these.' She drew her other arm from behind her back and held out the accompanying item. Black faux-leather trousers with lace-up sides greeted Noah, and his face dropped.

'You are one sick, sick individual,' he said, taking the hanger from her and beginning to undress. Beth made her way past him, intending to give him some privacy to change. Noah stopped her before she reached the door.

'Aren't you forgetting something?'

Beth tried to keep her eyes focused on his face, even though he was almost naked. He noticed her gaze inching downward. In one quick movement, he scooped up the dress she had discarded at the foot of the sheet-covered bed, and threw it so that it landed over her head. Beth balled it against her chest and left. As an afterthought, she snaked her hand back through the doorway and grabbed his discarded clothes from the floor. Beth thought she heard Noah mutter something that sounded like '*pervert*' as the door clicked shut, and she chuckled as she went to look for somewhere to change.

A door at the far end of the corridor revealed a large bathroom overlooking the rear of the building. The glass which had remained intact in the window was frosted, and so thickly coated with dirt that the view outside was mostly obscured. Vague shapes like aged, dead trees appeared in the near distance, the square outlines of other buildings farther away. The last slanting rays of daylight fought their way through the grime, and Beth sighed. There was no way they would be away from here before full-dark. They might as well get settled in for the night.

Oh well, she thought, *at least the roach will have time to recharge by tomorrow. That should give us enough power to reach the base.*

Beth wriggled out of her worn clothes, her boots thudding heavily onto the cracked floor tiles. She slipped her jersey over her head, letting it fall on top of her boots and jeans. Picking up the yellow abomination, Beth held it at arm's length and inspected it. It was a couple of sizes too big for her, but that was hardly the worst thing about it. She lifted it over her head, tucking the halter strap around her neck and pulling the loose fabric down the length of her body. Looking down at the spray of sequins around the neckline, it looked like she had vomited glitter over herself. The dress split at thigh-level, allowing the many layers of ruffles to fan out to a fishtail hem.

Gross.

Beth scanned the room around her, hoping – and also not hoping – to find a full-length mirror to check her reflection. The only mirror she could find was attached to the medicine cabinet above the sink. She stood in front of it, rising onto her tiptoes to try and get a better look at herself. Beth screwed the fabric into a knot at her lower back. She did the same with the halter neck, tightening it until it fitted her better. She paused before removing the loosely holstered gun, which was causing an unsightly bulge at her hipline, and strapped it to her thigh instead.

It's not ideal, she thought, *but at least it doesn't ruin the line of the dress.*

Catching sight of her own face scrunched up in concentration as she continued to make her adjustments, Beth burst out laughing.

'Noah!' she yelled. There was no answer. She listened for sounds of movement in the house, but heard none. 'Noah?'

Beth opened the bathroom door slowly, and stepped out into the corridor. She walked its length, pausing at the open door to the bedroom where she had left him. He wasn't there. She carried on, stopping to listen at the top of the stairs.

Hearing nothing, Beth held up the hem of her dress and crept downstairs. As she reached the ground floor, she heard the slow creaking of a loose floorboard nearby. Beth tiptoed across the lobby to the open door at the back of the building. The sound was no longer there, but Beth felt the presence of someone standing on the opposite side of the door. Whether it was Noah, or someone else, she couldn't tell.

'Noah?' she called softly this time.

'I'm in here.' His voice carried through the open doorway, and Beth exhaled in a rush. She skipped into the dusty kitchen, forgetting for the moment to brace herself for his reaction.

Noah was leaning against the kitchen counter, the dining table in front of him.

'Oh,' was all he managed to say before the grin spread across his face. Beth didn't understand it immediately, then felt the odd sensation of the fabric swirling at her ankles. She looked down, embarrassed. She hadn't even taken time to check out Noah's appearance in his ridiculous clothing.

Noah stepped out from behind the dining table, spreading his arms wide so that Beth could fully appreciate his ensemble.

'So?' He turned in a circle, his abundant shirt sleeves billowing. She was about to make a flippant remark when she caught sight of his naked behind poking through the twin cut-outs in the faux leather.

'I … I…' She couldn't continue. Beth laughed until tears streamed from her eyes, and she slid back against the unit, holding her stomach as though it might explode if she released it.

Noah turned to face her again, his brow creased in mock-disapproval. 'Whoever lived here had really, *really* weird taste.'

'Sorry,' was all Beth managed to say before she creased over again and sank against his chest, muffling the sound of her laughter in the ruffles of his shirt.

Noah laid his hands lightly at her waist, then pulled her even closer to him. Beth looked up to find herself caught in his gaze. Any lingering amusement vanished; all she saw was her own image reflected in his eyes.

'I know you,' she said. It was true, but not what she had meant to say.

Noah traced her lower lip with his thumb. Then they were kissing, as though they had kissed a hundred times and it was written in their DNA. Noah pulled away as he felt her face tighten, pain once again etched across it.

'What is it? Did I hurt you?'

He cupped Beth's chin with one hand and she shook her head minutely.

'Just another migraine,' Beth answered, a tight smile forced across her mouth.

'Is it the same as usual? Or worse since you banged your head?' he checked her pupils again as he asked, and she laughed at the sight of his head bobbing from side to side centimetres in front of her.

'It's not worse,' she promised. 'I'm fine, honestly. It's practically gone now.'

Noah scrutinised her a few seconds longer.

First of all when she was drinking, then when we were breaking down doors ... now, when I kissed her. What's the common thread there? Noah wondered.

Aversion triggers, the voice in his head whispered.

'Do you think it's wrong to drink alcohol?' he asked her, suddenly.

Beth raised her eyebrows. 'No, not really.'

'Even though you're underage?'

She gave a sharp laugh of surprise. 'Are you going to turn me in to the police?'

He shook his head once, impatiently. 'Look, just answer honestly, please? I'll explain why in a minute.'

'All right. Yes, I suppose it is wrong for me to drink alcohol, given that it's against the law.'

'And this building belongs to someone, right?'

'Yeah.'

'So it's wrong of us to break in and take their things?'

'Yes.' Beth had begun to look a little mortified. 'What are you driving at? That I'm a bad person?'

'No, I don't mean that at all. Can you tell me what you were thinking about just now, when we were kissing?' Noah continued studying her face, and she looked away, embarrassed by such close scrutiny. 'Please,' he urged her.

She still didn't look at him as she answered. 'I was thinking I didn't want to stop.'

'And?'

She looked at him in exasperation. 'And what?'

'What else were you thinking? Or maybe even *feeling*?'

'Are you really going to make me say this?' Beth paused for him to respond, but he just waited quietly for her answer. 'Fine. I was thinking about … doing *other* stuff. With you.'

Noah tried to hold back his smile, but didn't entirely succeed. 'But you didn't.'

'No.'

'Why?'

'Because we don't really know each other that well, I guess.' Beth blushed as she gritted her teeth.

'And as you thought this, your migraine set in?'

'What's your point?' Beth was annoyed now, and Noah sensed that he shouldn't push her any further before explaining the reason behind his questions.

'I think there's something in your head that's trying to manipulate you to behave a certain way. I think that's why your head hurts – because you're doing, or thinking about doing, something you believe is *wrong*.'

Beth's eyes narrowed sceptically. 'Really?'

'Let me try something,' Noah said. 'I'm going to kiss you. I just want you to keep thinking about the fact that this is *me* doing it, not you. All you're doing is staying perfectly still.'

Beth did as he asked, standing stiffly as she concentrated, waiting for the pain to resurface. Noah kissed her lightly, his mouth just brushing against hers at first, then lingering, his teeth softly grazing her lower lip. He heard her breath catch, and pulled away.

'Migraine?' he asked, frowning as she held her eyes closed. She didn't move.

'Do it again,' she whispered.

He chuckled. 'I'll take that as a *no*, then.'

Beth's eyes opened, and she smiled. 'No migraine. Did I pass your test?'

'I think so. It seems *my* actions, *my* decisions, don't cause your pain to flare up. It's only when *you* do something that your migraine kicks in.'

'So that proves…?'

Noah shrugged. 'That it's somehow focused on your behaviour, not just kissing and stealing stuff in general.'

She laughed. 'So something, some evil migraine goblin, is punishing me for being sinful?'

'*Sinful?*' he repeated the word curiously. 'Interesting idea.'

'Now, if you've finished dissecting me, can we please eat? I'm starving.'

Noah turned to the cupboard he'd been about to search when Beth came in, and tugged open the door with a creak of disused hinges. He looked inside and lurched back, knocking into the dining table. Beth peered over his shoulder.

'What the hell *is* that?' she said.

Inside the cupboard, there were no tins or mouldy food packets, or even empty shelves. There was a swirling mass of pixels, shrinking and expanding like a beating heart. But this was no living thing.

Noah reached out a hand, skimming his fingertips across the outer edges of the swirl. Where he touched, his fingers appeared to dissolve. Beth yanked his arm back with a shriek.

'It's not real,' Noah said, and flexed his hand in front of her so she could see his fingers were again intact. 'None of this is real.'

CHAPTER TWENTY-FIVE

Alteria Community

'Are you sure you can't just wait for her to get out on her own?' Frank said.

I'd known it wasn't going to be easy to convince him to go along with the plan, but as he hadn't outright refused, I had a glimmer of hope.

'Frank,' I said, sighing, 'she's being tortured in there, and she's trapped with a murderer. I really don't see why that's so difficult to understand. And you know it's not even her fault she's in there.' I could tell he felt guilty over the ink being found in his overalls, and maybe it made me a shit to use that against him, but I was desperate.

'Well, there's no need to get pissy,' he grumbled. 'I'm just trying to make sure you've thought this through.'

'I have.'

It was true: I'd thought about nothing else since my initial plans were laid with Dallan in the arboretum. Frank would hide Dallan in Deep Blue while I was in the tube, seeing as Dallan couldn't very well go walking around

Alteria when he was meant to be in rehab. From Deep Blue, Dallan would be able to use the crawlspace to access the rehab computer systems directly, and feed messages through my implant whenever he could get away with it.

'So will you do it?' I said. 'Will you help me get Eden out of there?'

Frank ran a hand over his bushy moustache and sighed. 'Fine. But I don't like it, Mason. I don't like it at all.'

I knew I was putting him in a compromising position. I knew it, but I was doing it anyway. 'I promise, if anything goes wrong, I'll keep your name out of it.'

He raised an eyebrow like he doubted I could keep that promise. 'Just don't let anything go wrong,' he said.

Back in my quarters, I recorded a series of messages to send to my sister every couple of days in the hope that she'd just think we kept missing each other. The last thing I wanted was for her to realise I'd gone AWOL.

'Hey, thought you'd be back from work by now. Just heading down to Deep Blue for my shift, so I'll catch you later.'

'Hi, Ari. Did we have breakfast plans today? Can't remember, and I need to dash to my counselling session. I'll call you back.'

'Wow, it's getting harder and harder to catch you these days…'

As long as I wasn't in the programme for more than a week or so, she probably wouldn't even miss me.

Dallan had also been busy since our meeting. Entering the crawlspace system from Deep Blue, he had gone up to the storage levels and accessed Eden's file so that he would be able to help me figure out what her exit trigger was. While he was there, he set up a 'sleeper programme', as he called it, to override whatever rehab he was meant to complete.

Dallan had also, courtesy of a short-lived trip on Frank's ink capsules and the super-sensitive Alterian sensor system, managed to get himself ordered back into the tube. So far, all the building blocks of the plan were shifting neatly into place.

My own preparations were simple by comparison. I buzzed my hair into the same spiky, cropped style as Dallan's, scowling at the result in the bathroom mirror. I went back to my bedroom and snagged the photosensitivity goggles I'd stashed at the back of the closet, then recorded a final message to Ariadne – to be delivered only if something went hideously wrong. I was hopeful our plan would work out, but my long list of past fuck-ups urged me to cover my bases.

I was about to head down to Deep Blue when my eyes caught on the covered easel Eden had set up near the window. I knew she hadn't wanted me to see it until it was finished, but that same instinct that had made me record the goodbye message to Ari told me I might not get another chance to look. Catching the corner of the sheet,

I peeled it back. The image she'd painted made my throat close up.

Legs – two pairs, horizontal and perfectly tangled – against a bed of pale sand. Each grain had been picked out in a different colour, giving it a crystalline appearance I could never have imagined without seeing it through her eyes.

This was the new world she had created for us. I wanted it, so badly. And maybe we would still get to roll around on a beach on New Earth. We still had a chance.

I swung the cover back over the easel and tucked the goggles into my pocket. I was ready.

I checked the time display on my vox. Only a few minutes to go.

Huddled in the crawlspace, I peered through the tiny crack where I had opened the hatchway looking out onto the pod where Dallan – or rather *I* – was about to be imprisoned. At any moment now he would arrive with the medical tech. I started taking off my clothes, removing everything but the dark goggles, and left them in a neat pile behind the hatch for Dallan to use after the switch.

After what felt a lot longer than two minutes, footsteps hammered across the grille floor plating. I could identify three pairs of feet, not two as I'd expected. There were two techs instead of the usual one.

This was not good. The plan had been for Frank to

distract the tech to allow Dallan and me time to switch places without being seen. Frank wouldn't be expecting to have to distract two of them.

I ferreted through my discarded clothes, looking for my vox, but as I found it I saw that Dallan and the techs were now too close for me to place the call. They would most certainly hear the sound of my voice echoing from inside the walls.

I froze as they came to stand in front of the pod marked *24N*, trying to think of some way I could distract the techs.

'Shall I take your goggles?' one said to Dallan.

'Thanks, but the doctor said I have to keep them on,' Dallan lied smoothly. 'The artificial light in the tube was too strong last time, and stopped my eyes healing properly.'

Right on cue, the incoming call alert sounded from a panel somewhere on the far side of the room.

The tech who had already spoken sighed. 'Sorry, I'd better get this. Jonah?' It sounded as though he was addressing the other guy. 'Stay with Dallan until I return. I should only be a moment.'

'Yes, sir,' Jonah replied.

Hmm ... I thought, *must be new. Nobody calls the techs 'sir', no matter what level they are.*

I heard Dallan start freestyling with his lies, trying to convince Jonah to leave him alone for a moment.

'I just need to gather my thoughts, you know…?'

The unprepared lie wasn't half as convincing as the first

had been. Jonah stood his ground. Then an idea came to me. Not a *good* one, but it would do. I hoped.

I tapped on my vox and placed a call to one of the terminals on the far side of the level. Hopefully Jonah would follow his colleague's lead, and see taking the call as being more important than guarding Dallan, who for all he knew had no way of escaping the level without a security pass – especially not in the nude.

The alert sounded, and I heard Jonah's feet shuffle as though uncertain whether to answer it or not. Finally, the insistent ring of the incoming call alert won out, and he stepped quickly away from Dallan and the pod, muttering something I didn't catch.

I hurried through the hatch, leaving it open for Dallan to make his getaway. He strode towards me, grinning beneath his dark goggles. I saw myself reflected in the glass – same goggles, same hair, same pale, naked skin. It was scary how much we looked alike. Perhaps not enough to fool Ari or his parents if they decided to pay a visit, but certainly close enough to fool almost anyone else.

'Remember, I'll be feeding you messages whenever I can,' he whispered, giving my hair a quick scruff as he passed. 'Good luck.'

I took my place facing the glowing cylinder, trying to relax my posture. But nobody would expect me – Dallan – to look relaxed, so I let my buttocks clench as they pleased.

'Mase!' Dallan's hiss seemed to wrap around the forest of glass cylinders before it reached me. He was still at the hatch.

The hatch that was now closed.

CHAPTER TWENTY-SIX

Alteria Community

I padded across the grille floor, trying not to let my footsteps echo. 'What are you doing?'

'The bloody thing swung closed! I think it's stuck,' he said as he tried to work his fingertips around the edges of the hatch. But I could already see why it had jammed – the cuff of my discarded shirt was poking out from under the door.

'Shitting hell!' I tried to help, feeling the sting of a fingernail tearing as I tried to prise the hatch open with him, but it was as if it had suddenly been welded shut. I braced my leg against the wall, yanking and shaking it. It did no good.

Dallan looked as nut-shrinkingly terrified as I felt. If the techs caught us – two naked lookalikes in dark goggles jiggling against a metal door – I couldn't imagine they would react well.

'I can't go back in there, Mase,' Dallan said, and I saw that tic pinching his cheek again. 'I can't, I…'

'It's all right,' I said and pointed to another access hatch at the far side of the room. 'Hide until after the techs are gone, then use that hatch to get down to Deep Blue.'

As soon as I'd finished speaking, footsteps vibrated through the metal flooring behind us.

'Go!' I whispered, and hurried back to the spot where the techs had left Dallan. I skidded to a halt just as the junior tech returned, frowning. For a second I thought he'd noticed the switch, or my near-stumble.

'Looks like whoever was calling changed their mind,' he said, shaking his head. I grinned awkwardly and shrugged, eyes darting back towards the jammed hatch. There was no sign of Dallan there now. I couldn't see him through any of the clear casings, either, so he'd managed to find somewhere to hide. I let myself breathe, finally.

The senior tech was muttering to himself when he returned moments later, annoyed by whatever Frank had kept him talking about. The other guy and I both turned to face him, and my eyes went wide in horror. The glass cylinder behind the senior tech had been empty a minute ago. Now, Dallan stood in the empty pod, his goggles gone and eyes shut. At a glance, he looked the same as any of the others floating in the tubes around us. But even from across the room I could see him shaking. One look, and the techs would notice there was no liquid in his pod, and he was not, in fact, floating.

'Uh…' I began, forgetting that they might know Dallan's

voice, and having no clue what to say, anyway. But both techs were looking at me now, and I had to do something. So I fainted.

'Hey now…'

The junior tech gripped my arms, keeping me from pulling off a complete crumple. I made myself sway, ducking my head so they wouldn't get a good look at my face. The senior tech barely glanced at me anyway, just sighed and checked the time on his wrist. But neither of them was looking at Dallan. I tried to focus on that small win instead of the fact that I'd just made a total bellend out of myself.

'Let's get this done, then,' the senior tech said, putting a hand on my shoulder as he attached something sharp to the back of my neck. 'Now go ahead.'

He guided me towards the open casing of the tube. I tried not to catch my breath, pretending I knew the drill. I'd avoided looking at them head-on so far, but once I'd stepped into the cylinder I had to turn. If they were going to realise I wasn't Dallan, now was the time.

Jonah watched his superior tap in some commands to the interface on the side of the pod. Slowly, the casing closed with a hiss as the vacuum seal engaged. I tried not to wince at the ugly sound grating inside my head.

The senior tech spoke to me through the clear casing. His voice was muffled by the barrier, but I had no trouble reading his lips.

'You know what's coming, so try not to hold your breath. Just let your lungs fill, and you'll be under and relaxed in no time.'

I nodded once, and they both stepped back. Liquid gurgled up through a hole beneath me as the inlet sequence began, surprisingly thick and syrupy as it spilled into the cylinder. It was the exact temperature of my skin, although I supposed that might have been because I was in the throes of a fairly magnificent cold sweat. My breathing grew terse. The sound bounced back at me from all directions in the confined space, and I focused all my energy on not vomiting into the rising goo.

It ran in quickly, and was already up to my knees. My lungs filled, then refused to deflate. I sucked in more air, more. *Shit.* I was going to hyperventilate, probably drown in a mix of body-temperature ooze and my own piss. I tried to hold perfectly still, beginning my mental list.

1) I came up with a hare-brained scheme with my friends to try and be some kind of hero for Eden.

2) I failed to get her out of the crawlspace in time, and broke my promise to her.

3) I didn't make sure she was safe before I went into the crawlspace.

4) I fell in love with a girl.

My chest relaxed until I could breathe – if not normally, then at least tolerably. The liquid rose above the level of my thighs, and I let my fingers trail through it. It reached my chest. I felt the weight of it constricting around me, and instinctively closed my mouth until it passed my chin. Then I remembered what I'd been told, and forced my jaw to relax. The liquid filled my mouth, but it tasted of nothing. I held my breath for a few seconds, unable to completely surrender just yet.

As it reached eye level, I risked one final glance towards the pod where Dallan was hiding. He was still inside, looking like a wax statue. Just as the goo crept up to cover my goggles he gave me a quick thumbs-up, and vanished in a liquid blur. He was on his own now, and so was I.

I felt the top of my head being engulfed. I was completely submerged, and my lungs started raging for air.

My head whipped around, panic driving me to look for some way out. How had I ever thought I could do this? I would die, and Eden would still be trapped, and when she got out she'd want nothing to do with me...

The sharp object on the back of my neck suddenly prickled – some kind of current, I guessed. My muscles went limp, and I floated weightlessly in the gel as it finally seeped down my throat and into my lungs. The last few bubbles of air forced their way from my mouth and travelled up towards the surface. I remembered seeing Alteria's hull from the sub that first day, the bubbles forming and fleeing upwards like they knew something I didn't.

I blinked a few times, but my eyelids were heavy.

I had one final coherent thought as my mind sank under the surface with the rest of me: *I wonder if they have beaches in the programme...*

CHAPTER TWENTY-SEVEN

Sector 24

Noah woke to an odd sound in the distance. At first he thought it was the roll of thunder, but the sound was too even, too fast. Somewhere between a man sprinting and a pneumatic drill.

Finally, the sound moved on, and he looked at Beth as she lay sleeping next to him on the large, dusty bed, her hair tangled around her face. Noah slid off the bed, careful not to wake her, and walked to the window overlooking the main road. The sound of the engine had gone by now, and there was no sign of life on the street outside. Noah watched for a few minutes, in case the vehicle should happen to return.

'Noah?'

He turned at the sound of his name. With his eyes unaccustomed to the darker interior of the room, his feet met the frame of the bed without warning and he went sprawling across it. Beth let out a gasp of surprise as he landed fully on top of her.

'Are you okay?' The smile was audible in her voice.

'Sorry, I tripped – I didn't hurt you, did I?'

'No, don't worry about it.' She was quiet while he resettled himself next to her on the bed. 'What were you looking at outside?'

'It was nothing.' He didn't want her worrying that they were going to be attacked in their sleep, especially as whoever had been out there had moved on. If he was right, and this was all a simulation, that didn't mean the other people in Sector 24 weren't real. It didn't mean they weren't dangerous.

Noah stared at the ceiling as he turned it all over in his head, Beth breathing steadily next to him. He thought she was asleep until she spoke softly in the darkness, her words rushed as though she had to get them out before they grew too large to contain.

'I've been thinking about what happened earlier, and you might be on to something. I mean, this place, Michael, everything we're told about Sector 24 … it feels wrong somehow, doesn't it? Like a picture someone's drawn, but they've forgotten to sketch in the details right. Damn, I'm not explaining this well.' She sighed. 'I've never seen the enemy, you know. I've seen the bombs, the damage they cause, but I've never actually seen one of them. And where is the government Michael supposedly answers to? Who gives him his orders? The more I question everything, the more I see the cracks. Not literally – I mean, apart from that weird hole in the kitchen cupboard, but now I don't know what to believe. But I definitely think you were right about my migraines – they're some kind of behavioural conditioning. Ever since you told me that, and I started to believe it, the pain has completely gone, even when I think about doing something ... *bad*. I think it's because I now know that whatever I do here isn't real, so it can't really be bad. Does that make sense?'

'I think so. But does that mean you think I'm not real?'

Beth's tone was suddenly sharp. 'Are you laughing at me?'

'No,' Noah said. 'I just wanted to know whether you thought I was a part of this illusion. I'm honestly curious. I don't know the answer myself.'

'Oh.' Beth paused. 'I believe you're real, but you're stuck in here, like me.'

'So how do we get out?' Noah asked, rolling onto his side, his head propped on his hand so he could see her face in the dim light shining through the window.

'I don't know...' Beth started to say, but Noah heard another voice.

She must trust you, the voice said. *That's her final exit trigger.*

How can I make her do that? Noah thought, but the voice didn't offer any further insight.

'Do we really want to get out?' Beth asked, quietly.

'Don't you?'

289

She hesitated before she answered. 'Well, I *do*, but what will we be escaping to? What if we never find each other out there?'

'I will find you,' Noah said with certainty. He wrapped his arm around her, letting his head drop to the pillow beside hers as he thought about their situation. Beth rolled towards him, nestling into the contours of his body, her head against his chest. Noah watched her face, her lips parted as her breathing settled into the steady rhythm of sleep. He brushed a stray strand of hair away from her cheek, and she moved into the heat of his touch. Beth muttered softly, but this time Noah knew she was asleep.

'I'll find a way,' he whispered. 'I promise we'll get out of here, and I will find you again.'

As soon as he had uttered the words, it was as if a light slowly turned on in the room. He looked to the window first, anxious that the passing vehicle had returned, but the light wasn't coming from out there. It was coming from Beth.

Where her head rested on his chest, he no longer felt any weight. Her skin had a faint translucent glow which grew with each passing second. Noah watched, fascinated and afraid to move in case he ruined the phenomenon.

Say goodbye, the voice urged him.

Noah skimmed his fingertips across her cheek, but there was no sensation of contact. His fingers passed through her as though she were no more tangible than a

290

ray of light. Noah understood what was happening at last. Beth had heard him, and believed him.

You kept your promise, the voice said as the light began to fade, taking Beth with it.

Now I just need to get the hell out of here and find Beth again, Noah thought.

Noah stood in the grey light of early dawn, letting the cold air wrap around his bare torso. Standing in a small courtyard behind the building, he wore his own scruffy jeans again, his feet and upper body still bare while he ate an unappetising breakfast of pickled beets.

Looking at the sky, Noah's eyes met a featureless grey sheet smoothing over the cracked lives beneath. He hoped that Beth was looking at a brighter sky than this now, not the fractured light of a lie.

Noah dropped his fork into the empty jar and went back inside. There was no reason to hurry now, but he was still impatient to get moving again. He dressed quickly, pausing to look at Beth's discarded clothing. *She won't be needing these again.* Noah picked up her gun and tucked it into the belt of his jeans.

He gathered what little food he found tucked away in dusty corners of the house, wrapping the cans in a sheet to take back to the roach. Opening the rear hatch, he threw the makeshift food sack onto one of the rear bunks and made his way to the driver's seat. He sealed the rear hatch and fired up the engine. Beth had been right – the cells had recharged.

'So, where to now?' Noah addressed the voice in his head.

Find your father, it replied. Noah chuckled softly to himself, thrusting the roach into gear and almost tipping the vehicle as he pulled it in a tight loop and set off for the southernmost point of the sector.

The odd creak Michael had developed in one knee had kept him distracted for the last few kilometres, but he slowed his stride as the gates of the military base came into view.

Michael scanned for signs of the roach but saw none, although he reasoned it might be parked behind the building. The tracks could easily have been lost to the swirling dust.

He strode up to the gate and held his wrist to the sensor. But instead of flashing green and allowing him entry, a voice blared from the speaker unit.

'Android Michael, serial number S24-0006-24-05-12 identified. State your purpose.'

My purpose? he raged silently.

'My charges are expected to arrive at this facility, and I need to see them urgently.' He recited Noah and Beth's serial numbers for the disembodied voice and waited.

'Access denied. Please leave the base immediately.'

'Are they here? At least tell me that.'

There was a silence as though the owner of the voice was considering his answer. 'They have not yet arrived, though the General is expecting his son presently.'

The General. His superior. A man with answers.

'I need to speak with the General as well. I have vital information about his son.'

There was another silence, this one stretching almost two minutes before the voice returned – presumably having received a response from someone higher in the chain.

'You may enter.' The light flashed green and the door swung open. There was nobody waiting to greet Michael on the other side, only an empty corridor cast in a red glow from the overhead lights. Then a panel flashed next to him, and the same disembodied voice said, 'Turn left at the end of the corridor, then take the second door on your right.'

When no further instructions followed, Michael set off to find the General.

The door opened into a room with luxurious fixtures such as Michael had only seen in photographs. Thick carpet, comfortable-looking sofas, and an ornately carved table surrounded the hearth where a fire blazed merrily. Burning wood, no less.

In front of the fireplace sat the General. Michael had to admit to himself that Noah at least *looked* like the General's son. He was a tall man, fitting perfectly into the high-backed chair, his eyes fixed on the fire. He didn't even glance up as Michael entered the room and took a seat on one of the sofas.

'Excuse me, General?'

The man finally looked up, his eyes boring into Michael as though they had been drawing heat from the fire. 'I'm waiting for my son.'

'He isn't here yet. But I … I have questions for you,' Michael said.

'I have no answers for you. You are not my son.' The General's gaze settled back on the fire. A long silence followed, with both men staring at the flames drawing in the life from the room, burning everything they touched to ash. To dust.

'I killed a man today. A man it was my duty to protect and to save,' Michael said. The General gave no response, so he continued. 'My very first memory is of waking up and thinking I was in heaven. Isn't that ridiculous? My first conscious thought, and I believed I had already earned my place there. Everywhere was so green, so alive and bursting with promise … but then it all changed. The war came, and this place became a wasteland in the blink of an eye. But still, I had my purpose. I knew that I had to help this man, and any others who were sent to my care. I have helped *so many*, seen so many pass into the light. But not him. I couldn't save him, and in the end I killed him. Why am I here if I could not save him?'

Michael waited, but he was met with silence. A quiet desperation seized him. It was almost as though he could hear some distant tidal wave roaring a path to claim him while he searched for an anchor – anything to cling to.

'Why won't you answer me?'

Michael went to stand in front of the fire, facing the General. But still the man's eyes stared blankly ahead, as though Michael were no more significant than the ashes gathering in the hearth. Michael picked up the iron-tipped poker from the fireplace and swept it in front of the General's face.

'Stop ignoring me!'

Before Michael could think about what he was doing, he jabbed forward with the poker, planting it firmly in the General's chest. The man's eyes met Michael's at last, but they were no less distant.

'I'm so sorry, I didn't mean…' Michael breathed, his voice barely a whisper. The wave roared closer, ready to swallow him.

The General pulled the poker from his chest with a grunt and tossed it across the room. When he looked at Michael again, it was as though the android's synthetic skin had become consumed by the fire behind him, now glowing with its own light.

'I have no answers for you. You are not my son. And this place has no further use for you,' the General said, just as the wave which had been threatening finally rolled through the programme and through Michael's body. 'You will be purged.'

Michael vanished in a burst of light.

CHAPTER TWENTY-EIGHT

Alteria Community

Michael opened his eyes. He was covered in a strange substance, and something was in front of his face, stopping him seeing clearly. Raising his hand to investigate the phenomenon, Michael felt his hair floating around his head. He brushed it aside, but his vision was still clouded by the clear gel.

As it drained away, his head first of all cleared the surface, and he gagged as he became aware of his need to breathe.

Wait, breathe…?

He started choking, the liquid pumping up from his lungs as he fought to replace it with air. *How am I in a human body?*

Michael opened his eyes again, finding an unfamiliar face looking back at him through the clear casing of the cylinder. The young woman appeared to be very small and slight, her white-blonde hair framing an angular face. She held his eye for a moment, and Michael saw the disconnected power cable in her hand. He tried to figure out what this meant, but couldn't.

I've left the programme...?

From his hiding place, Dallan watched Ari drop the power cable she had disconnected from Saul's pod. Seeing only the man who had killed her father, she seemed to feel no remorse as she spat against the clear casing of the pod before striding away towards the main door, leaving the restricted area.

Stepping out from behind the cylinder nearest the access terminal, Dallan assessed the situation. Ari stopped, only vaguely surprised to see him, and waited for him to speak.

Dallan saw the man he had known as Saul stumbling from the now empty pod. He had been automatically ejected when Ariadne disconnected the power, leaving no time for the reintegration process to be initialised to restore Saul's memory.

Saul had been completely purged. What now lay on the metal grille of the floor, gasping and vomiting, was, Dallan thought, no more than an empty shell.

'How did you know he was here?' he asked.

Ariadne pulled a data pad from her pocket, and held it out to him. He saw the goodbye message – the one which was only meant to be sent in case things went horribly wrong. The one which told Ari everything; about the mission to save Eden, about Ari's father's killer being in Alteria all the time she had been living there.

'Oh, no.' Dallan looked at her pained expression. 'I'm sorry, you weren't meant to see that. Wait – how did you get it?'

Ari looked at him, her eyes and mouth set resolutely. 'When I saw Eden without my brother, and she couldn't tell me where he was, I searched through his communication logs. I found this one encrypted, and I broke through the code.' She shrugged. 'It told me everything. I knew what I had to do.'

Dallan rubbed his forehead, a pained expression crossing his face. 'Mason's not trapped in there. At least I don't think he is … is that why you pulled the plug on Saul?'

Ariadne's eyes closed briefly, but her expression didn't change. 'That bastard killed our father, *ruined* both our lives. I couldn't just wait and see what else he might do to my brother.' Her voice lowered to a whisper. 'Can you help him? He's all I've got left, Dallan.'

'I'll do what I can,' he said. 'But you need to get out of here. *Now.*'

Ariadne looked at him for a moment, then hurried away.

Dallan returned to the access terminal, erasing the log of Ariadne's visit. Creating a false security entry, he placed her in her quarters at the time the programme had been illegally terminated. He looked for the command to silence the alarm he knew would have been triggered on the Command Deck, but it was too late.

Dallan looked from Saul's prostrate form to the access terminal. At this point, he knew Noah would be arriving to see the General in the programme, and if he left the access terminal, he wouldn't be able to steer the encounter to release Noah as he had planned. But the alarm would have alerted the techs to Saul's release by now, and they would be coming through the main doors at any moment.

He had no choice.

Dallan made his way to the hatch that led into the crawlspace, then paused. He darted back to the access terminal and typed in another false log, grinning to himself.

Unauthorised entry to Section 24 at 2120 hours: Citizen Lyle.

Dallan locked the terminal just as the main entry door swooshed open, and disappeared into the crawlspace.

CHAPTER TWENTY-NINE

Sector 24

Noah arrived at the military base with the roach running on empty. He stopped at the gate and waited for the guard to clear his entry to the compound, then followed the same route to the General's quarters that Michael had walked just twenty minutes earlier. Striding ahead of the guard who let him in, Noah knocked on the door.

'Hello,' he said, looking up at the General – as perfect a representation of Mason's father as Dallan had been able to compile within such a short timeframe.

'I'm so glad you're here,' he said, ushering Noah inside.

'Thank you for agreeing to see me,' Noah replied awkwardly. He had been concentrating so intently on getting there, following the oddly circumlocutory directions the roach's onboard computer had given him, that he hadn't given any thought to what he would actually say when he arrived.

Noah watched the General as he moved towards an armchair and lowered himself with a grunt that sounded like pain.

'Are you all right?'

The General's face was pale, and had a pinched look about it. He smiled with effort. 'Don't worry about me, boy. Just old, that's all.'

Noah studied his father's face. He didn't look especially *old*, just exhausted. The General adjusted himself in his seat, and as he did so his jacket fell open, revealing a strange shadow against the shirt underneath. The General pulled his jacket back into place.

'You're bleeding,' Noah said as the realisation dawned on him.

'It's all right,' his father said.

'Do you need me to get someone…'

The General cut him off with a wave of his hand. 'It doesn't matter right now.'

This is weird, Noah thought to himself, *like some strange dream.* This impression was reinforced as he took in his surroundings properly – the oddly lavish decor, the roaring fire, and a photograph above the fireplace which caught his attention as soon as his eyes fell on it.

Noah rose from his seat on the ruby sofa and picked up the photograph. His father and a woman stood together in the picture – his mother, he assumed. They looked happy.

'You look exactly as I thought you would,' his father said, making Noah jump.

'Is this my mother?' Noah held out the photograph to his father.

'Her name was Elin. I'm sorry you never had the chance to know her properly.'

'What is your name? Sorry, I never thought to ask.'

'My name is Arthur.'

'Arthur,' Noah rolled the name around in his mind, wondering whether that felt familiar. He couldn't say whether it did, or if he just wanted it to.

'I expect you have a lot that you would like to ask me,' Arthur prompted. Noah replaced the photograph on the fireplace and turned so that his back was to the fire.

'Not really.'

He had expected his father to look surprised, or even offended, but instead he laughed.

'Then how about we have a drink together?' Arthur moved to lift himself from his chair, but stopped abruptly, wincing and clutching his side where the shadow bled. He looked up at Noah and forced a smile. 'Perhaps you wouldn't mind doing the honours?' He gestured towards a cabinet in the corner of the room, set with a decanter and two glasses.

Noah poured the golden liquid into one of them. 'Alcohol doesn't really agree with me.'

'Something else, then?'

'No, I'm fine, thank you,' Noah replied, handing the drink to his father. For the first time since he'd woken up in Sector 24, that was true – he was neither hungry nor cold. He was beginning to feel like *himself*, somehow. Noah sat on the sofa near his father.

'An android called Michael was here earlier,' Arthur said after a moment's pause. 'But he's gone now.'

The conversation had resumed that strange, dreamlike quality Noah had felt before.

'Is he the one who hurt you?' Noah asked, wondering about the bloodstain.

Arthur nodded.

'And was he looking for me? I'm so sorry, I had no idea he would follow me here.'

'It's not your fault.' He caught Noah's eye in a way that told him there was more behind his words than appeared on the surface. 'I don't blame you for what happened.'

'Are you sure you wouldn't like me to call someone to come and look at it?' Noah was concerned, but found it difficult to frame his thoughts logically. He knew he should try to help his father, but somehow it was more important to stay here, to remain with him, at least for the moment.

'We don't have much time.'

Noah looked at his father, his vision almost glowing with the reflected blaze of the fire.

'I know,' he said. It was as though he had always known their time together was a stolen fragment, somehow separate from everything else, and fleeting. 'This is goodbye, isn't it?'

'Yes. Our chance to part properly, with no guilt on either side.'

'Guilt?' Noah asked. *Yes, guilt – like it's always been there. This dream is truly bizarre*, he thought. He felt different parts of his mind sliding into place, like tumblers aligning within the mechanism of a lock.

'You aren't responsible for anything that happens to me,' his father said pointedly. 'Do you understand that?'

'Yes.'

Noah moved his fingers, bright white next to the flames.

Arthur smiled. 'You're ready to move on – can't you feel it?'

Noah saw then that the glow of his skin was not a reflection of the fire – it was the same beautiful iridescence that had taken Beth. It was time to find her again.

'Dad, I...' Noah's words cut short as he looked at the General again. Behind him, a crack had appeared in the wall. Only it wasn't a crack. The wallpaper flickered at the edges of a void, a black chasm growing bigger by the second. From it, Noah thought he heard a low buzzing, like static from a radio, or some kind of insect swarm.

Another glitch, Noah thought, and now he wasn't sure if the voice in his head was his own, or the one that had guided him since his arrival. The void stretched, yawning wider.

'Dad?' The General hadn't moved, hadn't even glanced towards the hissing fissure at his back. Then Noah noticed that the flames in the fireplace were not moving, either.

The tingling glow continued to spread through Noah,

at once setting his nerves alight and numbing him to the world around him. The only other movement was from the void – and the figure now emerging from it.

It swirled and coalesced to form the outline of a man, glittering darkly like it was made of smoke and beetle shells. And this was a man Noah knew.

'Saul!' he gasped as the face took shape, its hard, black eyes glaring at him. 'What … what are you?'

The mouth opened into a snarling hole as Saul spoke. 'I'm the thing that lives inside your nightmares,' he – *it* – said, the voice grating like a knife being sharpened.

Saul moved closer. The figure hummed and shifted where his legs should be, moving him forward in a way that had nothing to do with nature. Noah would have liked to back away from him, from this *thing*, but Saul was within arm's length of his father now. Perhaps the General wasn't real, but Noah couldn't run while his father remained frozen.

As if he sensed Noah's conflict, an arm formed from the vibrating swarm, whipping out to wrap around Arthur's throat. The General jerked.

'Stop!' Noah stepped towards Saul and grabbed for the whip-like arm. His glowing hand passed right through it like a laser. Noah had felt nothing – only the cool numbness of the glow building in him – but Saul shrank back, his severed arm coming apart in a spray of black sparks before blinking into nothingness.

Saul's face morphed into a mask of rage. The arm was reforming – Noah could see it.

Noah lunged for his father, aiming to shove him clear of Saul's reach, but found himself passing through the space where the General had been. He whirled around, but there was no sign of the General now. The fire in the hearth had vanished, too – no ashes or coals to show it had ever been lit. Something was happening, and it wasn't any programming glitch.

A slithering hiss sounded behind him. Noah already knew what he would find when he turned around, and he faced the pulsating monster Saul had become. Its eyes shone like embers in oil.

'What happened to you?' Noah whispered.

'*You* happened!'

Saul's arm lashed around Noah's throat, but it was as though Noah were made of air, of light.

He can't hurt me now, Noah thought. *He can't hurt me anymore.*

Saul's arm disintegrated wherever it made contact with Noah, but within seconds the limb re-grew. Saul stabbed it towards Noah's chest. Again, it burst in a shower of jet sparks. And still Noah felt no pain. Felt nothing at all, except the tingling sensation spreading inward to the very heart of him.

He heard Saul's scream of rage, but Noah couldn't see him now. His transformation, his escape – whatever this was – wrapped around him like a cocoon. The room faded, Saul's mutant form lost to darkness, and Noah felt himself being pulled free.

He pictured Beth's face as he grew lighter. Then Noah closed his eyes, and was gone.

CHAPTER THIRTY

Alteria Community

It is perhaps the most unusual experience of all, being born for the second time in one lifetime.

This time, though, as all the tumblers fell into place, and those separate poles of my existence merged, I felt complete. This wasn't really being born, thrust shrieking into the alien expanse. It was more like the reversal of death – having everything you knew and wanted given back.

Noah – the version of him I had lived – was a part of me now. The programme had been a nightmare, even with Dallan's modifications helping me out. But I'd gotten to know a part of Eden I would never have seen otherwise, and the chance to say goodbye to my father. I clung to those two things, used them to force back the memory of the fear and loneliness I'd felt in Lyle's nightmare world. It was the only way I could even begin to forgive him, and what his programme had turned Saul into. What it might have turned me into, given the chance.

As I stumbled from the cylinder, two pairs of arms caught me – one seemed to belong to myself, and the other to my father – making me some kind of unholy ghost, I supposed. Looking up into their faces, I recognised Dallan and Frank grinning down at me. Frank carefully removed my dark goggles, and I squinted against the light.

'Well done, Mase,' Dallan said, reaching around the back of my head and detaching the sharp interface node from my neck, then applying it to his own with a quick grimace. 'You got her out. Eden's fine. She's waiting for you upstairs.'

I coughed again. 'What about Lyle? I need to keep him away from…'

'Already taken care of,' Dallan cut me off, his attention drawn by the sound of approaching footsteps. 'Frank, you'd better get going.'

Dallan clapped me on the back and took my place next to the open mouth of the cylinder, waiting for the techs to take him, once again, to transition therapy. Frank pulled me to the hatch in the rear wall. Once we were inside the crawlspace, he dried me roughly with a towel and helped me into a set of clothes he'd left waiting. Frank half-watched me, trying to allow me some privacy while still making sure I was all right. I tried to look reassuring.

'Frank, can we please get out of here?'

He laughed, and it echoed inside the crawlspace. 'I take it you feel well enough to climb down a few levels?'

'Sure.' My body wasn't feeling a hundred per cent, but I was damn sure I'd make it down to Deep Blue.

We crawled and climbed until we exited the crawlspace on the lowest level of Alteria. I looked around at the control panels, the rubberised flooring, and felt like a soldier returning from a war. My world was exactly the same as I had left it, but my perspective had shifted permanently. The one constant was *her*.

'I need to see Eden,' I said.

Frank smiled in understanding, and led me out to the lift. 'You'll be all right from here?' I nodded as I stepped inside, entering directions for it to take me to Level 26. It seemed to move in slow motion as I counted off the levels in my head. I barely noticed the harmonics changing as I rose above sea level, up from the depths.

Eden lay across my bed, breathing in the regular rhythm of sleep. I saw her eyelids flutter, signalling that she was dreaming. The door swooshed closed behind me, the purge unit removing the remaining residue of the biomedical gel from my skin, and I felt my way towards her in the half-light.

It was the most bizarre feeling, approaching someone I knew so well, but hadn't seen in such a long time. I caught her scent, as sweet and faint as her breathing.

'Mason?' Eden sensed my presence almost immediately, or maybe she was dreaming. Either way, I had to be near her.

'Eden,' I answered, bumping into the bed frame. She sat bolt upright, and then her arms were around me.

'It's you,' she said, her lips finding mine. The connection that bound us was more tangible than ever, and my heartbeat raced in time with hers.

'I missed you – I missed you so much. Are you…' I hesitated, cupping her face in my hands. I could feel her pulse thrumming against my fingers, but I couldn't see her eyes, couldn't read her expression. Had the programme altered her? Made her into someone else, someone who wasn't my Eden? 'Are you still my girl?' I said at last, the words spilling from me like white heat. I felt her smile.

'Of course I am.'

My hands tangled in her hair, pulling her closer, seeing both sides of the girl I loved now merged. She was everything.

'Eden, I…' It was like a valve had been opened between us, and everything we had been unable to say for so long came rushing out in stolen breaths.

'I love you, Mason. I tried to tell you before the water got too high…'

'I know. I'm so sorry I didn't reach you in time.' I breathed in Eden's scent, her warmth, feeling everything I had so nearly lost come back to me. 'I didn't know he was your brother, or that he'd do that…'

'It wasn't your fault. And he won't be bothering me for a while.'

'I'm still sorry.'

'Sorry for what?' she asked, kissing my chest.

My voice came out very quietly when I spoke. 'I didn't keep my promise.'

Eden stopped moving, then looked up at me.

'What do you mean?'

I sighed. 'I couldn't stop them putting you into the programme, even though I promised I would.' That was why Eden – Beth – had felt that gnawing sense of betrayal, I was sure of it.

Eden let out a deep breath. 'Oh, that.' She shook her head. 'That's not what it was about, you know – the trust thing. Remember, it was Lyle who programmed my exit trigger. *He* thought I had trust issues, because I wouldn't open up to him in my counselling sessions. He's always been a creep, doesn't get that there are some boundaries a brother shouldn't cross.' She shuddered, and I held her tighter. Just the mention of Lyle gave me a bad taste in my mouth. 'But I don't want to talk about him. I don't want to talk at all.'

Eden kissed me, her hand running over my hair. She paused for a moment to examine me in the dark.

'You cut your hair.' It was a complaint, and I laughed.

'It'll grow back,' I reassured her.

Eden activated the lights on a dim setting, blinking her hazel eyes into focus. Her hair was wild around her, messy from sleep, and her lips pouted where the blood rushed to them.

'It *is* you,' she said softly. 'I…'

'Be quiet now,' I cut her off. All traces of humour vanished. I couldn't stand not to touch her for a single second longer. She squeaked as I threw her back down onto the bed and moved over her, looking into her eyes for a moment before I leaned in and kissed her. Not the breathless, hungry kisses of a moment ago, but with all the intensity of what she meant to me.

Eden's hands moved under my shirt, sliding up my back as she drew me to her and deepened the kiss. With one hand I dragged the shirt over my head and tossed it, giving her better access. Every touch made me burn hotter, harder. I traced a path down the smooth line of her jaw with my lips, kissing her neck before moving lower to place an open-mouthed kiss just above the lacy edge of her cami top.

Then I hesitated.

I'd just got her back, been given a second chance, and no way in hell was I going to ruin that by rushing her.

'Uh-uh,' she said, a smile in her voice. 'Don't even think about stopping now.' Then one hand slid under the waistband of my jeans, and I think my eyes actually rolled back in my head.

'You're sure?'

Her answer was a hot clash of lips and tongues, and a wiggle of her hips underneath me as she shimmied out of her underwear.

She was right. Stopping then would have been just plain wrong.

CHAPTER THIRTY-ONE

Alteria Community

I sent Ari a message asking her to meet me in the refectory for breakfast.

'Would you like to come?' I asked Eden as I dressed. 'I really want you to meet her.'

Eden stretched on the bed, shuddering as her muscles strained.

'I would like to come. But actually, we *have* met.' She opened one eye and looked at me. 'I hope you don't mind. We kind of ran into each other in the corridor a few days ago. She's lovely.'

I stopped midway through buttoning my shirt. 'What did you two talk about?'

She smiled, looking wicked. 'You, mostly.'

Heat rushed into my face. 'What about me?'

Eden laughed, then grabbed one of the pillows from the bed and launched it at my head. I dodged it easily.

'We hardly even talked. Just introductions really …

Ariadne said she looked forward to getting to know me. So it wasn't all about you, vain boy.' Eden laughed at the scowl I could feel pinching my face, and she suddenly looked very much like Beth. I supposed she had always been there, but it was going to take some getting used to, seeing them both in the same skin.

Any witty response I'd been about to make was rudely interrupted by the sound of the incoming communication alert.

'That's probably her,' I said to Eden, pointedly. Not that I was hiding anything from either of them, but I still thought it would be better to spare my sister the evidence of our nocturnal activities. Eden jumped off the bed and headed for the wet room. I quickly smoothed the bedsheets into a more respectable state of disarray, then accepted the call.

The face that popped up onto the screen wasn't the one I'd been expecting. It was Eli.

'Mase, how's it going? You glad to be back in the real world?' He was pleased to see me, judging by the way his eyes creased up at the corners.

I raised an eyebrow. 'This is the real world?'

'As real as it gets. Listen, I had a message from Dallan yesterday. He said if all went well, he'd be going through transition right now, and you'd be making up for lost time with Eden.'

I saw him peering over my shoulder towards the bed.

'She's in the shower,' I said.

Eli's smirk settled into a more thoughtful look. 'How is Dallan? Do you think he'll be okay?'

Dallan had left me a message as well, explaining what had happened when he'd had to disconnect his interface with the programme after Ariadne had come to pull the plug on Saul's pod. I wasn't shedding any tears over the fact that Saul had been completely purged.

'I think Dallan's cleared things up in his head now,' I said. 'His parents have arranged to stay here permanently, so I guess I'll be able to keep an eye on him, seeing as I'm staying too.' I decided to lighten the tone a bit. 'So how are things in the lab?'

Eli's eyes narrowed. 'Wait, you're staying there?'

'Well, yeah. I'd always planned to switch out to whichever community was ready for launch first, but since Eden doesn't want to leave her people, I guess we're staying. At least I think that's still the plan. Eden and I haven't had a chance to talk about it since we got out of rehab, but I'm not leaving here without her.'

'What's up?' Eden's voice sounded right next to me, making me jump. 'Oh, hey, Eli.' She waved her hand at the monitor. 'Did you tell him your news?'

Eli laughed. 'No, he hasn't got around to asking me about my news yet.'

'Actually, I did ask, but you ignored me,' I interrupted, 'and your life's so boring anyway...'

'I find it's generally better for me if I ignore you,' he countered. 'Far less trouble.'

'Will you tell him already!' Eden cut in.

'All right!' Eli hissed through his teeth, making Eden laugh. 'I'm being transferred to Alteria.'

'Here?' I said, surprise evident in my voice. 'How come?'

Eli looked miffed. 'Well, don't strain yourself with enthusiasm, will you?'

'Sorry,' I said, 'of course that's great news. I'm just surprised, that's all.'

He shook his head, dismissing the apology. 'It's a work transfer. I'm going to be developing new tech that's tied in with the rehab facility.' He gave me a knowing smile. 'There are some security issues with the biotech down there, and they want me to redesign some hardware before it's time…'

I caught Eden giving him a quick shake of the head, and he shut up immediately.

'Oh. That's great?' I hadn't meant it to sound like a question, but it did, purely because of what he was going to be working on. Eden reprimanded me with her eyes, looking beautiful and cross. I was transfixed by her, almost forgetting that I was mid-conversation with Eli.

'I'm looking forward to meeting you in person,' Eden said to him, beaming.

'No doubt. If you think I'm a handsome devil now, wait until you see me in the flesh. These monitors aren't flattering, you know, and I'm sure Mason puts me on widescreen on purpose…' I glanced his way for a second. 'Ah, you are still with us, then? I was about to ask Eden if she would wipe the drool from your chin.'

Eli wasn't far wrong. I'd been staring at her for an obscene amount of time.

'Stop flirting with my girlfriend,' I said. 'You're really awful at it.'

'Anyway,' he continued, ignoring me, 'I can see I'm losing my audience, so I'll leave you to it.' He reached forward to deactivate the monitor, then paused and looked at us with a grin. 'Eli out.'

The screen went black.

'Come on,' Eden said, taking my hand and pulling me towards the door before I could respond. 'We're going to be late for breakfast with your sister.'

Just as we were about to walk out of the door the incoming call alert sounded again.

'I'd better just get this…'

She smiled, shaking her head. 'I'll meet you down at the refectory. Don't be long, though.' She kissed me, lingering a second too long for me to remember why I was letting her leave my quarters. As she pulled away, the alert once again demanded my attention and I answered it as the door swooshed closed after her.

Dallan's face flashed up on the screen. He looked happy, which made me instantly suspicious.

'You all right, mate?'

I wondered whether he'd been taking Pi again, which I didn't think would be a good idea, given what he'd done the last time.

'I'm great, Mase. They've let me out already.'

I hadn't expected to hear from him so soon. The last time he'd come out of rehab, it had taken four days in transition before they'd released him.

'I'm really glad,' I said, and meant it. Dallan had sacrificed a lot to help me get Eden out, and I knew it would take me a long time to make it up to him. 'Dallan, thanks for everything you did. You were – it was…'

He smiled lopsidedly. 'You didn't mind about the whole Arthur thing? I thought that was something you might actually find useful in there.'

'It was,' I agreed. 'It was good to kind of see him again.'

He looked at me seriously for a moment, his head tilted to one side. 'The way it ended, though, with that freak Saul appearing and Arthur glitching out – you know that wasn't me, right? I wouldn't have set it up to end that way, man.'

I laughed, but it sounded hollow. 'Yeah. I kind of figured you didn't set out to torture me.'

'Anyway, I'm glad we're both free men again. Frank's cool and all, but I'd have preferred to spend my time checking out the cute boys here, now that I'm sticking around.'

I laughed. 'You just reminded me, I have a breakfast date. Catch you later?'

'Sure,' Dallan smiled briefly, and the screen went dark. He was even worse at goodbyes than I was.

I made my way down to the refectory. Eden stood waiting just outside. We went in together, her hand sliding into mine like it'd been made to fit. Ari was waiting at a table when we went in. She practically pounced on me and Eden, enveloping us in a double-hug.

I kissed the top of her head as she released us.

'Don't ever do that to me again,' Ari said, her voice trembling. 'I thought I'd lost you, too.'

'Can I take your order, or would you like another moment?'

'Another minute ... *Saul*?' My skin seemed to shrink at the sight of the man who stood next to our table – the face that had haunted me for years, even though I hadn't recognised him in the programme. 'What the hell are you doing here?'

I jerked to my feet, and everyone at the tables around us fell into a hushed silence. The man backed away, clutching a data pad to his chest like a shield.

'No, I ... I'll give you another minute.'

He hurried away, and I stared after him, unable to believe what I'd just seen. It had looked like my father's killer. But there was something different about him, something I couldn't quite put my finger on.

'Mason, stop it! Everyone's staring.' Ari tugged at my sleeve until I sat down, and the tables around us resumed their chatter. 'There's something I need to explain.'

She told me what had happened while I was in the programme – about finding Saul's tube, and making sure his memories from before the programme would never be reintegrated. 'That man is gone now, Mason. He's as good as dead.'

I took a deep breath, mulling it over. I'd seen Saul disembodied in the programme – was that why? If so, who – or what – was walking around wearing his skin?

'Will there be any … repercussions … for what you did?'

Ariadne shook her head, and continued in a whisper. 'I'm not exactly thrilled about what Dallan did to cover for me…'

Eden interrupted her. 'If you mean what he did to Lyle, don't feel bad. Seriously, he had it coming.'

'What did Dallan do to Lyle?' I said. It was Ari who answered.

'He planted evidence to make it look like Lyle pulled the plug, not me. He's been put into rehab.'

I tried not to grin, really I did. But the thought of that wanker being trapped inside the hell he'd inflicted on Eden and me was just too good.

'Don't be too smug about it,' Eden said, trying to hide her own smirk. 'Lyle basically wrote the programme. He'll probably be out within a week.'

I shrugged. Maybe it would only be a week, but it would feel much longer than that to Lyle.

'Still, I didn't plan on letting anyone else take the blame for what I did,' Ari said, frowning into her coffee cup, 'but I can hardly come forward now. It would get you and Dallan into trouble, and I think you've had enough to deal with already.'

'I think we all have,' Eden said. 'It's the perfect time for a fresh start, don't you think?' She grinned wickedly at my sister.

'Oh, yes. Most definitely.' Ari said, smiling now.

I looked from one to the other. 'What are you two up to?' They continued to glance at one another shiftily. 'Aw, come on!'

'All right, all right!' Ari held up her hands in defeat. She turned to Eden. 'I don't know how you put up with his impatience.'

'I'm probably worse than he is,' Eden admitted.

My sister shook her head as if that was impossible. 'I've been asked to oversee the engineering team for the launch project here at Alteria.'

'Okay…' I waited to see where this was leading.

'I took a look at what's been done so far with the development and it's … well, we're practically ready to go.' Ari paused, waiting for my reaction. I leaned back.

'Seriously? Like, how close?' I asked finally.

Eden squeezed my hand, unable to contain her

excitement. 'Four weeks!' I looked to Ari for confirmation, finding the same excitement shining in her eyes.

'So who gets to go?' I tried to hide the uncomfortable undertone to my question. After all, I had my Citizen card now, and Eden and Dallan were both free of the programme, so did I care what the Alterians really had planned for the other inmates? As much as I wanted to say no, the lead brick in my stomach said otherwise.

'You'll both be coming, along with everyone else who's already in the community. Frank's heading up his section of the crew, and he's asked for you to work with him full-time. He made it a condition, actually, when he agreed to work on it.' Ari was positively beaming now.

'What about you?' I asked Eden. 'Are you going to be working on this too?'

'Eden's got her own role in the project,' Ari answered for her. 'She's working with the botany team.'

'I did tell you I was good at growing things,' she said, coyly.

'But not that you're a botany specialist!' I took a deep breath, then let it out slowly. 'You knew Alteria was close, didn't you?' I looked at Eden. She reached up to run her fingers along my jaw.

'I didn't *know*,' she said. 'But sometimes it pays to have a little faith.'

Sector 24

Lyle climbed the steps onto the front porch with heavy footfalls, noticing the programme had reset the roach outside the house. The six-legged vehicle seemed to sneer down at him – the man who had created this desolation, and had now become a part of it.

'*Where is your God now?*'

Lyle jumped at the serpent-like hiss, searching for the owner of the voice. But there was nobody out on the porch with him, nobody anywhere that he could see. He entered the house, the door swinging shut behind him with a snap as though he had underestimated his own strength.

He wandered through the rooms on ground level – the parlour where a fire had recently burned to ash in the hearth, a bedroom with sheets that had been slept in no more than a few days ago. In the kitchen he found everything where it should be. Cans of food were stacked in rows in the cupboards, the cutlery laid neatly in the drawer. All signs pointed to this place being occupied very recently, yet the roach was outside and not a soul was in the house. Lyle shouldn't have expected there to be; shouldn't have known this place at all. His memory should have been purged the moment the neural connection engaged. There was no way to bypass that part of the process – he'd certainly tried when he redesigned the programme.

'Why do I still remember who I am?' Lyle wondered aloud, his voice sounding strange in the false confines of the kitchen. He backed out into the hallway, blinking as something dark moved in his peripheral vision, but it was gone by the time his eyes reached the spot where it had been.

'*You're more useful to me this way,*' the voice whispered, turning Lyle in a full circle as he searched for the source. He stopped, surprised by his own speed, and caught sight of himself in the cracked mirror further down the hallway. Moving closer, Lyle saw why his movements felt so unnatural, so alien.

The carbon-copy features of an android reflected back at him, the eyes as soulless as a puppet's.

This is not a part of my design!

The wooden siding cracked as Lyle jerked backwards, his body feeling no pain, only an awareness of the impact. Then it was as though his action had shaken loose the dust ingrained in the building. It billowed out in a vibrating swarm until Lyle was surrounded by it, covered in it. The darkness wasn't a part of the programme Lyle had created, either. But it fit into this hell like it was meant to be there.

'What in God's light *is* this?'

His question drew a hollow, mocking laugh from the darkness now engulfing him.

'We're going to have so much fun together.'

Acknowledgements

Mason's journey has changed a lot since the first dirty draft I wrote of this book some years ago. *Purge* has had many readers and supporters since then, and each one has helped shape it.

Huge thanks to Leana Van Rensburg and Norma Reece for their expertise and insight into the realities of Mason's deafness, and to all those on the cochlear implant forums who shared their experiences so graciously. Your help was invaluable, and the responsibility for any inaccuracies or creative leaps I have taken rests squarely on my shoulders.

My earliest readers were Ian Ellis, Julie Owen, Alex Lidster, Rhian Desmond, Gabrielle Lloyd, James Ellis, and Helen Ellis – I'm so grateful for your feedback and enthusiasm, and for not telling me to toss it in the bin. Thanks to Jani Grey, Ian Hiatt, Caitlin Greer, Misty Provencher, and Marieke Nijkamp for reading, critiquing, and cheerleading. Very special thanks to Bellamy (formerly known as Bridget) Shepherd, who not only gave me great feedback at several stages, but also created the most wonderful fan art of my characters. Dawn Kurtagich, whose books and 'business lunches' always leave me feeling excited to write – you are a little belter.

To Penny Thomas, Janet Thomas, and Megan Farr at Firefly Press: thank you for seeing the heart of my story, making it shine, and getting it out into the world! And thanks to designer Anne Glenn for creating the perfect cover. I'm very fortunate to work with such an amazing publishing team.

Purge connected me with my brilliant agent, Molly Ker Hawn, without whom this book wouldn't exist. You are a champion of dreams, Molly. Thank you so, so much for all that you do.

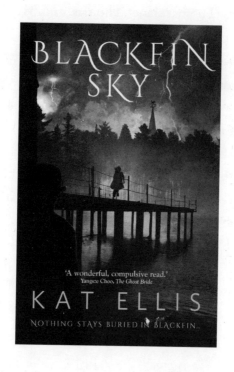

www.fireflypress.co.uk